Tietam Brown

Tietam Brown

Mick Foley

LARGE PRINT

This large print edition published in 2003 by
RB Large Print
A division of
Recorded Books
A Haights Cross Communications Company
270 Skipjack Road
Prince Frederick, MD 20678

First published by Alfred A. Knopf, 2003

Grateful acknowledgment is made to *Grubmam Indursky & Schindler, P.C.* for
permission to reprint excerpts from the song lyric "Backstreets" by Bruce
Springsteen. Copyright © 1975 by Bruce Springsteen (ASCAP). All rights
reserved. Reprinted by permission of Grubman Indursky & Schindler, P.C.
on behalf of Bruce Springsteen.

Publisher's Cataloging In Publication Data
(Prepared by Donohue Group, Inc.)

Foley, Mick.
  Tietam Brown : a novel / Mick Foley.

    p. ; cm.

  ISBN: 1–4025–5698–5

1. Young men—Fiction. 2. Large type books. 3. New York (State)—Fiction.
4. Bildungsroman. I. Title.

PS3556.039173 T54 2003b
813/.54

Typeset by Palimpsest Book Production Limited
Polmont, Stirlingshire, Scotland
Printed in the United States of America
by Bang Printing
3323 Oak Street
Brainerd, Minnesota 56401

For my mother,
who always thought I could write
one of these things

OCTOBER 23, 1985

She had wanted me to kiss her. No doubt about it. The realization hit me as I navigated my dad's '79 Fairmont through the back roads of Conestoga, New York, a small town about thirty miles south of Syracuse.

To tell the truth, a high school senior with one functioning hand really had no business operating a motor vehicle in the first place, let alone a one-functioning-hand high school senior without a license or even a half a thimbleful of experience behind the wheel.

Unfortunately, my father had refused to drive me. Not out of meanness, however—no, my dad felt like he was doing me a favor. "Hey Andy, a kid only goes on one first date," he'd said. "You've gotta make it count. Besides, kid, it's kind of tough to cop a feel in the backseat when you've got your old man behind the wheel." Maybe it was that last bit of paternal sentiment that sold me on the driving idea, and at approximately 7:40 p.m. on a cool autumn evening, I held the door open for Miss Terri Lynn Johnson as she slipped ever so gracefully into the cracked burgundy interior of the

1

piece-of-crap Fairmont that my dad had insisted on lending me. No, a feel was not copped on that night, nor was one even attempted, but that didn't make the night any less glorious, because after all . . . she had wanted me to kiss her. And that was a fact, or at least a pretty strong gut feeling that was worth celebrating . . . with music.

A red light at the intersection of Elm and Broadhurst, only a half a mile from Conestoga High, where I'd met Terri only six weeks earlier, gave me the respite from my driving duties that was necessary in selecting the perfect postrevelatory music. Unfortunately, even a red-light respite isn't much good when trying to fumble with some clunky old eight-tracks with a hand that hasn't closed, clasped, grabbed, or done anything meaningful since Gerald Ford was in office.

I had barely managed to clear my dad's blue fuzzy dice from the glove box when the light turned green. Yeah, my dad had fuzzy dice all right, only they didn't usually reside in the glove box. No, those bad boys swung proudly from the rearview, and served to separate my dad's machine from all other pieces-of-crap '79 Fairmonts on the road. So with the light instructing me to go, and a late-model Ford pickup truck's blaring horn adding to the urgency of such a moment, I reached into the glove box with my left hand, the good hand, and pulled out the first eight-track I felt. Then, with a hint of defiance, I popped that mother in, pushed my curly dark hair back in the general vicinity of where my right ear used to be, and stepped on the gas, as the opening strains of *Barry Manilow Live* drowned out both the horn of the Ford and the shouts of the driver within.

What's wrong? Oh you don't think Barry is appropriate for such an occasion? Sure, it might not have been my first choice, or even in my top couple hundred. And true, the sky blue jumpsuit Barry sported on the cover of the live album, or eight-track in this case, may have been a tad inappropriate. But don't try denying that "Mandy" and "Could It Be Magic" are classic compositions that still hold up well today. Jumpsuit or no jumpsuit, they held up just fine on that night in 1985, and as my voice joined Barry's in belting out, "Baby, I love you now, now, now, and hold on fast, could this be the magic at last," I reflected back on what was at that point the greatest night of my young life.

Terri was several leagues out of my ballpark. Not that I was a horrible-looking guy or anything, but a missing ear and a useless hand tend to cramp a guy's style at that age, and the style-cramping perpetuated itself in an awkward shyness that had invited a lifetime of bullies to boost their self-esteem, or at least try to, at my expense. Sometimes they succeeded, sometimes, as I'll explain later, they didn't. Come to think of it, a lifetime of foster homes, orphanages, and juvenile detention centers hadn't done a whole lot for my sense of self, either.

Terri, on the other hand, was drop-dead gorgeous.

3

Just a beautiful creature. Her beauty was beyond compare, with flaming locks of auburn hair, ivory skin, and eyes of emerald green. Actually, that description is straight out of the Dolly Parton song "Jolene," but that was Terri. Statuesque, but not slutty like some of the other girls who graced Conestoga's halls, she carried herself with a maturity that belied her years. It was really only on game days, when the cheerleading squad sported their official blue-and-orange Conestoga cheerleading sweaters, that her physical attributes really screamed for attention. And in doing so, made me think of the word "maturity" in a whole new light.

She literally could have had her pick of any boy she wanted. Any man for that matter. Her father headed up the local Assembly of God, where his fiery demeanor and hell-and-brimstone sermons contrasted sharply with her gentle nature and overall acceptance of everyone not as fortunate as herself—which pretty much meant everyone.

Her father's vocation, combined with her natural gifts, had given birth to a rather unusual challenge that was spoken of in almost reverent tones among the boys at Conestoga High. No one, it seemed, had gotten into Terri Johnson's pants, or for that matter anywhere even remotely close. Personally, I found the whole subject of Terri's pants to be disrespectful. A creature as beautiful as she deserved better than to have her pants, and what was underneath them, a subject of horny teenage speculation, let alone a prize to be claimed.

How we got together is beyond me. It was actually all her doing. It was she who laughed at my first dumb joke in Mr. Hanrahan's social studies class. It was she who had gone out of her way to say "Hi Andy" in the halls. It was she who insisted on studying together in the library, where she showed off such unique talents as wiggling her nose and ears while I fell hopelessly in love. I know, you're not supposed to fall that quickly, and that the L word should be used sparingly, if at all, during the high school years. But in the fall of 1985 with Terri Lynn Johnson in the library, between the wiggling nose and ears and the sweater, and the wonders that lie beneath the blue-and-orange wool, my heart offered very little resistance. I was a goner. A one-eared, one-handed goner.

And in the one day it took from when Terri asked me to the movies until the entire student body of Conestoga High found out, I went from being a nobody to being the most hated kid in school.

Sure, it was Terri who had laid the foundation for that first date, but in my own defense, it was I who acted on it, and went into overdrive in order to give this vision of loveliness a date she would never forget. The other young lovers were heading to the new mall over by the river, to "the Seven Valley Twelve," as the theaters were officially known, but I had different plans. The Twelve may have been new, enriched with stereophonic sound and equipped with a state-of-the-art snack bar that served different foods from around the globe, but it didn't have the character of the century-old Lincoln Theater, named after, you got it, President Lincoln, who would soon go on to play an unlikely but important role in my life. Yes, when it came to a first date, nothing came close to character as a prerequisite. Except for price, which of course was miles ahead of that whole character thing, especially for a guy who'd come into town with exactly nineteen bucks to his name. My financial woes looked to be easing soon, courtesy of a glamorous minimum-wage dishwashing job at Frank 'n' Mary's diner, a venerable establishment that was home to a myriad of small-town life-forms, from blue-collar locals, to drunk college kids, to on-the-road truckers who needed a little shot of caffeine or cholesterol.

So with my finances in mind, the Lincoln's 85-cent admission made even the specter of seeing *Rambo: First Blood Part II* on a first date sound pretty good. The Lincoln's price policy, you see, was derived directly from whatever year happened to be taking place. In 1984, the price was 84 cents; in '85, it was 85. Guess what it was in '83? If you guessed 83 cents you'd be wrong. Back in '83 when the Lincoln was still the only game in town, a flick cost four bucks, but with the advent of the multiplex, the ancient cinematic institution was forced to make changes to survive. They stopped showing first-run movies. They lowered their prices. They cut down on the variety of candy and on the freshness of the popcorn. And they stopped doing the little things, like cleaning the floor.

So after spending $1.70 on two admissions, and the total of $3.50 on two Cokes and a medium popcorn that we decided we'd share, I escorted the most beautiful girl I had ever seen into a dingy cave of a theater, where she would see a plethora of people perish on-screen in the ensuing ninety-five minutes. But her smile never waned, and she somehow managed to be the picture of class, even as a previously chewed piece of gum formed a bond with her designer jeans, and her slim and gorgeous feet got acquainted with a floor that had known no mop in quite some time.

My mind began to wander at about the time the eleventh person died in the first coming-attraction preview. My father had been so happy for me on the eve of my first date. He had wanted to make sure that everything was perfect. The car had been a very nice gesture, fuzzy dice or no fuzzy dice. "Andy, my boy," he'd said with a big grin and an "I've got a secret" wink in his eye, and a secretive hand held behind his back. "Hold out your hand and close your eyes and I'll give you a big surprise." So I held out my hand and closed my eyes, and I'll be damned if my father didn't give me a big surprise. "Just a little something to make sure that you and your girl have a good time tonight," he said with a laugh that sounded as if it had been lifted from a used car salesman.

When I first closed my hand around my dad's surprise and felt the rustle and crinkle, I had a premonition that a ten-dollar bill had found its way into my hand. My premonition was wrong. A ten-dollar bill would have placed me and Terri inside the Seven Valley Twelve, where people on the screen might actually do things besides kill each other. A ten-dollar bill would have spared Terri the union of her ass and a wad of chewing gum. But it was not to be.

I moved my foot slightly and found it nearly glued to the floor. At that point I experienced what can only be called a flashback, as the sticking of my shoe at the Lincoln gave way to the memory of the sticking of my shoe at the Pussycat Cinema in eastern Pennsylvania two months earlier, although I'd be willing to bet that the substances causing the stickiness were altogether different.

The Pussycat had been my dad's idea, when he showed up at the Northern Virginia Juvenile Detention Center near Richmond on my seventeenth birthday, after an absence from my life of only sixteen years and nine months. I'd received a postcard a few months earlier that in its entirety read, "See you in a few . . . Dad." A few. I had no idea what "a few" meant, so I waited a few hours, then a few days, then a few months, and then finally, on the day of my release, without a clue as to what to do with the rest of my life, I set eyes on my father, Antietam Brown IV. "Come on, kid," was all he said. "I'm taking you home."

I had no idea the "home" of which he spoke meant Conestoga, New York. Home to me had always been Virginia, with the exception of my life's first three months, which had been spent in a suburb of Tampa, until my dad got tired of the Mr. Mom routine and shipped me off.

We drove on through Maryland that first night, with my dad insisting that I drink my first beer, and then my second, and so on and so forth until I was so drunk that his words became increasingly incoherent, which was probably a good thing. He said nothing about his work, and even less about my mom, opting instead to spend our inaugural night together regaling me with details about his past sexual conquests. As the miles flew by and the beers, at his urging, flew south, those details became fuzzier and fuzzier, until the fuzzy dice started spinning in unison with my stomach and I mustered the fortitude to blurt out, "Pull over," which my dad did a split second before those birthday beers came barreling up my throat, and into the green grass and wildflowers that bordered that particular section of Highway 95.

"Thatta boy," my dad laughed as the vomiting process reached its conclusion, and a thick stew of spit and puke adorned my chin, like some strange new goatee. "Never let it be said that ol' Tietam Brown doesn't know how to show his son a good time!" Then, after a pause, "I'm proud of you, boy," with a rugged slap on the back for added emphasis.

The Pussycat Cinema was the first thing I saw when I awoke that next day. "Look over there, kid," my dad said as the Fairmont screeched to a stop, kicking up a cloud of dust and jolting me awake to find that I was in the middle of nowhere, with a massive headache and the vile taste of stale vomit to remind me of my Happy Birthday.

"Where?" I asked, which seemed an appropriate response, as from my vantage point, all I could see was a ramshackle trailer enhanced by the timeless beauty of a rusted-out Pinto on cement blocks on display in what passed for a front yard. "Not there, kid . . . *there*," he said, and with that he was out the door and headed for the Pussycat at a trot. I followed suit, afraid to be seen but a little intrigued.

"Andy, these babies are a dying breed," my dad said, his voice heavy with nostalgia. "Might as well check one out before they turn it into a hardware store or some damn thing." And with that I headed into the plush surroundings of the theater itself, my feet sounding like quacking ducks as I made my own way down the aisle, while a lone man in the back appeared to be furiously cleaning his glasses underneath a long trench coat on a hot August afternoon.

There we sat, father and son, estranged no longer, watching a pretty but not beautiful blonde, with a face that was somehow far too sweet for that line of business, having odd deeds done to her while Antietam Brown IV nudged me in the ribs and doled out words of wisdom like "That's what's known as the 'money shot.'"

Two tickets . . . ten dollars. A flat Coke and a box of stale Jujy-fruits . . . four dollars. Spending an afternoon with your dad in a scuzzy porn theater . . . priceless.

I was jolted back to the present with the gentle touch of a manicured hand on the knee of my tattered jeans. "Andy . . . Andy . . . are you all right?" I glanced quickly at the screen to see a ripped and pumped Sylvester Stallone, who by all accounts seemed to have adapted well to the rigors of chain gang life. "Andy, are you all right," Terri repeated, and her hand gently squeezed my knee in a gesture of concern. "Yeah, oh, uh, yeah," I said, and at that very moment, with her hand upon my knee and all her attention directed right at me, the truth was, I had never been better. "I was just thinking."

"And what, may I ask, were you thinking?" she said.

I opened my mouth, and my voice cracked. Honestly. A legitimate Peter Brady voice crack. Then, mustering all that was left of my pride, I opened up my mouth again and gave that talking thing another try. "Um, um, Terri, I was just thinking that maybe you would have liked another movie better at another theater."

She smiled and her gentle clasp on my knee became the softest of caresses. Then she squinted in mock Clint Eastwood toughness, sneered a bit like early Mick Jagger, and said, "First of all, I love Rambo," and then, with her voice losing its humor, continued, "and second, I don't care about the theater, I just like being with you."

My Adam's apple suddenly turned into an Adam's watermelon, and I couldn't speak. Hell, I couldn't breathe. I think all my body functions stopped. All except my tear ducts, which produced enough water in the next few seconds to irrigate the Sahara. God, I tried not to let those tears fall, as, after all, crying isn't really crying unless the tears actually leave the eyes. My eyes had welled up many times over the years in Virginia, but it had been ten years since I'd actually let one fall. But try as I might, and believe me, I tried, that ten-year dry streak came to an end at the Lincoln Theater as Colonel Trautman sprang Rambo from the clink in order to aid his country in a double secret mission.

And what a tear it was too. A big fat solitary drop, which made a slow journey from the right corner of my eye down the side of my flushed face. Terri saw it, she had to have, but said nothing, until breaking the silence a good minute later with a simple but daunting request. "Andy, give me your hand."

Oh no, not the hand. I had sat on her left-hand side, meaning that the hand in question, the hand in demand, the hand she wanted, was the dead one. I panicked, and for a moment thought that the single solitary tear might well be joined by a parade of his brothers, before calming down sufficiently to risk a daring strategy . . . the truth.

"Terri."

"Yes."

"Um, Terri."

"Yes, Andy."

"Um, my right hand, um, doesn't work."

The declaration was met with silence, and surprise, but, turning my head, I was relieved to see, not with disgust.

I continued, "It was an accident when I was little."

She smiled sadly and said, "The same accident as the ear?" I nodded in silence. She knew of my ear, or lack thereof, indeed it was the subject of my missing ear which had led to her laugh and our first mutual smile in Hanrahan's class. Hey, if she wasn't turned off by my stump of an ear, then maybe she wouldn't mind the dead hand, either.

"Andy?"

"Yeah."

"How about the other hand?"

"What about it?"

"Does it work?"

"Yeah, it does."

And with that she stood up, oblivious to the fact that Rambo was now in mortal danger, and, like Jesse Owens claiming Olympic gold in the high hurdles in Berlin in '36, deftly vaulted over my lap, pirouetted, and dropped into the seat to the left of me. She then lifted my curly locks and playfully, just a tad seductively, whispered into my good ear, "So how about it?"

I should have known what she was talking about, but I'll admit right now to being somewhat distracted by the pleasant tingling that her whisper had caused in my penile area. So I said the only thing I could think of. "How about what?"

"How about giving me that hand, big boy," she said, and before I could reply, her hand was entwined with mine, in what was the most romantic moment of my young life, with all due respect to the two young men who tried to forcibly sodomize me during my stay at the Petersburg Home for Boys.

But on that night, at the dilapidated Lincoln Theater, those two young men, attempted sodomy, and the first seventeen years of my troubled life were a distant memory. Because on that night, the world was right. John Rambo was making the world safe for democracy, and Terri Johnson was holding my hand, her head leaning on my shoulder, with just the slightest hint of a beautiful, wonderful breast touching my arm.

And then I saw it. The mere sight of it repulsed me. It was terrible. The lump in my jeans. No, not that lump, which if detected might prove slightly embarrassing, but not necessarily repulsive or terrible. And truth be told, that lump was not all that prominent. It wasn't the quarters in my right pocket that concerned me either. No, the lump that terrified me was in the left front pocket of my jeans, and if detected, it would certainly spell the end of my one-hour-old romance with Terri. How could I have forgotten to have thrown it out, after my dad had handed it to me? I literally prayed that her hand wouldn't move one inch and a half up and two inches to the right. Terri, I'm sure, could have forgiven me for having a first-date boner while she held my hand at the Lincoln Theater. Forgiveness would not be so easy, or even borderline conceivable, if she discovered that I had brought three rubbers with me on my first date.

Over the years, there have been times I have doubted God's existence, and there have been times I have cursed his very name, but the night of October 23, 1985, I had no doubt that he was smiling down on me, willing Terri's hand not to touch the foil three-pack that housed my dad's Trojans with their helpful reservoir tips and spermicidal jelly for added protection. Yes, God was with me, and not only did he provide protection from my protection being detected, but he seemed to bestow upon me the ability to not be a total bonehead when we got into the Fairmont and headed for home.

Indeed, the conversation flowed inside that crappy car, and I was not only comfortable, but I was funny as well. Actually, I'd always had a decent sense of humor, but I usually brandished it almost as a defense, as if a self-deprecating wit could smooth over the fact that most of my life had pretty much sucked. But on this night, my humor was different. It was irreverent, it was topical, and it elicited genuine laughs from Terri. Big, wonderful laughs.

I wished that ride, like the night itself, could have lasted forever, for besides loving Terri's company, I loved the unique feeling of liking myself. So when I pulled that Fairmont into the Johnson driveway that led to her estate-like home surrounded by her huge manicured lawn, the vehicle seemed to be filled with love. "I had a great time tonight, Terri," I said, and I stuck out my hand. As in the customary good-night hand-shake.

She stared at me for what seemed like minutes, with a flabbergasted look, then regained her composure, and accepted my hand in the gesture of respect and friendship that it symbolized. And a fine handshake it was at that. "I had a great time too, Andy," she said, while I shook that hand as if I'd just sold her an insurance policy. "I'd like to do it again."

"Me too," I said.

Then the handshake ended and she got out of the car. It didn't dawn on me to open the car door, or to walk her to her house, maybe because dating etiquette hadn't been covered all that well at the Northern Virginia Juvenile Detention Center.

"Good night, Andy."

"Good night."

"I'll see you on Monday, okay?"

"Okay."

And then she was gone, at least momentarily, for as I put the Fairmont in reverse, she reemerged in a flash and headed for my window, which I was kind enough to open. In a blur of auburn hair, she moved her face within inches of mine, to the point where she was actually leaning into the car. Her breathing was a little labored, as if she'd just run a lap around the track instead of hopping down two steps and walking ten yards.

"Andy," she said, so close that I could almost taste the sweetness of her breath.

"Yeah."

"I just wanted to make sure that you didn't get lost on your way home. Do you know the way?"

"Yeah, sure," I said with a shrug, "I live off this same road. I'll be okay."

"You sure?"

"Yeah, I'm sure, but thanks for checking on me." And to show her my appreciation, I stuck that left hand out the window and we shared another good shake. She paused momentarily, and I gave her a wink, and then she turned and walked back to her house. And as I watched her go, I couldn't help but wonder, Why would I need directions? Then she turned, waved, opened the door, and disappeared.

Strange indeed. I mean, I couldn't possibly get lost. Sure it was a back road, and sure there was that one fork with the red light to contend with,

17

but it was still the same road. I shrugged my shoulders and headed out, and somewhere between a sixteenth and an eighth of a mile from the Johnson house, I suddenly figured it all out. Oh my goodness. She had wanted me to kiss her!

I was singing along with Barry when I pulled into my own drive, which led to a much less illustrious house, surrounded by a much less manicured lawn. "Now, now, now, and hold on fast—could this be the magic AT LAST!" So I'd screwed up. I didn't kiss her. It was a big screwup, but one that I felt confident I could redeem. Hands down, there had not been a better night in the history of my life, and there was only one way to celebrate it. A half gallon of vanilla ice cream and the scratchy old Nat King Cole Christmas album that still carried my mother's maiden name on it. Kathy Collins. It was the only thing, memories included, that I had of her to call my own.

Nothing could have ruined that night for me, but the next moment came pretty close. For in that moment, I saw my father's silhouette in our living room window, moving up and down, up and down, doing a steady stream of deep knee bends. My father was "doing the deck," which could only mean one thing.

"Hey Andy," my father's voice called out as the front door opened to herald my return from the world of first dates. "Just a sec, kid, I want to talk to you." Then, with his body continuing its up-

and-down motion, he called out the last repetitions of the card he'd drawn. "Fourteen. Fifteen."

With that my father picked up his Genesee Light Beer, to be known hereafter as a "Genny," took a gargantuan swig, and set it down. "Hold on, Andy, sit down, I'm almost through my second deck."

He turned another card, a joker, and let out a loud sigh. "Oh man, they're killing me," he said with a snort, and then commenced to drop down to the ground and reel off twenty-five textbook push-ups, followed by the cracking open of what looked to be about his tenth Genny, which he proceeded to not so much drink as inhale.

"How was the big date, kid . . . any action?" he said, but before I could answer he turned another card, a king, reeled off another fifteen deep knee bends, and just about polished off another Genny.

"No, no action, Dad, but we had a really—"

"Hold on there, Andy, I've only got two cards left to go, and then I want you to tell your dad all about it." He turned up a card. "Three, well damn, that's no challenge." He dropped down, did three push-ups, with a casual clap in between each one, rose up, took a small sip on the Genny, and turned over the last card. A queen.

I watched my dad rise up and down, up and down, as he concluded his solitary ritual. For many years he'd been doing this routine, shuffling his deck of cards and then turning them one by one, alternating between push-ups and what he called Hindu squats, with the numbers on the

19

cards dictating the number of repetitions he performed. I never did the math, but completing a deck meant doing hundreds of repetitions of both exercises. I tried it on my own one day and barely made it through half a deck before my legs betrayed me, turning to jelly during the twenty-five Hindus the joker required of me.

My dad's legs never betrayed him, however, seeming instead to get stronger with each turn of the card, and with each drink of the Genny. With only one huge exception, doing the deck was the only time I saw my dad drink.

Looking at him in action, my dad seemed not so much human as machinelike in function, his sinewy muscles popping through his lean frame like steel cords. The kind of guy who looked almost wimpy in a baggy sweatshirt and jeans, but whose muscles stood out like a relief map of the human anatomy when in the nude. And I should know, for whenever he was "in the deck" Tietam Brown was in the nude. Yeah, maybe I should have mentioned that earlier, because it does tend to alter the perception of his exercise regimen just a bit.

You see, for Tietam Brown, doing the deck wasn't just about exercise. It was about a whole lot more. Exercise, sure. Beer drinking, yeah. But for my father doing the deck was primarily about sex.

Doing the deck was a sure sign that intermission was under way. That the second act of a long passion play was about to commence. "The first one's for them, Andy," he'd told me once, "but

20

the second one is all about ol' Tietam, even though by the sound of things they seem to have a pretty good time too."

I'll say they did. As the inhabitant of the room next door to his, I would say that was an understatement.

Usually the commencement of his ritual would send my dad bounding up the stairs to begin act two immediately, a very sweaty, very drunk, very physically fit, and very horny man. But this night was special. His son had just had his first date and he wanted to spend some quality time right there in the Brown living room, surrounded by the odd potpourri of sweat, beer, and sex.

"So Andy," he said as he dried the sweat off his balding head with a dish towel, "tell me about the big night."

His smile was big and happy, and I had to smile back, not just in reflection of the momentous night I'd just had but also at the walking, talking, drinking, Hindu-squatting contradiction that stood before me.

"Dad, it was probably the best night of my life, I mean we had the—"

He cut me off. "Which means you used the Trojans, didn't you, kid?"

The guy was actually beaming, he was so happy. I considered humoring him, but couldn't bear to stain Terri's reputation with even a phantom sexual encounter. "Actually, Dad, I didn't use any of them." With that the huge smile became a mask of concern.

21

"Don't tell me you rode bareback, Andy, not in this day and age. You know they've got that AIDS thing floating around."

"No, Dad, I didn't ride bareback, I just—"

He cut me off again. "Oh, did you opt for a little—"

I interrupted him as he was making the universal hand-and-tongue signal for oral sex. "No, Dad, we didn't do anything, we didn't even kiss, but I had a great time, I really like her . . . and she . . . she held my hand."

"Whoa! Ho ho! Whew! Sheeeew!" my dad laughed. "We've got a wild man on our hands. Watch him, officer, he's a hand holder!" Then, in an instant, I saw his expression change. I can't call it compassion, but it seemed almost to border on understanding. "Andy," he said softly.

"Yeah."

"Do you like this girl?"

"Yeah."

"And did it feel nice when you held her hand?"

"Yeah it did, Dad, it felt nice."

"Well that's what counts, kid. You'll have plenty of time to do that other stuff later." Then he stepped forward, and for the first time he hugged me. I hesitated just for a moment, just to make sure that it wasn't a joke. It wasn't. Then I hugged him back. I hugged my drunk, naked father . . . and how many kids can say that?

My dad stepped away, not embarrassed, but obviously not used to this father-son bonding thing.

He put his hand on my shoulder and said, "I'm glad you didn't use those condoms tonight, son."

I didn't quite know what to say, so I opted not to say anything. In the wake of my silence, my dad finished his thought. "Because I'm all out, and that broad upstairs would never forgive me if I didn't plow her field another time."

"Hey Dad," I said, smiling in preparation for what I had to say next.

"Yeah, kid."

"I thought you said the second one was all about ol' Tietam."

With that my father grabbed me and tousled my hair the way he might have if I'd been ten and hit the winning home run in Little League, or any other number of reasons that fathers who don't disappear for sixteen years and nine months might have for tousling their son's hair. He then followed the hair tousle with a bit of verbiage that most children won't hear from their dads in their lifetimes. "Now give me those condoms, you little muskrat."

Then he was off, condoms in hand, bounding up the stairs, gold medallion slapping off his chest, middle-aged balls slapping off his thighs. "Hey Gloria," he yelled as he opened the door, "let's just hold hands tonight!" Gloria laughed.

Gloria, I knew, meant Gloria Sugling, as in next-door neighbor Gloria Sugling, whose cop husband Charlie worked the midnight shift in Cortland, keeping the streets safe while my father, in his own words, plowed his wife's field.

23

By my own count, this was Mrs. Sugling's third visit to Tietam Brown's bed, which meant, whether she knew it or not, it was also her last, in accordance with my dad's "three strikes, you're out" rule. As I pulled the half gallon of vanilla out of the freezer, I couldn't help but think my dad was right. Over the sound of bouncing bedsprings and the thumping of the headboard, I could hear Mrs. Sugling's voice, and she certainly did seem to be having a good time. Or maybe she was just agreeing strongly with whatever my dad had to say.

I lay down in my little bed with my half gallon of vanilla, and Nat King Cole's angelic voice competing with the not-so-angelic acts in the room next door. It took a couple of flips of the album, but then the headboard and bedsprings stopped, and Mrs. Sugling headed down the stairs and out our door for the very last time, and now Nat had the room to himself. I closed my eyes and listened in the darkness, the last taste of vanilla ice cream still cool upon my tongue. I listened to the beautiful voice sing about "the dear Savior's birth," and I listened to each sacred scar and crack of my mother's old LP, each one as beautiful to me as the music itself. With my eyes still closed, I thought of Terri, her head against my shoulder, her hand holding mine, and even that slightest hint of her breast against my arm. And then, for the second time in ten years, a tear rolled down my cheek. I slipped into a beautiful dreamless sleep with one last thought . . . she had wanted me to kiss her.

THE RAGE / 1973

My mother died giving birth to me in 1968, and after Antietam Brown IV realized that changing diapers and warming bottles wasn't his heart's desire, I was sent to live with Maria DelGratto, the wonderful woman I would come to call Auntie M, my mother's best friend in the town of Boyer, just outside of Richmond.

She was a big buxom woman, my Auntie M, and Italian to the core. Indeed, my initial remembrance as a part of this world was not one of sight or sound, but of smell, taking in the fragrance of her culinary efforts, which never seemed to end, as she cradled her ladles, spoons, and spices with one hand and took turns cradling me and her one-year-old son Johnny with the other.

A year later, little Rachel was born, and Maria DelGratto took turns handing out generous portions of love, attention, and her patented big-boob hugs. When she pulled me close, I would close my eyes and nestle in real deep, and there was not a place in the world that I would rather be. Come on now, don't read too much into it, I was just a baby. I didn't equate those boobs with sex, but with warmth, comfort, and most of all safety. And safety, unfortunately, was often a scarce commodity in the DelGratto house once Big Vinnie came home.

I'm not sure what Vinnie did for a living, but he was out the door every morning at eight with a cheery "Better have supper waiting!" and back every evening at six with an equally chipper "Get me my dinner." No, I'm not sure what he did to put that food he was so concerned about on the table, but if he could have thrown a baseball half as well as he threw plates and glasses around the house, he would have been a twenty-game winner for the Yankees for sure.

Any little thing seemed to set him off. A toy in the kitchen? Yeah, that was reason enough. The monthly mortgage? Like clockwork. Even the faintest smell of poop drifting from one of our little baby butts could set off an eruption of rage that included not only the throwing of objects but the whipping of those little baby butts, extreme verbal abuse directed at anyone in his path, and the occasional stinging backhand that left Auntie M bruised and bleeding at intervals that became more frequent as time marched on.

And always, she'd hold us. Against those breasts. Those warm, soft, safe breasts. Hold us until the fear was gone, until the anger was gone. Until it was just Big Vinnie sitting in front of the TV, a ball game on, wondering where the hell his beer was.

I cried a lot back in those days, especially

between the ages of two and three, when I realized there really were monsters in the world, the worst of which slept in the bedroom down the hall. God, I shed a lot of tears back then. Tears in the form of loud screams when he was hitting any one of us. Tears in the form of silent sobs when I'd hear his loud and drunken sexual escapades down the hall. Escapades that, by the sound of things, my Auntie M neither wanted nor enjoyed.

And always, always, always, my tears were met with a big hug, even those silent sobs were soothed by a visit to the tiny bedroom that housed all three of us kids, where one by one she'd hold us close and kiss our tears away. "Andy, Andy, it'll be okay," she'd whisper as she rocked me in her bosom. "Don't cry now, Andy, I'll make everything okay."

It was Auntie M who took to calling me Andy, derived, I guess from my full name, Antietam Brown V, in honor of my great-great-great-grandfather Sean Brown, who died defending the Union on the battlefield of Antietam, in Sharpsburg, Maryland, in 1862. The battle, I was told, was the bloodiest single day of the Civil War, with the number of dead bodies far outpacing the army's ability to bury them. So Sean Brown, nineteen, only a year off the boat from his native County Clare in Ireland, was rewarded for his heroic efforts by being torn to pieces by the wild boars who ravaged the blood-soaked fields that ran along each side of Antietam Creek. I would later find out that the wild boar incident was one that my father had never forgiven, a character trait of his that had already altered the course of my life and would continue to as well.

Not to be outdone, Big Vinnie had his own nickname for me—little bastard. The name seemed to bring him joy, and as a result he used it often, to the point where for a while I thought it really was my name. It was a name for all seasons, a multipurpose phrase, I guess you could say, kind of like "aloha" is to Hawaiian people.

School started in late August in Boyer, so on a cool summer's eve, with big sheets of rain pouring down, Big Vinnie DelGratto packed his wife, two kids, and little bastard into his '65 Cadillac and drove to the five-and-dime for a year's worth of school supplies. I don't think Big Vinnie gave a damn about his kids' education, and I knew he couldn't care less about mine, but he wasn't about to let his wife drive his puke green pride and joy. Not out of any concern for her safety, but instead out of a firm belief that a woman's place was not behind the wheel. He even drove her to the grocery store every Wednesday, where he passed the time with the newspaper's sports section and a six-pack of Bud.

"We'll be right back," said Maria in a cheerful tone that was met with a Big Vinnie grumble, a newspaper rustle, and a cracking of that first Bud. If a grocery trip meant a six-pack, then I guessed that Vinnie was probably good for three by the time we collected our black marble composition pads and number two pencils.

I was wrong. For on our return, Vinnie DelGratto was already soaking his liver in Bud number five and cursing out loud at the fate of his beloved Atlanta Braves. "Goddamn, Aaron," he yelled, "home-run king my guinea ass. Strikeout king is more like it." When Auntie M finished squeezing her sizable frame into the Caddy, Big Vinnie took off, ran a red light at the edge of the parking lot, made a sharp left at the next stop sign, and passed by row after row of neat little 1930s-era houses en route to our eleven-hundred-square-foot home on the far end of town. The trip averaged about ten minutes, but even with the rain pouring down and visibility damn near nil, Big Vinnie seemed intent on making it in five.

I looked at Johnny to the immediate right of me in the Caddy's backseat, fumbling with the bags, a frown on his face. Little Rachel peered in from the far right as if not to be shut out of some big secret, and said, "Whatcha looking for, Johnny?" in her cute, four-year-old way.

"Get away, Rachel," said Johnny, who turned his back to his sister and continued his search. "Mom, I can't find my protractor."

I heard Vinnie grunt as he turned up the radio, which was broadcasting the tail end of an embarrassing Braves loss.

Rachel persisted. "Whatcha looking for, Johnny?"

she repeated, and attempted to reach into the bag.

"Stop it, Rachel," Johnny yelled, and called for his mom to get Rachel to end her reaching ways.

Auntie M, as usual, was the voice of reason and attempted to stop their sibling quarrel. "Come on now, Johnny," she said, "don't talk to your sister like that."

"But Mom, I can't find my protractor."

This time Big Vinnie spoke up as he gunned the car's motor and made his voice rise above the rain, and the radio. "Goddammit," he yelled, "I'm trying to listen to a ball game."

"But Dad, I don't have my protractor."

"Shut up."

"I need one for school."

"Shut up."

If there ever was a time not to speak, it was then, for Big Vinnie was in full scumbag mode, and even though I was seated behind him and could not see his face, I could see the fat on the back of his neck twitching, a sure sign that he was about to prove his manhood by smacking a small child.

Johnny leaned forward to plead his case, but before the one syllable of "Dad" was even finished, his father caught him in the face with a stiff back-hand swat. For the first time since I'd known her, Maria DelGratto got mad. "How dare you?" she yelled, which caught Big Vinnie off guard, but before another word could be heard, Vinnie DelGratto, her husband, filled the air of the Caddy with the loud cracking sound of fist meeting nose. I saw Auntie M sag down from the force of the blow, and something happened inside of me.

I heard Johnny scream, I heard Rachel cry. I heard Vinnie laugh. I said not a word, but that something inside me happened all the same. And for the first time in my life, I felt that rage take over.

I stood up in that seat, and as Vinnie admired his wife-beating hand, I reached both my five-year-old arms over his head, felt them graze over the flesh of both his chins, clenched both hands together, and pulled back on that fat bastard's larynx with everything I had.

Johnny still screamed, Rachel still cried, and the radio still played, but now Auntie M joined in the cacophonous roar, but her pleading fell on ears that were deaf to all but Vinnie DelGratto's fading gasps.

I leaned over, intent on seeing life fade from his face, and when I did he grabbed hold of my head and, in a last desperate move, pulled my fifty-two-pound body over his shoulder and onto his lap.

Then I felt a huge fist smash down on my jaw, and I saw Maria grab hold of her husband's arm and make a plea for some sense.

"Please stop the car! Just please stop the car. You're going to kill us! Just please stop the car!"

For a moment, just a moment, I thought Vinnie might just grant her wish, but that crucial moment only seemed to help him make a conscious decision. He could stop the car and save his family, or he could continue to pummel. He chose the latter.

"Die, you little bastard!" he screamed, and brought down that big fist with enough force to jolt me off his lap and down his knees, so that my legs waved awkwardly in the air and the right side of my face became wedged on the accelerator.

I heard little Rachel's voice cry out, "We're all going to die!" and though that thought turned out to be not entirely true, it seemed a good bet, and with consciousness fading quickly, I reached up with my right hand and closed it real tight on Vinnie DelGratto's balls.

The green Caddy finally stopped, courtesy of a huge oak tree that was nearly ripped out, roots and all, from the impact of an automobile decelerating from ninety to zero in a fraction of a second. Just enough time to see Johnny's body fly through the windshield like a sixty-pound missile, and I knew he was gone.

Time seemed to stand still as I lay in that car, until Rachel's small screams filled the Caddy's steaming carcass with hope. "Mommy, Mommy," she yelled over and over, her first word on this earth now the only one worth knowing. "Mommy," she cried again, but Mommy was gone. Not gone in the way that Johnny was gone, but gone in the sense that she was no longer in the Caddy's right front seat.

I struggled to get out of the would-be green coffin, and found the going tough. Big Vinnie's fists had done a number on my face, leaving my eyes swollen grotesquely, my mouth barely able to move. I eased my hand out of the area of Vinnie's crotch and felt like the hand was going to explode. Literally. Then all feeling was gone, my nerves having shut down like a faulty fuse box.

I kicked with both legs against Vinnie's big gut, planning to exit the floorboard as I had entered it, through his lap. Not a chance. The steering wheel was embedded in his chest, and his lifeless head hung over the wheel, dripping blood onto my shoulder. I pushed off the left door and wriggled my way into Auntie M's passenger side, hoping to exit the same way she had. I noticed that blood was cascading down the right side of my face, beating down on the rubber floor mat in a rhythm that blended with the falling rain. I felt the right side of my face with my functioning left hand, and felt only a stub where my right ear should have been. For a moment I panicked, not out of pain, but from the illogical fear that I might get in trouble for losing my ear. So my left hand darted out and searched the floorboard where my body had been, found the ear in question, and tucked it neatly in the right pocket of my shirt, which had turned from white to deep red over the past half a minute. It was only years later that I learned that my right ear had never been found. Apparently I had placed Vinnie DelGratto's tongue in my shirt.

"Mommy, Mommy," Rachel cried on, and I tried

my best to calm her. Maybe my words were wise, maybe not, but they were inaudible amid the sounds of that horrible night. Rachel's cries, the sounds of the still-blaring radio, the whine of police sirens that now entered the night with their flashing blue strobes, shedding some semblance of light on the whole grisly scene.

Then I saw her. Auntie M. Reaching out for me. Her face. Bruised but smiling. The blue lights danced off her big round frame, and I thought I'd never see anything more comforting in my life. God, I wanted her to hug me. In the rain, in the mud, with blood streaming out of the hole where my ear had been. One hug, and I'd be safe again. With the last of my strength I met her outstretched hand with mine, threw my body on top of hers, and held my sad, beaten face between the mounds of her warm, safe breasts. I looked up and saw her smile at me, the most peaceful smile I had ever seen. Then I put my head back into the safety of her bosom, and cried tears of joy until a man touched my shoulder and said "Son, you have to go." I cried some more. "Son," the man said again, this time a little louder, "it's time to go." I looked up and saw the last remnants of her peaceful smile being gently covered by a sheet. "It's too late, son, it's too late," the voice said, and then I was being lifted off her body, my little face never to feel her safe breasts again. I looked again at the sheet, hoping for one last glimpse of her smile, and noticed that her severed head lay a good three feet from her body.

A week had gone by since my first date with Terri, and I had yet to redeem myself for my wasted kissing opportunity. But I knew that when the time was right, I would be ready. I'd been practicing. Yeah, that's right, practicing. By taking what I'd seen on Dallas and Dynasty, and applying those same physiological principles to my pillow, I had come up with a technique that was sure to please.

At Conestoga, I saw kissing every day, but they were sloppy kisses, public kisses, kisses that almost shouted out, Look, we're kissing! I didn't want to be part of those. My kisses would be different. Smooth, precise, and downright SEXY! Despite the fact that not a single soul could vouch for me, I knew I'd be good when I got the chance.

For her part, Terri looked at ease with her shy, one-eared, one-handed boyfriend, but I found myself feeling somewhat less so. Not that I wasn't proud and in love and thanking my lucky stars on a nightly basis, but the smug smirks and snide comments were starting to get to me. And of all the smug smirks and snide comments, no smirks were smugger, and no comments snider, than those of Mr. Hanrahan, our seventh-period history teacher who doubled as the school's legendary football coach.

I would watch him as he taught his class in his own unique style: reading directly out of the textbook, head down, no eye contact, with his hulking physique stretching mightily at his two-sizes too-small silk shirts. He sported a mullet-style hairdo that looked ridiculous even by the standards of 1985; a look that did nothing to conceal a Frankenstein forehead that seemed to grow larger every day. One day, just for kicks, I went down to the library (this was before Terri showcased her nose-and-ear wiggling abilities) and thumbed through the archives of past yearbooks just to get a look at Hanrahan's ever-expanding brow. Sure he taught history, but he would have made a wonderful guest speaker for astronomy class, pulling down his pants and showing off his own unique galaxy of constellations that his hypodermic plunges were sure to have left.

Not that he would have been embarrassed. On the contrary, anabolic steroids were like a rite of passage for Hanrahan's dedicated gridiron warriors, their usage encouraged by parents concerned more with visions of glory than with livers that functioned. Size and strength were the prize, but even the side effects of an expanded brow and a deep boil-like back acne was a symbol of status among the football elite, and the girls that adored them.

Two things were a given in every single lecture he gave: (1) he would mention his five years in the NFL, (2) he would hurt someone's feelings in a way that teachers who had never played in the NFL wouldn't dare.

He was like a big cat in that way, searching his class for weaknesses using whatever tools were at his disposal before pouncing, the more damage the better, as long as it got a laugh out of his players, who made up about half the class.

But in an odd way, I had Mr. Hanrahan to thank for meeting Terri. My very first day in school, as Hanrahan called off the roll.

"Anderson, Jung, where is Jung Anderson?" he called. A tiny Oriental girl raised a meek hand and said, "Here."

"Anderson?" Hanrahan said again, this time in loud sarcastic disbelief. "Anderson? How did a Chink like you get a name like Anderson?" A couple of uncomfortable chuckles from the class, but uproarious laughter from the steroid studs. Then a pause before Hanrahan smiled and went for the kill. "What, did your mother bang a GI in 'Nam?" I bit my lip in anger as the football team turned the classroom into their own little end-zone celebration and Hanrahan shot both arms into the air and yelled "Touchdown!" I looked at Jung Anderson as she put her head on her desk, but the coach wasn't through yet. "Pow, pow, boys,

I got her there!" he said, and then in the lamest and most stereotypical of Asian accents said, "Me so horny, GI, me love you long time." I looked at Clem Baskin, Conestoga's all-conference fullback, and thought his head might explode. His face, always red from the chemicals he shot into his buttocks, was now purple and getting darker by the second as he roared his approval to Hanrahan's delight and Jung Anderson's dismay.

I knew I was next, my last name starting with B. "Brown, Antietam," the football god said, and I looked at his eyes as he contemplated the best way to strike. "Antietam," he said again, clearly pondering the odd name. "I know that name from somewhere." I let forth a small laugh that I knew right away was a mistake, but the idea that a teacher of history couldn't place the word "Antietam" was ludicrous to me. I saw a quick blank expression in his eyes, as I guessed he was not used to being laughed at, then he recovered and said, "What's so funny Ann Tietam, ha ha, how's that, Annnnnn Tietam, how 'bout I just call you Annie for short." Then "How's that sound, boys?" The boys were clearly in favor, and from that moment on I was just plain Annie.

Hanrahan smiled, clearly pleased with himself, and was about to stab into another fragile adolescent psyche when Clem Baskin stood up. "That's him, coach," he said, "the kid from wood shop, the one I told you about." And with that helpful hint, Hanrahan glared at me once more, clearly intending to have himself another heaping helping of Annie Brown.

I was indeed the kid from wood shop, second-period wood shop to be exact. The kid who couldn't wear safety glasses because they kept sliding down the right side of his face, there being, of course, no ear there to support them. The incident might have gone unnoticed had Baskin not heard me explaining my unique auditory circumstances to the shop teacher, at which point Baskin, like a beacon in the sawdust, yelled out, "Oh gross, this kid's got no ear."

So there I was, the new kid in a new town, on the first day of class with a 270-pound behemoth in my face, thirsting for blood. "So . . . Annie," he said, so close to my face that I could almost taste the Anavar he'd eaten for breakfast, "Mr. Baskin here tells me that you're missing an ear." There was a gasp from the general student population, and an anticipatory hum from the team as they took note of the verbal noose that Hanrahan had slipped around my neck, awaiting the hanging that my answer would bring.

For just a split second, I grabbed hold of my quarters, then let them loose with a jingle and went on the defensive instead. "Well, Mr. Hanrahan . . ." Dead silence for a moment and then I brought up my shield. "It may be gone, but I don't miss it."

It took only a second for that laugh to ring out. But that laugh was a wonderful sound, like a solitary trumpet blast amid a symphony of silence. I turned, we all turned, to see its source, and to my wonder, that source was Terri Johnson. Then, as if Terri's reaction had given the okay, a few more kids joined in. But not the squad, which kept a respectful silence in honor of their momentarily fallen leader.

But Hanrahan got up, dusted himself off, and immediately took the low road. "Okay, okay, that's enough out of you, Big Tits," and then an "I got her there, boys." Which elicited a few weak laughs, solely out of courtesy, from the team.

Then his attention was back on me, for, after all, Terri was a cheerleader, and therefore an extension of the team, and even though her social dealings with Hanrahan's 'roid warriors were minimal, there was no use picking on her when there were so many easier, weaker targets to choose from.

"Congratulations, Annie, you just made my shit list," Hanrahan said. "And you did it in record time."

Maybe I had, but as the local sports legend turned and picked out his next victim, I turned back to look at the girl with the auburn hair and smiled. And she smiled back.

So I had put up with the Annie stuff, and though I may not have liked it, I tried not to give it much thought, even as the name grew in popularity among the general student ranks, and my name, which had been given to honor a fallen soldier, became a big joke. But other than the name,

Hanrahan gave me some space, and concentrated his main efforts on prey that didn't talk back.

But this strange new romance between the school's homecoming queen and the earless guy had clearly renewed Hanrahan's interest in Annie Brown. So he began firing back, showing the tenacity that had made him a Pro Bowl nose tackle, before a knee operation sent him into early retirement with a full disability package to cushion the fall.

On this particular day, he was giving Bill Bradford a particularly hard time. Bradford was a soccer player, a fact that placed him just slightly below the common earthworm in Hanrahan's eyes. As the goalkeeper on a team that was in dead-last place, Bradford was easy pickings for a man whose football team was 6–0 and was steamrolling its way toward a third consecutive sectional title. We were now studying the Civil War, and amazingly Hanrahan still hadn't figured out the Antietam significance.

"Bradford? Bradford? . . . Is that name Swiss?" Hanrahan asked in a transparent act of interest.

"No, Mr. Hanrahan, I think it's English," Bradford said.

"Are you sure, Bradford?"

"Pretty sure, sir."

"Well you looked like you were Swiss in yesterday's game, Bradford . . . like you were Swiss cheese, that is!"

The team went into their celebration and

41

Hanrahan ruled the joke to be a touchdown, and even I had to admit to myself that it wasn't half bad. But Hanrahan wasn't through.

"Maybe your coach ought to sit you on the bench, Bradford, how's that sound? Yeah, sit you on the bench and let Jesus Christ take your place. Yeah, put Jesus in the goal, Bradford, how's that sound?"

Bradford thought for a second and then said what was on just about everybody's mind. "Sir, I don't know what you mean."

"You don't, Bradford?" Hanrahan said with a smile, and I could tell that he was just biding his time waiting for the perfect moment, looking for that cheap shot which had been his forte on the gridiron. "Well, you see I heard . . . that . . . Jesus saves! Get it? Jesus saves!"

And with that the team roared and Hanrahan traded in his referee's hat for a goalie's stance, pretending to bat down shots while he yelled "Save, save." He waited for the laughter to die down, which took a good while, as the sight of his huge body, his veins bulging like garden hoses through cantaloupe biceps, was actually quite funny to behold. Then he turned his gaze to Terri and focused it there, long enough for the entire class to sense tension. For Terri wasn't laughing; to her the subject wasn't a joke, a fact that wasn't lost on the coach as he lowered his gaze from her face to her breasts. And kept it there. Then, while still staring, he said in a just barely audible voice,

"Isn't that right. Doesn't he save? Just ask your father about Jesus. He'll tell you."

He then looked up from her breasts and glared at her, savoring the discomfort that his words had caused. Quietly, with great restraint, Terri spoke. "Mr. Hanrahan, I would appreciate it if you would keep the subject of my family's faith out of your classroom."

Hanrahan just stared, and Terri stared back, until he broke the silence at my expense. "Uh-oh, I'd better watch out or she'll sic her boyfriend on me." A cheap easy laugh. I grabbed for my quarters and held on to them tight as Hanrahan loaded more ammo and fired. "Hey Annie, there's a thread hanging off your sleeve . . . Oh I'm sorry, that's your arm!" He laughed with the class, hit a quick biceps pose, and then fired again. "Halloween's coming up, Annie, maybe you can close one eye and go trick or treat as a needle."

He ruled it a touchdown, and then used both outstretched hands to high-five players, who all hailed their leader, until the bell rang, signifying enough blood had been let for one day. Hanrahan called for attention and yelled out his homework assignments, which he liked to term "Han Jobs."

"Okay, okay, class, you've got one week to complete the following Han Job. Give me a thousand words on the Emancipation Proclamation." He then pointed to Russell Peterson, a child of African-American heritage, who in addition to being on the soccer team with Bradford also washed dishes with me twice a week at Frank 'n' Mary's, and said, "Peterson, I expect yours to be extra good. Let's face it, without that proclamation you'd be picking cotton."

Terri charged out of the class and called for me to follow. Through the cafeteria and into the courtyard, where she let out a bona fide scream. She clenched her fists, opened, then clenched again, and tried to talk but just let out a breath of air. Then, regaining her composure, she said, "How could he, Andy, how could he?

"He's met my father one time. Once. For dinner after last year's big game. Hasn't even stepped foot in the door of my father's church. So where does he get the nerve to criticize him?"

"Terri, if you can't stand Hanrahan and you don't like Clem Baskin and that bunch, why in the world do you cheer for their team?"

She mulled it over for a second, because in reality I'd hit the nail on the head. Terri didn't even like football, had only one or two friends on the team, was ostracized by her fellow cheerleaders for being a prude or a "CT," as they called her (a phrase that took me a while to decipher), and hated the coach's guts. Then she smiled and gave me an answer that was hard to refute. "Because I know you like the way I look in the sweater, big boy." And when I blushed and looked down, she picked up her offense. "Come on, Andy, admit it. You might as well. Because I saw you staring that very

44

first week. Staring at my boobies, Andy. Yes you were, you bad boy."

Now she was reprimanding me as if I was an untrained pup caught in the act of chewing his master's new shoe. I loved every second of it.

"Come on, Andy," she continued, "tell me your thoughts, you naughty young boy, why were you staring at my boobies?"

Maybe you had to be there to understand, but trust me when I say that the tone was not sexual in the least. It was fun, and gentle and innocent, and when she told me to be careful, because they were actually dangerous weapons, well who was I to disagree. And when she ran after me with both boobs in her hands, yelling in sixties-horror-film-style, "GONNA PUT THEM ON YOU ANDY . . . GONNA PUT THEM ON YOUUUU!" I had no choice but to run.

When I looked back at her, as strange as it sounds, it wasn't the dangerous boobies that first caught my eye. It was her smile. The happiest, friendliest smile in the world.

OCTOBER 30, 1985 / EVENING

Tietam Brown looked out the front window, his arm pulling the curtain back, his face pressed to the glass like that of a five-year-old looking for the faint glow of Rudolph's red nose on Christmas Eve. He stood in that position for so long that I became a little concerned. "Dad . . . Dad, are you okay?" I said, and then waited for about a minute for some type of reply. Without moving his face from the glass, he finally said, "Will you look at that, Andy, will you look at that?"

"Look at what, Dad?" I replied, and Tietam Brown just said, "Damn Sugling," and continued his long stare before adding, "Always trying to show me up . . . damn Sugling." Finally he turned away and summoned me to his special reconnaissance perch, where the glass was still fogged from his breath.

I looked, expecting some type of small emergency, and instead saw Charlie and Gloria Sugling erecting a small scarecrow, surrounded by a couple of simple pyramids of pumpkins, outside on their front lawn. Behind me, I heard my dad say, "Can you believe it?" and I wondered in silence just what the hell he was talking about.

He then whispered, as if we were caught up in some web of conspiracy, "Always trying to get one up on ol' Tietam, Andy, always trying to stick it to your old man." Finally I couldn't take it anymore, let out a nervous laugh, turned from the window, and said, "Dad."

"Yeah, Andy?"

"You're starting to scare me a little."

"Why's that, kid?"

"Because I have no clue what you're talking about. All I see is Mr. and Mrs. Sugling decorating their yard."

Tietam put his palm to his balding head, joined me by the window, put his arm loosely around my neck, and said, "Exactly. That's exactly what I'm talking about. They're decorating their yard."

Great. That cleared up everything. Now my dad really was starting to scare me.

"Andy," he said, "last year, before we got back together, I put up a hell of a Christmas display. Lights, an electrical Santa Claus, the works. Then Sugling, who had never so much as had a tree in his house, decides he's going to become Thomas Allen Edison and light up his whole house like it's Yankee Stadium. People were coming around in their cars just to look. So now here it is, October, I put out a hell of a Halloween display, and Sugling, who last year didn't even buy candy for the kids, and then hid in his house with the lights off so no one would knock, decides one day before Halloween that he's the Great Pumpkin or some damn thing and tries to outdo me again. Well screw them, I'm tired of the Suglings screwing Tietam Brown all the time."

I tried not to laugh, but man, it was hard. The veins in my father's neck were bulging out, and his hands were shaking he was so mad, and I didn't have the nerve to burst his bubble and tell him that his big speech was about the most ridiculous thing I'd ever heard.

First he'd talked about how he and I had "got back together," as if we were Simon and Garfunkel planning a reunion concert instead of a father and son who hadn't seen each other in seventeen years. Then he'd mispronounced a middle name that most ten-year-olds would know, before talking about his "hell of a Halloween display" as if our house was the set for *The Shining* or something. The guy had literally put a pumpkin on each side of the front steps, and a sign that said "Boo" on our front yard. Total time invested . . . maybe three minutes.

But most ridiculous of all was his contention that the Suglings were always screwing him. Because how I saw it a week earlier, or I guess "how I heard it" might be more accurate, it had been Tietam Brown screwing the Suglings . . . or at least one of them.

My dad's face lightened up a little, and his veins disappeared back under his skin, and he shook his head and said, "Not anymore, Andy, not anymore. You know why?" I shrugged my shoulders. "Because this Christmas, Andy, we'll have a setup that you won't believe. People will drive by to see *our* house, Andy, and as for Charlie Sugling and that little wife of his, well they'll just have to live with it."

He looked up just slightly, as if picturing this whole scene on our living room wall, and said, "I don't know how yet, Andy, but we're going to do it. And they'll just have to live with it."

I looked up at the same spot on the wall, briefly tried to envision this holiday extravaganza, and had to admit to myself that it sounded pretty good. I'd been listening to Nat sing the season's virtues for years, but had pretty much been void of any Christmas cheer for the last decade or so.

A nudge from my dad brought me back. "I nailed her, you know," he said, and when my mind drew a blank, he filled it right in. "Mrs. Sugling, I nailed her."

"I know, Dad," I replied, and looked at him looking at me, a big smile on his face, as if he was a child who'd just handed his mom a good report card and was waiting for a pat on the head. "I know you did, Dad."

"And," Tietam said.

"And what, Dad?"

"And . . . did she sound like she loved it?"

"Yeah, it sounded that way to me, Dad."

Satisfied, he adjusted the curtain, patted me on

the back, and walked up the stairs. Triumphantly. Then he walked halfway back down, looked down at me, laughed, and said, "You're damn right she did, Andy, you're damn right she did."

Later over dinner, a microwavable monstrosity that was barely edible, he became the vision of the concerned parent. "So Andy, tell me about this big dance."

I told him about the Superdance, an annual all-night affair that the school held to raise money for muscular dystrophy.

"Man," he said, "that's a lot of dancing. You ever danced before, Andy?"

"No, how about you, Dad?"

"Only between the sheets, kid. Only between the sheets." Then, while chewing a piece of chicken that looked to be tougher than the Pittsburgh Steelers front line, he said, "When does it start?"

"In about an hour."

"Need a ride?"

"Yeah, Dad, that would be great."

He swallowed hard, put his elbow on the table, and rested his chin on his hand as if he were Rodin's *The Thinker.*

"Andy," he said.

"Yeah, Dad."

"Maybe you can have the car for the night."

"Really?"

"Sure, I've got some work to do anyway. Besides, this is a big night, but hey, no drinking, all right?"

Man, this was pretty cool. Real interest in my

life, real honest-to-goodness parental concern, and the keys to the car for eight hours of Terri. So what if I'd never danced. I could always learn, right?

Then Tietam spoke, and as was becoming his custom, he was right there to seize the special moment with just the perfect sentiment. "You might want to get her to polish your knob while you're driving, kid. No feeling like it in the world."

Sometimes I kind of envied the little world my father seemed to live in. A world where making a scarecrow was a bigger sin than nailing the next-door neighbor's wife and where drinking behind the wheel was no good, but a one-handed kid with no license, spasming wildly while trying to drive along unlit back roads, was okay. I thanked him for the suggestion and told him maybe I'd try, and he slid me the keys and wished me good luck.

I put the keys in my pocket and headed up the stairs, where I turned on the shower. I stepped in and replayed the day in my mind, smiling a big goofy smile as the room turned to fog and the water beat down on my neck.

I thought about Hanrahan's class, and how not even his Neanderthal ways or his football cronies could ruin the day. I thought about Terri, and how she'd stayed so calm and strong on the outside even while boiling within. Then I thought about that wonderful smile, while she laughed and chased me with her breasts, and all of a sudden the thought of her holding her breasts while

51

chasing me didn't seem so gentle or innocent. No indeed, it seemed pretty damn sexy, and I closed my eyes and imagined that same scene, except in this scene she was naked, and I wasn't running away. No, I was running right toward her, running hard. Literally.

I looked down and something about me had changed physically. Had changed quite a bit. I assessed the situation a moment longer, and, with the help of a handful of my dad's pale blue Head & Shoulders, participated in the ritual that so many millions of teenage boys before me have performed, and that so many million have likely performed since. But unlike those horny teenagers, who were just obeying their hormones, I was accomplishing a whole lot more. I was practicing. Practicing and building up endurance, getting ready for the day when I wouldn't be the only one involved in my sexual encounters. And when that time came, I knew I'd be ready. And that I'd be good.

The nuns at the Petersburg Home for Boys had referred to it as "touching oneself in an impure way." One, Sister Fahey, had even tried to explain nocturnal emissions by likening our equipment to a kettle that just occasionally "boils over" as we sleep. I was thirteen at the time, and honestly had yet to touch myself in an impure way. To me, this boiling-over process sounded a little scary, and so I instantly concocted a solution that made a whole lot more sense, not to mention would ruin a whole lot less undies.

"Excuse me," I said, "but if we know that our kettle is going to boil over, wouldn't it make sense for us to pour some water out ourselves before we go to sleep?"

The class roared with laughter, and I received a rap on the palm with a ruler and a lesson about "the sin of Onan" from the nun. But my hand didn't hurt because she had smacked the dead one, and to tell the truth I had loved the laughter from the class, as it was usually the only gesture of acceptance that I received. So a moment later I raised my hand, and shared with the class my biblical knowledge.

"Yes, Mr. Brown," Sister Fahey said.

"Um, ma'am," I began with a completely straight face, knowing that the consequences of my next words would be heavy, but that I was more than willing to pay them. "I do believe that the sin of Onan is not about touching one's self, but about the act of coitus interruptus."

Bam! I caught a slap in the face.

I looked at the class, and they were howling. Even Richie Majors and Mel Stolsky, who only a few days later would attempt to forcibly sodomize me, seemed to be enjoying the moment.

I waltzed down the stairs a clean man, in body and conscience, despite what the nuns would have thought of me. Tietam Brown was waiting for me with a smile and another blue three-pack. He slipped the rubbers into the shirt pocket of my green-and-black plaid flannel, laughed a big fake laugh, and said, "What took you so long in there, kid?"

I thought I would die.

"Getting extra clean?" he said with playful sarcasm.

"I guess so, Dad."

"Or were you doing something just a little naughty in there?" with the last four words spoken in a singsong voice so that they were extra painful.

I said nothing, but looked for a spare hole in the middle of the living room that I could dive right into.

"Hey don't be embarrassed, kid, we all do it, even ol' Tietam, just to keep my bald-headed champion in fighting condition."

I haven't really enjoyed a boxing match since.

Then, as I was headed out the door, where I hoped the crisp October night might kill some of the heebie-jeebies my dad had just let loose on me, ol' Tietam let fly with some helpful advice.

"Don't take the dice down this time, son . . . Women love them."

I hopped in the car and took the dice down immediately, but as I did so I thought of him calling me "son" for the first time, and realized that I liked it.

Eight hours with Terri, I thought, and it was going to be awesome. More like seven hours by this point, but still plenty of dancing to do. It was going to be a special night.

A special night deserves a special song, and I didn't want to get caught unprepared with only Barry Manilow to celebrate with . . . even if, as I've mentioned, "Mandy" and "Could It Be Magic" do still hold up well. But with all due respect to Barry, he had to go.

I looked in the eight-track player and saw that Barry had been replaced by KC & the Sunshine Band. I contemplated its possibilities. Nope, it wouldn't do. Then again, "Do a little dance, make a little love" was not bad advice.

No, wasn't right.

I opened the glove box with my good hand and pawed through the selections. Village People. Nope. Paper Lace? What the hell was that? ABBA? Was my father caught in some type of time warp or what? This was 1985, not 1975. Only two selections left. I reached in again and pulled out Manilow, who I believed might get the decision by process of elimination. Then, with hope fading, I pulled out the last of the ancient eight-tracks, and bingo! Springsteen. *Born to Run*. No offense to *Born in the U.S.A.*, which was all over the radio in '85, but *Born to Run* was, is, and always will be *the* Springsteen album to have.

I backed out of the drive, saw my father waving to me, and wished that I'd left the fuzzy dice up until I was at least out of sight.

By the time I heard the piano on "Thunder

Road," I was over it. I took a slight detour en route to Conestoga High, opting to cruise past Terri's house for a little added inspiration.

I was handling that Fairmont like a pro, and had my right arm draped over the passenger seat, wishing my fingers could move so I could stroke Terri's imaginary hair, while I carried on an imaginary conversation complete with imaginary laughs. When it came to imaginary conversations, I kicked ass big-time.

Suddenly I had a premonition, and took my hand off the wheel to press the forward button on the stereo. In an instant I heard Bruce Springsteen singing my life story. "One soft infested summer me and Terry became friends, trying in vain to breathe the fire we was born in." I didn't really know what that breathing-the-fire thing was all about, but that part about me and Terri was perfect.

I knew as I barreled past Terri's house one last time that this was meant to be our song, even if we'd never actually done the things that Bruce and his Terry had done, such as sleeping in an old abandoned beach house and getting wasted in the heat. I listened again as I passed by Terri's house again, this time being the last for real, but couldn't really get all that much of it, partially because the Fairmont's speakers shook anytime the volume was up past 5, and partially because, well, honestly, Bruce sounds like he's singing in a cave on that one.

It was eight-thirty by now, or about six and a half hours left, when I stepped into the high school gym. I looked around for Terri and saw instead a jumbled mass of about a thousand bodies, moving seemingly in unison to a song I can't quite remember. Actually I can't quite remember anything, except that my heart was pounding, and that I was possibly the most hated guy on the planet, or at least in Conestoga High at the time.

I saw a bright glow of red and tried to focus, which worked, and was relieved to see that it wasn't so bad, it was just Baskin's skin, attached to his face, which was asking Terri to dance. What the hell! Asking her to dance, gesturing at the dance floor with his big arms, his tight satin shirt nearly ripping at the seams. Terri was shaking her head, and she was looking around. Looking for me, but I didn't quite dare make myself seen.

Baskin was resilient, but still Terri declined, and for a split second I stepped forward, so as to approach and say, "Excuse me, the lady's with me," and escort her to the floor. But instead I felt weak and sat down, looking out in amazement at all the mullets surrounding me. They were every-where. Those short-in-the front, long-in-the-back, shaved-on-the-side horrible mullets. All around me. I saw a quick flash and imagined myself smack-dab in the middle of the Michael Jackson "Thriller" video, and it was horrible. I mean that video is always horrible, and Michael Jackson by himself is pretty scary, but instead of being surrounded by corpses and ghouls, he was surrounded by Conestoga High football players in mullets. And right in the front was Coach Hanrahan, with the most frightening mullet of all.

The flash went away, and so did the horror, and I looked for my Terri and saw her still looking. Looking for me. I wanted to just run to her, take her in my arms, and spin her around. And you know what? That's exactly what I was going to do. Just as soon as I went back to the car and listened to "Backstreets" one more time . . . for motivation.

I unlocked the car, hopped in, and played the song one more time. This time I thought I heard Bruce saying something about trying to walk like the heroes he thought he had to be. The song ended, and I decided I was ready to return to the gym. Almost. I checked out a different song.

I heard the opening chords of "She's the One," and I swear it was like music to my ears. Wait a second, that's got to be the dumbest analogy I've ever heard. Of course it was music to my ears. But when Bruce started singing, I felt that magic, and knew he was singing for just me and Terri once again.

Once again the Fairmont's speaker system didn't shed much light on just what Bruce was talking about, but by the time I made out "with her long hair falling and eyes that shine like a midnight sun" and Bruce launched into the Diddleyesque guitar solo, I found myself right outside the

Lincoln Theater, where for some reason that will never quite become apparent to me, I took in the last hour of *Rambo*.

"What do you want, John," Colonel Trautman asked Stallone as I tried to figure out just what "eyes that shine like a midnight sun" might look like.

"Just one time," Rambo/Stallone replied, "for our country to love *us* as much as we love *it*."

I got goose bumps. What a great line. Last time, I'd been too busy worrying about the rubbers in my pocket to fully appreciate it. My heart went weak. Those damn rubbers—they were in my pocket again! Quickly I threw them down to the sticky concrete where, chances are, they might still be today. Then I walked out of that theater, no longer simply motivated, but glad to be an American too. I fired up that Fairmont, opened the windows so that the fortyish or so air could further invigorate me, drove directly to the Conestoga High gym, walked into the gym with purpose, and immediately panicked again.

I was just about to bail out again when I heard Terri's voice.

"Andy, Andy, it's me, over here."

She ran to me with outstretched arms, hugged me tight, and kissed me three times in the cheek-to-temple area. She sighed deep and said, "I'm so glad you're here, are you okay?! I was so worried."

It took a second to answer, as I was trying to figure out if we had technically just had our first kiss. When I did answer, I wished I hadn't.

"Sure, sure, I just went to the movies."

"The movies," she said, somewhat taken aback. "Why would you go to the movies when you knew that I wanted to see you here?"

"Well, I did show up earlier—"

She intercepted, and said, "And you didn't see me so you left?"

With that interception she had given me my out: if I just agreed, I would be out of hot water, and better yet, I could place the blame on her for not being there for me. I told the truth instead. Damn.

"No, I saw you, but—"

"But you left anyway?"

"Well," I mumbled, "kinda."

"Andy, how do you think that makes me feel?" she said with both hurt and anger apparent in her words.

"I'm sorry," I said. "Really."

"What did you see?"

"*Rambo.*"

"*Rambo?*"

"*Rambo.*"

"Andy, that's our movie."

"I know."

"So."

"So?"

"What were you thinking?"

At this point I officially began to whine.

"Terri, I don't feel comfortable here, can't we just go somewhere?"

"No, Andy, I can't just go somewhere. I'm the

head of the Superdance committee. I have to be here."

"But Terri."

"But Terri what?"

"But."

"Yeah."

"I just, well, I just, you know, I just, um, don't think a lot of people like me here."

"Well Andy," she began in a loud voice that was near a yell but then settled down to a softness that could barely be heard above the throng of Superdancers and the sounds of KC & the Sunshine Band. Honestly. "Boogie Man." "Andy, you're going to have to decide for yourself, what's more important? Those people liking you"—she pointed to the mass of dancers—"or me."

I looked at her features continue to soften, and then she smiled.

"Look," she said, pointing my attention to Mr. Hanrahan, who was serving as a chaperone, and at the moment appeared to be getting a little too close with one of Terri's cheerleading associates. "There's your buddy. Do you want to hang out with him . . . or me?"

I smiled.

"Or him," she continued, and pointed to Clem Baskin, who now had his shirt off, so that the acne on his back stood out like a cluster of small red mountains amid a sea of white flesh. "Do you want to hang out with him?"

"No."

"Then I'll tell you what I want you to do, Andy. I want you to go home now, because I have a lot to do here without baby-sitting your emotions. Go home and think about what you really want. And if you decide that what you want is me, then we'll move on. And Andy . . ." She paused a moment and continued, "One of these days, you're going to have to kiss me."

My heart started pounding, and the watermelon returned in my throat, bigger than ever. I tried to read her mind. Was she trying to tell me to kiss her now? Did one of these days mean today, right now? I thought it did, decided to act, then saw the thousand strong in the Conestoga High gym. What if "one of these days" didn't mean today? Was I man enough to face a rejection right there, in front of so many witnesses? I decided that, no, I was not ready, and meekly, without the slightest hint of intestinal fortitude, said, "Don't worry, I will."

"Bye," she said.

"Okay, bye."

And while the speaker played "I'm gonna keep on lovin' you, 'cause it's the only thing I want to do," I slunk out of the high school gym, looking back once to see Terri waving, thinking that even from that distance, I could see a small tear in her eyes. Her eyes that shine like a midnight sun. Whatever the hell that means.

I got into the car and pulled *Born to Run* from its slot. Bruce, you'd let me down, man. Let me down bad. Slowly I opened the glove box and put the Boss away. I closed my eyes, pulled out another eight-track, and slid it in, sight unseen. Then, as I pulled out of the lot, I pushed it in with the palm of my right hand.

"Macho, macho man—I want to be a macho man."

I stopped the car. Ejected the tape. Opened the door. And threw that SOB as far into the woods as I possibly could.

Silence, I decided, was what I needed to hear.

OCTOBER 30, 1985 / 11:57 P.M.

I was in urgent need of a man-to-man talk. A talk with someone who could understand my feelings, with someone who knew about life and all the mysteries tucked away inside its many wrinkles. I chose instead to talk with my dad.

I walked inside our little home, kept oddly neat for a single man and his teenage son. The living room was bare, with not a painting adorning its walls or even a television to gather round. Indeed the room served only as my father's all-nude workout room, the deck of playing cards and a few dozen empty Gennys the only reminder that life actually transpired within its walls.

"Dad, Dad," I called, "I'm home." Silence. I gave it another try. "Dad, it's Andy, are you home?" Nothing. I knew that my father often spent hours on end inside his bedroom, the place he went to do his "work," which he often spoke of in the vaguest terms possible. So, with a heavy heart and a giant question mark for a brain, I headed up the stairs, nursing the tiny hope that Antietam Brown IV could shed some light on the last few hours of clouds that had formed over my life.

I knocked lightly and received no response, then again, and heard the faint sound of papers rustling from seemingly far away. I had never been in my dad's bedroom, as it was strictly off limits and kept most of the time under lock and key. "This is where the magic takes place, Andy," he'd once said. "And a good magician never reveals his secrets."

"Dad, it's Andy, are you in there?" I said, and I heard a door shut and footsteps approach.

"Andy?" he asked through the door.

"Yeah, Dad, it's me."

"What do you want, kid?"

"Well believe it or not, I just want to talk to you."

"I'm pretty busy here, Andy."

"It won't take too long, Dad . . . promise."

"I don't know, kid, like I said, I'm pretty . . . well what do you want to talk about anyway?"

I was hoping to maybe ease into the subject gently. Maybe with a little small talk. But small talk wasn't easy with a guy whose only real interest seemed to be his penis. I couldn't talk sports because he didn't watch them, couldn't talk business because it was, like his bedroom, off limits to me. I didn't even attempt to discuss schoolwork with him, because that might actually require thinking; a demand that might threaten his standing as the world's shallowest man. But what the hell, who was I going to talk to, Hanrahan? Mrs. Sugling? I gave Tietam Brown a shot.

65

"Uh Dad, I um, wanted to ask your advice on girls."

Instantly I had an answer. "I'll be right down."

I walked downstairs and waited about half a second before my dad came vaulting down the steps, two at a time, grinning from ear to ear, as giddy as a schoolboy. For a minute I thought I might have sold the old man a little short. Maybe everyone has got a special talent, and this subject would prove to be his. Maybe he would be my love doctor.

He sat down on the couch, relaxed but alert, clearly relishing the opportunity to help and looking like he might, just might, be able to.

I didn't know what to say, and for a moment I looked at my dad and thought about the push-ups, and the beer, and the Pussycat, and the rubbers, and thought I must be crazy. Then I closed my eyes and fired away.

"Dad, I'm having girl problems."

He resumed his dinner-table *Thinker* pose and stroked his chin. He squinted a little and then closed one eye, a study in concentration. Surely he was weighing all the options, drawing inevitable conclusions, and would momentarily come bubbling forth with a sparkling nugget of knowledge that could transform my life in an instant. Then again, this was the same guy who'd used the term "bald-headed champion" only a few hours earlier. What had I been thinking?

His initial analysis of the situation surprised me.

"Well Andy, taking into account that all women are by nature different, and taking into account that you have yet to introduce me to your friend Terri, I would have to first warn you that forming a specific game plan for your specific situation could prove somewhat difficult."

He sounded smart. My dad sounded smart! I could almost feel those clouds dispersing.

"With that in mind, there are some generalities, some strategies if you will, that do appear to be effective with most women I've encountered."

The anticipation was killing me. Sure my dad had his share of somewhat odd idiosyncrasies, and yeah, maybe he didn't do things that other dads did, but women did like the guy, and there had to be a reason. And I was pretty sure it wasn't the fuzzy dice. He opened his mouth. "Well Andy, whenever possible, get them to lick your ass."

The clouds in my mind that had seemed to disperse accumulated en masse and rained all over my parade. I waited for a big laugh, and then a pat on the back to let me know that I'd been had. We would share a good chuckle over the whole thing, and then he'd tutor me on the lessons of love.

Except he wasn't laughing. Or smiling. Not even a little. As a matter of fact, I'd never seen him quite this intense, not even when talking about the Suglings' scarecrow.

"That way, Andy, no matter what happens after that, you've always got something over them."

I tried to speak, but my jaw was locked in the open position, like one of those Dickens carolers, with their top hats and scarves. Ol' Tietam Brown, for his part, was beaming with pride. His great secret out, his seriousness left him and his demeanor became that of a buddy, a comrade, a pal.

"Andy, I can't tell you how many times I've been out on the town and I run into some babe who's had her three strikes, and you know what I'm thinking?"

My jaw was still locked, so Tietam kept the wisdom rolling without skipping a beat.

"I'm thinking, I know what she's thinking, and I sure as hell know what I'm thinking." He gave me a wink and plowed right ahead. "And do you know what she's thinking, Andy?"

I tried to talk once again, and after a few seconds of stammering answered his question the only way I knew how.

"Um, uh, she's thinking that she licked your ass?"

"There you go, son. Now what am I thinking?"

"That she licked your ass?"

"You're damn right she did, Andy, you're damn right she did. But hey kid, just remember that there's an art to it, okay?"

"An art to the licking?"

"Well, actually yes, but that's not what I'm getting at. I'm talking about talking her into doing it . . . that is an art."

"It is?"

"Sure, look, for me, I like to have had a good time, one, two, three strikes you're out, and then I have the comfort of knowing that I own them, but for you, you really like this girl, right?"

"Yeah."

"Even better. Once it's done, she can't break up with you. She can't because you've got the power."

"What power is that, Dad?"

"The power to tell people about it—it's the same principle that's kept our country safe since we blew those Jap bastards to holy hell to end the big one, World War Two. We had the bomb, we weren't afraid to use it, and everybody knew it. It's the same thing here. You've got the goods on her, you're not afraid to use it, and she knows it."

"But Dad, aren't our butts gross?"

"Well of course they are, Andy, of course they are. But that's their problem, not ours, right? I mean, personally, kid, I find all asses gross, females' included. But some guys can't get enough of them. Like to take the Hershey highway, if you know what I mean. I had a buddy like that. His name was Masters, Luke Masters. But you know what we called him?"

"Uh, let me see, uh . . . Ass Masters, Dad?"

"Yeah, Ass Masters," he laughed. "Ass Masters, that's a good one, huh?"

"Um, yeah Dad, it is pretty good. But all the same, I'm not so sure that I'd want Terri licking me . . . there . . . anyway. Do you have any . . . um . . . other advice?"

"Sure, sure, of course I do."

"Well . . ."

"Well here goes, kid. Don't treat women like sluts. It's cliché. It's unimaginative . . . What you want to do is get them to treat themselves like sluts."

"That sounds a little crazy, Dad."

"Crazy, Andy, crazy?" my dad exclaimed. "What's crazy is all these people who think sex is about the body. It's not. It's about the mind. Once you own their mind, their body will follow. And the only way you can own their mind is to get the ladies to tap into the slut that's inside of each one of them."

"Gee thanks, Dad."

"Listen Andy, when I'm upstairs, how many times do you hear the F word?"

"Lots of times," I said, thinking about a few particularly loud ones.

"But how many times have you heard it coming from me?"

I had to think on that one. For a while. And then said, "None."

"Exactly!" my dad said. "I don't have to, because I lead them to the F word like you lead a horse to water . . . Always remember, son, the F word is a verb. A strong, powerful verb. Use it sparingly, but use it with force. It's not a noun or an adjective, understand?"

"Yeah." And to tell you the truth, I thought that I did.

A strange look then crossed my father's face, a look of pride and knowledge. He put an arm around my neck and chuckled just a bit. He patted my head, then playfully grabbed me and gave me what kids used to refer to as "noogies." Maybe still do.

"Andy, my boy, I think it's time."

"Time for what?" I didn't have any inkling of what my father had on tap, but I knew it would be weird.

"Come on, let's head downstairs."

Downstairs meant the basement, with which I was familiar. Our washer and dryer lived down there, where I did the family laundry once a week, making sure to wash his nasty sheets, all by themselves so that they wouldn't touch my undies. The basement also had a separate room, which was always locked. On several occasions, my dad had made it quite clear that my entry into that room was forbidden.

But on this night, the forbidden zone was exactly where we went. Tietam fumbled with his key chain for a moment, then unlocked the door, insisting that I close my eyes before he swung it open. He escorted me into the room and pulled a string that turned on a bare lightbulb. He granted me permission to open up my eyes, which on first impression revealed relatively little.

A weathered furnace. A pair of old dumbbells,

collecting cobwebs on the concrete. A rusty ax leaned against the wall, casting a thin shadow on a large book, which lay unceremoniously amid two rattraps in the corner of the room.

I was disappointed momentarily. I had expected something more. Coming from my father, something much, much more. I turned to face my father, whose eyes were gazing upward. A happy gaze. A proud gaze. I decided that I too would gaze.

Within a fraction of a second, my disappointment disappeared. My expectations were surpassed. My faith in Tietam was restored.

Two ropes hung from the ceiling like an X, from which some clothes were hanging. Panties, hundreds of them, were hanging from these ropes.

"Not bad, huh, son?" said my father, sounding content and peaceful, bordering on serene.

I was unable to respond, my jaw being once again locked temporarily in Dickensian caroling mode.

"Andy, this here represents my hard work. Every girl I've Teitamized since I began collecting back in '76, our country's bicentennial. With the exception of a few who bitched so much that I let 'em have 'em back . . . Now, kid, what do you notice about these panties?"

Luckily, I had just concluded my silent carol, enabling me to offer up an astute observation. "Um, that there are a lot of them, I guess."

"You're damn right there are," ol' Tietam

gushed, but then quickly became serious. "What else, son?"

I shrugged my shoulders, unable to absorb the deeper meaning of the panties. My mind was starting to wander away from the collection, as magnificent as it may have been, and I found myself thinking about the book in the corner, wondering what it was. The increasing urgency in my father's tone brought me back.

"There is quality in almost every pair. This stuff isn't cheap. Hardly any cotton in the lot."

I nodded my head, but Tietam knew appeasement when he saw it, and it made him cry out in frustration.

"Ohhhh! Don't you get it? These aren't a bunch of strippers I'm banging here, these are high-class women. They're not sluts until I get them here, and then I turn them into . . ." His thought tailed off into the air, as if he saw that his cause was lost. Then a big smile filled his face and he shot a finger in the air.

"Never mind, come upstairs with me. I've got a better idea."

He turned off the light, closed the door, and took the basement steps two at a time. I followed him, a good deal slower, thinking about the book, and the door no one locked.

Tietam ushered me into the living room and told me to sit down. "I'll be right back," he announced, and he took off out the door. He sped off in the Fairmont to whereabouts unknown, and

I thought about my horrible, wonderful, miserable, ridiculous dad.

Five minutes passed. Where had he gone? Tietam's couch was saggy. Kind of ugly. My father didn't strike me as a reader. More of a look-at-the-pictures guy. I thought about the book in the basement. Oversized and thick. Like a scrapbook, possibly. A book that might shed some light on my father's past so that I could better understand my own.

Five more minutes passed. The book was calling to me. Like Poe's "Tell-Tale Heart," this book was a living thing; it wanted me to hear its stories, to see its ghosts, to share its secrets. I had to look. I took the stairs two at a time.

I pulled the bare bulb's string and followed the ax's shadow to the book. I took it gently from the floor, taking care not to disturb the rattraps as I did so. But the springs were snapped and caked with rust; their intended prey had taken refuge a long time ago. I brushed dust and rat poop from the book's brown leather cover. Old traps and new poop.

I opened up the cover, my pulse racing as I did. The first page fell out from its binding and fluttered to the floor. A black-and-white photo of a soldier. World War II I guessed. A soldier who now lay amid feces and mildew, underneath a canopy of panties. The soldier deserved better. I picked up the photo and placed it back inside the album. The photo had been torn in half and yellowed tape in thin neat strips served to reconcile the soldier's image. My grandfather? I looked for some family resemblance, but I couldn't really tell.

I turned the page. My father. No guessing here, although he was obviously a good deal younger. Maybe eighteen, nineteen, twenty at most, and in a fighting stance. Maybe he was a boxer, it would explain the scars and broken nose. But in this photo, Father Time and human hands hadn't yet left their mark on Tietam Brown. His smile was sly, and full of hope, as if there was no goal he couldn't reach. I think I could have stared for hours if not for the fear that I'd be caught. He could come home at any second. I had to proceed with rapid diligence.

A simple headline filled one page, reading RIOT IN MONTGOMERY. No story, no date, just three words.

A page from *Ebony* magazine came next, a strange choice for a white guy like my father. A guy who listened to Barry Manilow. Although I think there was a black guy in the Village People. I wasn't really looking when the eight-track went whistling out the window.

The picture was unsettling. The beaten face of a teenage boy who'd been killed in Mississippi. Why would my father have this photo in his scrapbook. Did he know the boy? Did he know the killer?

Another strange photograph, this one from an Augusta, Georgia, newspaper. A woman wrapped in a bloody sheet, talking to police. A headline reading PECAN HEIRESS FENDS OFF ATTACK, and a story I was in too big a rush to read. My heart was pounding beneath my flannel. Butterflies flapped inside my stomach. I couldn't let my father catch me here. What did all this mean? Was my father some kind of lunatic who kept photos of his victims, or just a practitioner of naked exercise who kept the panties of his conquests?

There were other articles, all from southern newspapers. Birmingham, Nashville, Greensboro, detailing the fight for civil rights. Sit-ins, marches, and a troubling one of a fireman with a fire hose blasting a black child off his feet.

Then the *New York Daily News*, the only entry from the North. A two-page story of a man who had moved up from Atlanta and was trying to feed the poor. A black man with quite a biceps on him, holding a small child. The man's name was Eddie Edwards. Maybe Tietam knew him. Maybe they had boxed together, even if the guy looked much bigger than my father.

Finally a story about the first landing on the moon. All in all quite interesting, although it wasn't quite what I had hoped. Not a single thing about my mother, or what my father did for work. Unless he'd been a boxer.

I put the book away exactly where I'd found it. I wouldn't mention coming down, but if he asked me, I'd admit it.

My heartbeat had just regained its rhythm when

the Fairmont came roaring back, a sleek, black Trans-Am close behind.

My father, who was now walking toward the door with his arm around a blonde, his free hand pointing to the "Boo" sign in our yard, had been gone for thirty minutes, give or take a few, and had come back with a female companion. Where had he gone, Sluts "R" Us? Except the woman was not your standard off-the-rack white-trash specimen, the type I imagined my dad did his best with. No way. She was beautiful, in a shimmering red dress that hugged her hips tight. Classy, too. Or at least as classy as you can be while still getting picked up in record time by a middle-aged bald guy who has fuzzy dice hanging from his piece-of-crap car.

Then Tietam and his new friend were in the door, at which point my dad ran into the kitchen and brought forth a glass, which he told me to "hold up against the wall, with your ear to the bottom." Then said, "Listen real close, kid, your dad's gonna put on a show."

"The hell he is," said the blonde, who turned to my dad with fire in her eyes. "You promised me a good time, not a circus sideshow, Tikki."

"Tietam," my dad corrected her, then turned on a charm that I can only describe as eerie, and said, "Hey, we will have a good time, baby, I promise, but look at the kid, he's lonesome and it's his birthday. He just wants to listen. He won't even be in our room. He'll be next door, just innocently . . . listening."

77

"Promise?" the blonde said.

"Promise."

The blonde grew defensive and said, "I wasn't talking to you, Tatum."

"Tietam," my dad said, correcting her again.

"Whatever," the blonde said with a shrug. "I'm talking about him. No surprises, kid, right?" I nodded. "You're not going to do anything stupid like try to join in, are you?"

"No, ma'am."

"Oh southern boy, huh?" she said, sounding a whole lot less repulsed than she had just eleven seconds earlier. I never have considered my accent to be all that strong, but apparently she disagreed. She sashayed over to me and put her thumb on my lip, rubbed it gently, and said, "Southern boy, you go ahead and listen all you want, and I'll try to put on a little show for you, okay?"

I nodded, and I'll admit right now that the thought of Terri Johnson was a long, long way away from me at that particular point.

"Happy birthday, southern boy."

"Thank you, maaoohh."

The word "ma'am" is a simple one to say, and a short one as well, but somehow right in the middle of spitting out that short, simple word, the blonde caught me in midsyllable with her lips, and she momentarily explored the inside of my mouth with her tongue.

"You go upstairs now and listen real close now . . . ya heah?" she said with those last two words done in a pretty convincing southern belle drawl.

I did as I was told, and went upstairs to my little room and put my glass against the wall so that Tietam Brown could explain the art of the deal.

"Speak into the tape recorder now," I heard my dad say. Wait just a second, 'Speak into the tape recorder'? Was this guy for real? How could you possibly get any lower than tape-recording women licking your ass? Unless of course you are standing next to a wall with your ear on a glass, listening to your father tape-recording women licking his ass. Which is, indeed, a little lower.

"What the hell was I thinking?" I said out loud to no one in particular except maybe my conscience, and put the glass on my desk and laid down on my bed, a pillow on each side of my head to drown out the weirdness. I lay in that position for a good five minutes, hoping that the night's session would be a brief one, and that I could get some rest after what can only be described as the strangest day in the history of my life.

I put down the pillows and sat up in bed, and thought for a moment that my house was the epicenter of a midsize earthquake, as the room was literally shaking. I rushed for my turntable, thinking that maybe Nat could drown out the show that was being put on for my benefit, but my hormones betrayed me and I turned from the turntable, and in a moment found myself up against the wall, my ear cupped to the glass.

"Tell me," Tietam said, "tell me what I'm doing to you." I'd returned just in time.

The blonde in the red dress, who I guessed was now simply "the Blonde," picked up on her cue and told my dad exactly what he wanted to hear. My goodness, that woman could swear. A group of drunken sailors would have covered their ears in the face of her verbal barrage. Just for a moment I turned from the wall to catch my breath, then went back to my observation post, where, to my amazement, the tide had turned. The blonde was no longer talking, being momentarily unable to for a reason I was about to discover.

"Worm that tongue, baby, yeah worm it real good," my dad commanded.

I had turned from that wall for at most fifteen seconds, and the deal had transpired in my absence. I had missed out on the art of the deal!

I wish I could say that the whole thing repulsed me, but I can't. I thought of the blonde in the red dress, a woman of money, a woman of beauty, but a woman so utterly lacking in that special some-thing in life that she had to find solace in my dad's hairy ass.

When the show was over, I waited for the sounds of Tietam Brown's special ritual, signaling inter-mission. The cracking of the Genny, the whoosh of his breathing, even the steady commentary he delivered as he defeated the decks. But the sounds of this night were new, and a little bit sad, and I found myself missing the stability of my father's strange ways. In a way, it was the only constant in my life, a constant that was now replaced by the sound of high heels clumsily navigating the stairs and the spray of the shower in the bathroom down the hall.

Perhaps my father was right. Maybe he'd just been helping the blonde in the red dress play out a role, and she'd return with new vigor to her husband and kids, or her job, or her mom, or whatever she did. I knew nothing about her, except I'd heard her bad words, and I'd tasted her tongue, and it smelled like strong whiskey and a life unfulfilled. Maybe my father wasn't doing any favors. Maybe, in fact, the favors were for him, filling a void in his own sorry life. I pictured my father in his room with his tapes, and the art of the deal. And then I thought of Hanrahan, and his putdowns and jokes. Maybe, I thought, they are almost like twins. Predators both.

I lay in the darkness thinking of Terri, how I would take my dad's great advice and throw it all out, like the Village People eight-track I'd sent hurtling to its wooded grave. I needed some guidance, but not from my dad, so I closed my eyes and asked for help from above, asked to be just slightly better than I currently was.

Then I turned to my pillow, closed my eyes, and saw Terri kissing my mouth with the gentlest of lips. But try as I might, her image started to wane, and the mouth of that pillow became the drunk blonde, and the gentlest of kisses became a

81

probing wet tongue. The same probing tongue that had forced upon me my first kiss. Then Terri was gone and I was alone with the blonde, thrashing and plunging, my pity replaced by the most primal of urges. For once those old nuns were right, for the touching that night underneath my white sheets was impure to the core. The kettle was ready to boil, but turned quickly to ice with the knock at my door.

A moment later, my dad entered the room wearing a T-shirt and sweatpants, and a look on his face that was a stranger to me. In his hand was an envelope.

"Can I sit down?" he said as he flipped on the light switch.

"Sure, Dad, can I get you a chair?"

"Actually, son, if it's all right with you, I'd like to sit here with you."

I gestured him to the bed, and he looked at me for a long time without speaking. The light by my bed created soft shadows on his face, enhancing the scars that creased both eyebrows, and for the first time, I thought, my father looked vulnerable. The corner of his mouth drew up into just the slightest of smiles, and in a voice that was new, he said, "I wasn't always like this. I want you to know that what you see here, you know, in me, is not how I was when I was . . ." and then his voice trailed off, and he held his envelope with both hands.

"When you were what, Dad?" I said. "When you were what?"

"When I was, um, with your mother, Andy. I wasn't like this. I fell in love from the moment I met her. She was a singer. In a club . . . In Japan. God, she made me feel . . . like I was . . . the only man in the world." He swallowed hard, then went on, his voice starting to shake, both of his eyes starting to well. "I thought you should know that." Then, extending his hand to offer the envelope, he said, "This is for you, I'll let you open it in peace," and as he got up to leave, I saw that his cheeks were bathed in fresh tears. "Good night, son," he said.

I opened the envelope and took out a faded black-and-white photograph. A beautiful woman, her hair long and blond, looking down at her hands, which were placed on a huge belly. Those hands cradling her belly as if it were the most precious gift in the world. And I instantly knew, my mother . . . and me, in a time when the future seemed like a friend to us both.

I've thought about that time, Tietam and me, alone on my bed, a great deal over the years, and I always come to those tears on his face. I was his son, and his tears were all real. After all of this time, those tears are still real.

THE RAGE / 1977

I still remember those fireworks. Man, they were impressive. Sure, it was only on television, but as I sat in the Delanors' cozy living room, I could almost feel the heat as blast after blast illuminated the July sky in honor of our country's independence. And when Mr. Delanor put his arm around me and patted me on the back, I felt for the first time in a long time that I really belonged.

The Delanors weren't my first foster parents since the death of the DelGrattos, but they were the first to act as if they actually liked having me around—indeed, during the spring and early summer of 1977, I will dare say that they seemed to love it.

Little Rachel had been adopted almost immediately following her parents' death. She was kind of like a blue-chip prospect. I, on the other hand, was like the last kid picked in gym class when it came to choosing up sides. It could have been the useless hand. It could have been the missing ear. Or maybe, just maybe, it could have been that nagging stigma of having single-handedly wiped out my last family.

So when the Delanors pointed to me on their visit to the Petersburg Home for Boys, I pretty much felt like I'd hit the lottery.

Mrs. Delanor wasn't home on the night of our country's two hundred and first birthday. She was at grief counseling. Her counseling generally took place on a weekly basis, but at certain times, like this night in question, when her sadness overwhelmed her, emergency counseling was made available to her.

Just a little over a year earlier, there was no sadness in Sandra Delanor's life. She had what seemed to be an ideal existence. Victorian house, picket fence, a golden retriever named Shakes, a husband who was a pillar of the community, and a ten-year-old son whom she adored. A ten-year-old son who had accidentally stumbled upon his father's pistol . . . and fired it.

Little Wilson Delanor's pictures were everywhere. Eight-by-tens documenting his elementary school years smiled down on me from every conceivable angle, and snapshots of family vacations seemed to occupy every spare nook and cranny in their spotless home.

With his dark curls and impish grin, Wilson Delanor looked a lot like me, even if I didn't let my impish grin out in the open very often. Enough like me so that passersby in their small town just north of Petersburg did double takes. Enough like me so that as time went by, I realized what my role was. I was the substitute kid. Which might have hurt my feelings if it hadn't been for the fact that Doug and Sandra Delanor were just so . . . damn . . . nice. Damn, they were nice. I know that sounds repetitive, but I really don't know how else to put it.

I can still picture Mrs. Delanor with her happy smile saying, "Andrew, would you like a piece of pie? I just baked it." Or "Andrew, would you like some help with your homework?" Always Andrew, and always with that happy smile. A smile that was betrayed only by the sadness in her eyes.

In many ways, she was Auntie M's exact opposite. She was slim, maybe even skinny, a problem which I guess was compounded by her seeming refusal to eat just about anything. With the exception of an occasional cigarette or drink that she held with shaking hands, I really can't remember anything that she put into her mouth.

Auntie M loved to hug. Maybe even lived to hug. Mrs. Delanor, on the other hand, made contact only with the slightest touch of a fingertip, and even then it seemed like she was forcing herself. Like she was trying to relearn a gesture that had once been so natural.

On one evening in late June of 1977, about four months after my arrival in their home, I had watched as she poured herself two or three glasses of sherry over her normal limit. Had watched as her hands shook less with each passing swig.

She sat down on the couch, and while Mr. Delanor looked intently at his paper, she looked intently at me as I played intently with Shakes the dog. The dog had originally been named Jebby when given to little Wilson on his seventh birthday, but the boy had done a switch in honor of the way the puppy emphatically shook his head anytime an object of any type found its way into his mouth.

On that June night, Shakes was having his way with one of Mr. Delanor's old slippers, and was really growling up a storm as I rubbed the dog's belly and tried to pull the slipper from the clenches of his stubborn jaw. I looked at Mrs. Delanor and saw her smile, which was not unusual. But something about her didn't seem quite right. And then I got it—realized what was different. Her eyes. For the first time, for the only time, her eyes were smiling too.

She tucked me in that night as she usually did, with a story—this one was about a little pony who joined the circus. But on this night, she touched my cheek with the faintest of fingertips and said three words that I thought were long extinct . . . "I love you."

She was already sobbing quietly when she closed my door, and she didn't leave her bed for the next three days, but I will never forget those fingertips or those words. Words that hurt her so much, but made me so happy.

Mr. Delanor was a fifth-grade teacher and coached cross-country, winter track, and track at the middle school. The man liked his running. At one point he'd been a hell of a runner himself, having held a Virginia high school record in the fifteen hundred meters that stood for nearly a decade.

Sometimes he'd take me running with him. I hated it but never had the nerve to tell him. I was afraid it might hurt his feelings, so I played the role of the happy runner, talking with great excitement about that happy day when I would run for his team. That sentiment always brought a smile to his face—a face that seemed to walk a very fine line between all-American good looks and outright nerdism. The strong chin and classic nose said "all-American." The oversized ears that supported thick black-framed glasses said "nerd" in a way that Potsie Weber or Ralph Malph couldn't even begin to approach.

Mr. Delanor didn't attend grief counseling with his wife. He said that he'd "come to terms with it" and that "someone had to be strong" in the family.

Mr. Delanor talked a lot about family. And never more so than on July 4, 1977, while we watched the red glare and bombs bursting in air.

"Hey sport," he said to me, utilizing one of the three nicknames he threw my way regularly in random order, the other two being "pal" and "chief." But at this particular moment, I was "sport."

"Hey sport?"

"Yes, Mr. Delanor?"

"Hey come on now, chief, you know you can call me Doug."

"Okay, Doug . . . sorry."

"Hey pal, nothing to be sorry about. Listen, chief, how do you like being part of this family?"

"Oh I like it a lot, Mr. Delanor."

"Doug . . . sport."

"Yes sir, I like it a lot . . . Doug."

"Well then, sport, what would you think about us making it official?"

"You mean . . . ?"

"That's exactly what I mean, pal. I mean you being our son, me being your dad."

I didn't know what to say, so I just nodded my head. Nodded my head while I watched Shakes shake his own head back and forth, a rubber chew toy paying the consequences.

Mr. Delanor said, "Think about it sport-o, think about how happy Mrs. Delanor will be."

I nodded again, thinking about her fingertips and her gentle voice . . . saying those magic words.

"But chief . . . Andrew, there's one thing I need to know before we can make this happen for real. One thing that's real important."

"Yes sir?"

"What I need to know, chief, is . . . can you . . . keep secrets?"

"Secrets?" I said.

"That's right, sport, secrets. Can you keep them?"

"You mean, keep them from . . . Mrs. Delanor?"

89

"Well yes, Andrew, sometimes we might need to keep a secret from your . . . mom . . . for her own good."

"Really?" I asked.

"Sure, sport. Look, I love my wife. And I think you love her too, don't you?"

I nodded my head.

"And chief?"

"Yes sir?"

"She loves you too. You know that, don't you?"

"Yes sir." My voice was but a mouse's squeak.

"But it hurt her to tell you. Do you know why?"

I shook my head slowly. "No sir."

"Because she's afraid she might lose you. She's afraid that you're going to leave her. Leave her like . . . our son did."

I felt tears welling up, but I fought them back. I fought hard. Then I yelled, "No I won't, Mr. Delanor. I won't leave her. I promise. I promise."

Mr. Delanor took it all in, then smiled and said, "Do you keep your promises, sport?"

"Yes, Mr. Delanor, I do, I swear I do."

"Well chief, if you're able to keep promises, then you won't ever have to call me Mr. Delanor again . . . or Doug for that matter. Do you know what you'll call me, pal?"

"Dad?"

"That's right, sport, you will call me Dad, and do you know what you'll call Mrs. Delanor?"

I took a second to fight back tears again, and then managed to squeak out, "Mom?"

90

"Yes, pal, you'll call her Mom . . . if you can keep a secret."

"But . . . um, Mr. Delanor—"

"Dad, call me Dad."

"Dad?"

"Yes, chief?"

"We don't have any secrets."

"No, not yet, but we will."

"When?"

"As soon as you promise . . . are you ready?"

"Yes, I guess so."

"Guessing isn't good enough, pal, I need you to promise. Can you do that?"

"Yes."

"Okay then, chief, here is the promise. Promise me that for the sake of your mother's health, you won't tell her about any of the things that you and I do together. Promise me."

"I promise."

Mr. Delanor smiled and nodded his head. He put his hand on my shoulder and kept smiling. Then he asked me to put out my hand, and when I did, he dropped a shiny new quarter into it. Then he stood up.

"Chief, put that quarter in your pocket. It's for being a good boy. Now you watch that television, and I'll be right back."

With that he turned and walked to his bedroom, leaving me to look at my shiny new quarter. A quarter that I slipped into my pocket just as Mr. Delanor was reemerging from his bedroom, looking to my naïve eight-year-old eyes like a ghost with a pointy white hat.

Mr. Delanor looked at me for a long time. A little too long, it seemed.

"Why are you dressed so funny?" I asked.

"Well, sport, it might look funny to you, but there's really nothing funny about this. No, sport, to the contrary this garment means that I belong to a very important club . . . a club that I want you . . . my son to join someday. Would you like to join the club?"

I thought he looked ridiculous, but again, I didn't want to hurt his feelings, so I nodded my head slowly. As I did, a car's headlights flooded our living room with light. Mrs. Delanor had returned. Mr. Delanor seemed to panic.

"Remember, pal," he said as he ran for the bedroom, "this is our secret."

In his haste he neglected to close his door completely, and from my spot on the couch I could see him slide his bed to the side, pull up a rug, uncover a small opening in the floorboards, and throw his wadded-up ghost outfit into it. He was just skidding the bed back into place when Mrs. Delanor, my soon-to-be mother, walked into the room with her warm smile and her sad eyes.

I woke up that next morning with the realization that I was going to have a mother, a real mother. And a father, a real father. A mother who had said she loved me, and a father who wanted me to join his special club when I got to be old enough. I looked on my nightstand in the room that still housed all of little Wilson's things, and tried to find my quarter. It was gone.

That afternoon, while Mrs. Delanor took her daily nap, Mr. Delanor asked to see my shiny new quarter. Sadly, I told him it was gone.

"Sport," he said, "if you want to join our club, you can't be losing things. That's irresponsible, understand?"

"Yes sir," I said.

"Now chief, if you can't be responsible, we can't have you in the club."

"But I can be responsible, Mr. Delanor. I swear I put it on my nightstand last night, but when I woke—"

"All right, chief," Mr. Delanor interjected, "I'm sure it was an honest mistake. So I'll tell you what . . . I'll give you another one, and to make sure you don't lose it, I'll put it in your pocket myself . . . okay?"

"Okay."

"And remember, don't tell your mother about this, all right?"

"All right."

"About any of it." And then he took the quarter and put it in my pocket. But before he let go of that quarter, I was pretty sure I felt his finger rubbing my testicle. He looked at me and smiled.

"How was that . . . son?"

"Um good," I said, happy to have the quarter,

but not sure of what had just gone on inside my trousers.

"Call me Dad," Mr. Delanor said, still smiling.

"Okay . . . Dad."

Within a week I had fourteen shiny new quarters to my collection, and an accumulated total of two and a half minutes of Mr. Delanor's clandestine pocket pool. The contact was no longer incidental, it was pretty obvious, and the duration was longer with each passing episode. It no longer consisted just of testicular tickling either. No, now my penis itself was part of the act as well. An act that always ended with Mr. Delanor and his goofy smile saying, "Remember, this is our secret."

I weighed the positives and the negatives of the situation. On the positive side, I now had a family. Mrs. Delanor had taken to calling me son, and had even echoed her three magic words after a bedtime story about a girl who had a hundred dresses. As she walked away, I had said, "I love you too, Mom," and she had raced back into my room and for the first time wrapped me in a tight hug, so that the mangled cartilage of my missing ear was crushed against her bony chest. Even so, for that brief moment, her breast seemed like the safest place in the world.

Now, the negatives. Let me see. Oh yeah, I was being molested by the guy I called Dad, and even at the age of almost nine, I knew that something about that was wrong. Sure, I'd made a cool $3.50

in the process, but I still had a hard time rationalizing Mr. Delanor's behavior. I wanted to tell his wife, but I knew I couldn't. She'd be devastated, and besides, I'd given my word.

I turned nine that August. I had a lot of money, 23 dollars and 75 cents to be exact, but my guilt far outweighed my income. I couldn't sleep. I couldn't eat. And most importantly, I couldn't tell anyone, because I'd given my word. To make matters worse, my real father, Antietam Brown IV, was legally fighting the Delanors' adoption efforts, despite the fact that he had shown no fatherly inclination in eight years and nine months. The legal proceedings were taking their toll on Mrs. Delanor, whose naps had become longer, whose drinks had become more frequent, and whose bedtime stories were becoming increasingly less coherent.

My birthday was supposed to be a good time for us. For our family. Dinner at Cappy's Catfish Shack followed by all the games I could play at Players II Arcade. Games that accepted quarters. Quarters that Mr. Delanor was more than happy to give me.

He came into my room that afternoon, while Mrs. Delanor was sleeping, holding a sack of quarters. A whole sack.

"This," he said with a great big animated smile, "is for us. First I'll give you some, just like . . . always, right, chief? And then we're going to try something different, okay, sport? You see, you're going to put quarters in my pocket."

He reached into his sack (of quarters, that is) and came out with two handfuls. He started singing "We're in the Money" in an overly nerdy type of way, a way that might have seemed funny if not for the ball handling that I knew was about to ensue. He danced up behind me and started singing that "money" song from *Cabaret* into my missing ear as he placed quarter after quarter into my pocket. Wow, what a birthday! Not only was I getting rich, but I also got to hear Mr. Delanor sing "Money makes the world go round, the world go round, the world go round" as he played Ping-Pong with my genitals.

Then he stopped. "Okay, chief, now it's your turn. Reach into that sack and start putting quarters into Daddy's pocket."

And I'll be damned if I didn't start to do it. If I didn't just reach right into that sack and pull out a handful of quarters. And truth be told, I guess I really was going to put them into Daddy's pocket.

But then I saw his face, still singing that... stupid *Cabaret* song, and I just instantly realized how wrong this whole thing was. And that if being a son meant having to have my balls felt by Doug Delanor, then I would rather be on my own. And that's when the rage hit me. For the second time in my life, I was overwhelmed by the idea of destroying human life.

So with those quarters clutched tightly in my left hand I instinctively drilled him as hard as I could. Hit him right in the solar plexus, and I heard all the wind leave his body, and I saw him double over, and saw that his head was now at about the same height as mine. And then I threw another punch, even harder than the first—a punch that caught the child-molesting prick in his left eye. Immediately I felt his glasses shatter, and then I heard screams of unparalleled anguish. He brought his hands up to his face and I saw red running through his fingers.

To tell you the truth, I was surprised he was still erect. And by erect, I mean still standing, as I'm pretty sure that whatever sexual sensation he had been feeling had been replaced by the rather unique sensation of glass sticking out of his eyeball.

I wasn't satisfied. I wanted to see him fall. I picked up the sack of quarters with my left hand and spun to my right in two tight circles, as if I were Olympic hero Bruce Jenner throwing the discus in Montreal. As I swung, I was vaguely aware of Mrs. Delanor opening the door to my room, just in time to see me catch her bleeding, screeching husband in the right temple with about sixty dollars' worth of quarters.

Mr. Delanor went down. Went down and stayed down, and with the exception of his left foot, which twitched involuntarily for a few seconds, he didn't move at all.

Mrs. Delanor called 911 and then returned to my room, the room that had once belonged to her son Wilson. She didn't yell at me or even cry. She just sat expressionless as she looked at her unconscious husband, a husband with a piece of glass embedded in one eye.

She never gave me away. Even as the paramedics were loading her husband into the ambulance, she maintained that she had no idea what had happened.

When the last car had left, I heard a knock at my door.

"Come in," I said, wanting to see her but dreading the hurt that I knew her eyes would carry.

She looked worse than I'd feared.

She sat down on my bed, my mattress barely registering her body weight.

Slowly, with great trepidation and pain, she spoke.

"Andrew?"

"Yes ma'am?"

"Please tell me what happened."

I felt my stomach rise into my voice box as I fought off tears. After several moments, I managed to speak, but just barely. "Um, Mrs. Delanor, I don't think I can."

"Andrew, my husband hasn't touched me in a very long time, not since before Wilson left us." A tear left her eye and traveled a long lazy route over her cheek and down her throat. "In a few years, you might know what that means . . . but what I want to say is that . . . whatever happened in here, I don't think it was your fault."

I took a deep breath and tried to talk. Failed. Took another breath and tried again.

"Mrs. Delanor, I can't."

"Please Andrew, please."

"But Mrs. Delanor, I promised."

"Andrew, I want you to . . . I need you to tell me."

"But if I tell, he said I can't be in his club."

"His club," she said, suddenly incensed. "Tell me about his club."

"I can't."

"Please Andrew, I need you to help me. If my husband is in a bad club, then I need to know."

"But it's not a bad club, Mrs. Delanor, it's a good club, where they dress up like ghosts with white pointy hats."

"Are you sure about this club, Andrew, are you absolutely sure?"

"Yes ma'am."

"Andrew?"

She took hold of my hand, squeezed it hard. Harder than I would have imagined she could. I longed for her gentle fingertips on my face. Longed to hear her three magic words again. But I had the sinking feeling that any words I had to offer would only hurt her.

"Andrew," she repeated. "Are you sure? If you're telling the truth I need to know. Are you sure, Andrew?"

"Yes ma'am."

"Can you prove it?"

I wanted to call her Mom again, I really did. But instead I trembled in fear and put my head down, ready, finally, to give in to my urge to cry. To just

99

open up the floodgates and let it all come flowing out. Then I felt her fingertips on my face. And her voice. Pleading softly. Saying, "Help me . . . please."

I told her everything I knew. About the quarters and the fondling and the secrets, and the trap-door in the floorboards underneath the rug underneath the bed.

She nodded her head throughout it all, and then slowly got up from my bed. As she opened my door to leave I found myself blurting out her name.

She turned and tried to smile. She tried to look happy but failed miserably.

"I love you, Mrs. Delanor," I said.

She said nothing but walked to my bed. Took hold of my hand and raised it to her cheek. Let me feel a tear that was in midstream. And then she was gone.

I heard her struggle with the bed, knew the effort had to be great for someone so weak and thin. For a few minutes, maybe five, I heard nothing, and then a single blast echoed throughout the immaculate house. The unmistakable sound of a gunshot.

I walked slowly, very slowly, to her room, thinking, I guess, that I could delay the inevitable.

I saw her lifeless body slumped over the robe of Doug Delanor's secret club, her skull oozing blood onto his stupid pointed hat.

Snapshots were strewn about the robe. Photos of a young boy in poses that no young boy should be in. For a moment, I thought the photos were of me. But they weren't. Just a child who looked like me.

NOVEMBER 6, 1985 / MORNING

"**W**ake up, wake the hell up!"
The demand woke me from a beautiful dream, one that played off the theme of the wonderful talk I'd shared with Terri that cleared the air and put us back on track as a couple.

"Damn it, wake up!" my dad yelled again, and I looked up to see him waving some papers in my face like a madman.

He yelled, "What is this?!" and as my eyes adjusted to the glow of the morning sun that streamed through my window, I could see that he held in his clenched hands my paper for history.

"What is this?!" he repeated.

My mind drew a blank as I reached for the obvious and said, "Um, my history report?"

"And what is it on?" The voice was still intense, but had lowered considerably in volume and had taken on an attorney's courtroom tone.

"It's on the Emancipation Proclamation, Dad."

"Oh the Emancipation Proclamation," he said, as if I'd just been caught in a lie upon cross-examination. "And what exactly did you refer to this proclamation as?"

"I'm not sure, Dad."

"Well let me clear it up for you, Andy. You called it, uh let me see, there, there it is, you called it the most important document in the annals of American history, didn't you?"

"Yeah, I guess," I said in a most puzzled voice.

"And?" my dad asked.

All of a sudden I thought I caught his drift, and although my dad's wake-up procedure and sudden interest in American history had caught me off guard, I adjusted quickly and said, "Well yeah, Dad, it is." It's funny, because for all my dad's shortcomings as a human being, which were monumental, I hadn't really considered him a bigot, his comment about the "no-good Jap bastards" notwithstanding. Maybe, however, he didn't think Lincoln's idea had been a good one. I decided to act.

I sat up in my bed and spoke with authority. "Dad, I'm sorry if you disagree, but even more than the Declaration of Independence, even more than the Constitution, I think that the Proclamation—"

"Shut up!"

"But Dad?"

"But Dad nothing, I told you to shut up!"

I heeded his demand, said nothing, and stared.

"Most important document in the annals of American history?" he said, sarcasm dripping all over his words.

I said nothing.

"The annals?" he said.

Said nothing still.

"This document," he said, "doesn't belong in history's *annals*, Andy, you know that?" I didn't reply. "No," he continued, "this document belongs in its *anals*, because it is a stinking, steaming piece of crap."

"It is?" I asked, and I realized that my voice had taken on the exact same inquisitive, innocent tone that I'd used during our last talk about the anal area.

My father then laughed and said, "Yeah it is," and for the next few minutes I listened with great interest as my father became a teacher, his philosophy debatable, but his integrity beyond reproach.

"Andy, what was the proclamation's main purpose?"

"To free the slaves, right?"

"No, just some of them, kid."

"Well which ones were those?"

"The ones he had no legal right to free, Andy. You see, the proclamation wasn't a moral issue, it was a political one, dressed up in morality. He only freed the ones in the South, the ones who were part of a country that didn't take orders from the US of A. Are you with me?"

I nodded I was.

"They were Confederate slaves he freed, Andy, which meant what?"

"Um, that none of them actually went free?"

"Not a one. But what about the slaves in the

Union? The Kentucky slaves, Maryland, Delaware, did they all go free?"

"Probably not."

"You're damn right they didn't, Andy, you're damn right they didn't."

"What should he have done, you know, Lincoln, about the slaves?"

"He should have grown some balls and just let them all go. Each godforsaken southern state. They've been weighing us down for the last hundred and twenty years, Andy. He should've just let them go."

I thought of this new Tietam Brown I'd just met, the one who had reared his head in between naked push-ups and perfecting the art of the deal. I liked him but he worried me, and he brought with him a tension that hung like a curtain between us.

Finally, after a minute of silence, I said, "So what should I do?"

"Do about what?"

"About my report?"

"Throw it in the garbage."

"But it's due by today."

"Just throw it out."

"But I'll have to—"

"Andy, take that report, just throw it out, lay back down and get your rest, and I'll take care of everything, okay?"

"Okay."

"Now throw out your report."

"I will."

"Now." A demand, but a gentle one, and like a nice Jonestown boy with a cup of Kool-Aid, I wadded up my papers and, without a thought to the consequences, tossed them away.

"Good boy," he said, and with a pat on my shoulder, he was out of the room, leaving me nearly drunk with the buzz of his words. He was weird, but he cared. What more could I want?

Then I snapped out of it, the reality of my predicament bringing me to like a fresh cup of hot joe.

What was I going to do? Tell Mr. Hanrahan that my father wouldn't let me bring my paper to class because the Emancipation Proclamation belonged up history's ass? I thought about Russell Peterson, the black boy from class, and how he would feel about my dad's thoughts. Who would Russell Peterson have found more offensive, Hanrahan or my dad? I wouldn't know, for although I washed dishes with Peterson and we talked all the time, our level of intimacy started and stopped with the Buffalo Bills. If you lived in Conestoga, you had to make a choice. The Giants, the Jets, or the Buffalo Bills. But all of those teams, and sometimes breathing itself, took a distant backseat to the town's undying love of its Conestoga Togas (yeah that really was their name) and their loyalty to their fearless leader, Coach Hanrahan.

A fearless leader who would eat me for lunch when I showed up for seventh period without my report.

Then in a twinkling, I heard on the roof the prancing and pawing of eight little hooves.

That's what went through my mind, although it's not quite right. But the sound of Tietam Brown on a typewriter, clicking away on those keys as if he were a pro, was as altogether happy and surprising as a visit from St. Nicholas.

Click, click, click, click for a good hour or so, and then while I ate cornflakes, my father came down and placed his work on the table, gave me a slap on the back, and said, "Well, what do you think?"

I pushed the cornflakes aside and picked up his work, and as I read through the words, I could hardly believe that this was the same guy who had spoken of "bald-headed champions." This guy was a scholar, who in just over an hour had poured forth a well-reasoned argument, complete with footnotes and quotes, that, while stopping short of painting Abraham Lincoln as a full-fledged racist, certainly cast a shadow of doubt on his long-heralded character.

For a moment, I just looked at him, then started to laugh and said, "Dad, this is great," and made my way out the door, but returned immediately to ask one brief editorial question. "Dad?"

"Yes, Andy." His face beamed with pride. A true father with a son.

"Can I really call Abraham Lincoln a cock-sucker?"

NOVEMBER 6, 1985 / AFTERNOON

"Great, Peterson, just great. I'm sure you realize that without the Emancipation Proclamation, you guys wouldn't be making millions of dollars in the NBA."

Hanrahan had struck again, somehow managing to give both a compliment and a racist insult within the same twenty-five words. "Thank you," Peterson said, but his words were lost amid the roar of Hanrahan's players' raucous laughter as the great coach and historian pretended to shoot jumpers at the front of the class.

After sinking a buzzer-beater with a three . . . two . . . one, swish, he turned his attention to me. "Annie Brown, Annie Brown, would you care to share your report with the class?"

"Yes sir, Mr. Hanrahan."

Which I proceeded to do, and with each passing sentence, I could feel Hanrahan's hatred growing around me in a steroid-filled haze. He took his feet off his desk and got up from his seat, glaring at me as I went into the homestretch, the really good meat at the end of Tietam Brown's thesis. I knew that I shouldn't but I just couldn't stop, and while Hanrahan hovered over me, just three feet to my left, I called Abraham Lincoln a cocksucker in a tone of voice that bordered on joy.

A hush filled the air of room 325, and I looked back at Terri, who was looking at me, a sly little grin on her face to let me know she was proud. Not at the words, but for having the guts to say them.

The rest of the class looked at Hanrahan as if he were the outlaw in an old western flick, the music having just stopped when he entered the saloon.

"Annie Brown," the coach said, "I've been teaching this class, as well as coaching this school to sectional championships, for the last eleven years, and that is the most vile, racist garbage that I've ever heard."

"Then, sir, it's a good thing that I live in America, where I'm entitled to say it."

Hanrahan seethed and yelled, "Not in this class you're not, because tomorrow morning I meet with the principal, and your name will come up, and I can guaran-damn-tee you that with just a snap of my fingers"—and he snapped them for emphasis—"you'll be out of this class. Out of this class and out of this school, so you can go back down to Georgia or wherever you came from, and you and your southern fag friends can all reminisce about how Abraham Lincoln kicked the asses of your gay southern granddaddies!"

The speech earned him a standing ovation from

his team, and even applause from some other lost souls who thought that kissing his ass might save them their turn at Hanrahan's gallows.

I raised my hand until the laughter died down, at which point a content Hanrahan said, "Yes, Annie Brown, and make this one good, because it's your very last words as a part of this class."

"Mr. Hanrahan, I just wanted to point out that my grandfather, or great-great-great-grandfather, fought on the side of the Union."

"The hell do you mean?" Hanrahan snorted.

"Well yeah, he did, otherwise my name would be Sharpsburg, wouldn't it?"

"The hell do you mean?" Hanrahan said again, obviously fond of those distinguished five words, although he spoke them this time with just a touch of befuddlement.

"He was killed in the battle of Antietam, the bloodiest day of the whole Civil War. It's where I got my name. The North always referred to the battlefields according to the closest body of water, in this case Antietam Creek." My voice was picking up steam. "The South used the names of the towns they fought near, which is why I am Antietam, and not Sharpsburg, Brown." I then measured up Hanrahan, who now glared directly over me, looked up at his fuming face, and let my final words fly. "Look it up in your book—it's called history. You. Dumb. Ignorant. Jerk!"

For just one single second, I owned that whole class. I heard quick sudden laughs, and I even heard cheers, undoubtedly from some who had just moments earlier been kissing some ass. Even the silence of Hanrahan's goons was like the sweet sound of vengeance, and I savored its ring. And Terri Johnson, whose laugh had first paved the way for our friendship, laughed hardest of all. And then a sickening thud replaced all of those sounds, and I went down like a shot from a crushing blow to my cheek, delivered from the closest of ranges by the strongest of men.

"Andy," Terri yelled, and she dove from her desk and cradled my head, which began streaming blood all over her hands. "Andy!"

The rest of the class just stared, even the football players, who seemed momentarily stunned by what had just transpired.

It was Hanrahan himself who broke the silence. "You little bastard, get out of this class. Take that redheaded bitch and get out of the class." I looked up through my fast-closing eye, through the blood and the goofy glow that exists along that fine line between incoherence and consciousness. I briefly pictured Vinnie DelGratto as Hanrahan went to his knees, but it was Hanrahan's voice that shook me out of my trance. "You son of a bitch, you get to your feet. You walk out of that door, and you don't say a word!" Then he stood and admonished the class, "Not one of you will say a single word. Not a word. Understood? Because I run this school, and if I get a report that one of you, just one, saw a thing, I will personally guarantee that you will know pain. Got it?" The class did.

I staggered down the hall and outside, with only Terri's arm and a good deal of guts to keep me up. "I'm okay, I'm okay," I just kept repeating, as if sheer repetition would make me believe my own words. My eye was now swollen shut, and it throbbed with pain with each beat of my heart. Terri, I saw through my one decent eye, was streaked with blood; her white cashmere sweater had turned a soft pink. But the sight of her face in all its concern made me feel that my eye was an awfully small price to pay for all her attention.

"Andy," she said, "I'm taking you home," and we walked to her car, our two bodies as one. We stopped at her car and she opened the door. She helped me climb in, then it was out of the lot and down Broadhurst Road until the school's visage was history, although the afternoon's memories were still open and raw.

She weaved her way toward Elm, holding my hand between the shifting of gears. I watched her drive, a vision of loveliness with a look of concern. Like the thrill of victory and the agony of defeat all wrapped up in one beautiful package. And that thought made me wonder. If I could take it all back, would I? The whole lousy day. The wake-up, the report, the reading-out-loud, the punch. Would I take it all back? Not on your life. Not if it meant missing the chance to bond with my dad, to stick it to Hanrahan, and, most of all, not if it meant missing this drive. I looked once again at her ivory hand, the drying blood turning to rust, and then looked up to see her passing my street.

"Terri," I said, "you just missed my house."

"I know," she replied, then she turned with a smile, let go of my hand, and shifted to fourth.

"But I thought that you were taking me home."

"I am taking you home—my home."

We pulled into her drive, to the estatelike manor with its lawn decked out in shrubs and bright vibrant mums of brilliant oranges and yellows. And pumpkins galore, all over the yard. I briefly thought of my father in all of his glory, and wondered if he thought the pumpkins were here just to screw with ol' Tietam.

"Andy, one of these days I want you to meet my parents," she said. "And one of these days, I want to meet your dad."

"That would be awesome," I said, although I instantly knew that "awesome" was probably not the best way of describing my feelings on the inevitable first meeting of Tietam and Terri.

I said, "Is your father home now?" and secretly thought, Oh please say no, oh please say no.

"Not today, no, both of them are at a meeting in Syracuse for the day." She opened the door, grabbed my arm, and said, "That's part of the reason that I brought you here now, big boy."

Her house was immaculate, and seemed to ooze money. The kitchen was spotless. Gleaming white countertops and real marble floors. The luxurious living room stood in bold contrast to mine. A real

Persian rug. The finest of furniture. And though I'm not a connoisseur of fine art, the paintings I knew must have cost a nice buck. Especially the black velvet Elvis that hung over the mantel. (Just kidding about that one.)

All of a sudden she became Florence Nightingale and cleaned up my wounds with sensitive hands, her mothering instincts clearly taking command. Next she went to the freezer and emptied two trays of ice cubes into a towel, which she put gently on my eye, telling me softly, "Just keep it there." She declared me "all healed," and then walked down the hall and emerged with a sweatshirt and a simple request. "Take that shirt off, Andy."

Oh man, this was embarrassing. I wasn't real big about changing in public, a fact that almost made me feel blessed that my hand cxempted me from phys ed and those post-workout showers that allowed pecker-checkers to size up the competition. I thought of a Kinks song where Ray Davies looks in the mirror at his pigeon chest and has to put on his clothes because it makes him depressed. I didn't really know what a pigeon chest was, but I was pretty sure I had one.

Thinking quickly, I said, "But it's your dad's shirt, won't he miss it?"

She laughed, "It's Winnie the Pooh. I got it three years ago for him, and he hasn't worn it yet. Go ahead, put it on."

I looked at Terri, who must have either read my mind or seen the fear written all over my face, and she said, "All right, all right, I'll turn around. But one of these days you're going to have to stop being so shy." A pause, and then, "Come on, I'll show you my room."

"But won't you be late for cheerleading prac- tice?" I said. Yeah, thataway, Andy. Add to your league-leading average in the "boneheaded plays" category.

"No," she said.

"Are you sure?"

"Yes."

"How come?"

"Because I just quit."

"You did . . . ? When?"

"When I walked to the car with you, Andy."

A sudden chill raced up my spine, and my legs nearly collapsed.

"You did that for me?"

"Yes, Andy, I did, for you and me both. That whole stupid team has given me nothing to cheer about. I'm just sorry I didn't decide on it sooner." She paused for a second, looking a bit sad, then looked up, gave a smile, and playfully said, "So my parents aren't here, I have nowhere to go, I'm alone in my house with nothing to do . . . Andy . . . why don't you . . . come to my room?"

Her room was a mixture of little-girl dreams and a teenager's tastes, as if she'd gone to bed at five and woken up at seventeen, with no record of the years in between.

But the room's centerpiece was the man in her

life. No, not me, but Jesus himself, who was well represented throughout the whole Johnson house, but particularly here, where his presence was known in several ways. Not least of which was a cross over her bed, where it hung so the Savior was staring at me, as if to say, Don't even think about it.

While I stared at the cross, Terri rummaged through her top dresser drawer and came out with a book that she handed to me.

"This is my diary, Andy. It's got all of my thoughts. I write things in here that I would never say in school, or even to my parents. No one's ever seen it, except for you now. I want you to look at just this one page that I wrote as soon as I got home from the big dance. You remember that dance?"

"Not all that well. I wasn't there long."

"But I bet you could tell me all about *Rambo*, couldn't you, Andy?" she said, and I put my head down and just shook it in shame.

"Andy?"

"Yeah."

"I'm going to jump into the shower so I can clean off your blood—no offense—and while I'm in there, I want you to read what I wrote. Okay?"

"Okay."

"But just that one page."

"You got it."

"I'll be right out. Now ready, set, read."

But I didn't read then, at least not right away.

Instead I thought of her saying "so I can clean off your blood" without even the slightest sign of revulsion. The shower turned on, and I heard her lightly step in and draw the curtain closed. I thought of that blood swirling around the drain— how absurd it was that Hanrahan's hatred had yielded this special time. Then I looked at the diary.

Dear Diary,

What a disaster this whole evening was. The Superdance was a Superdud, and I spent most of my time dodging the football team and wishing Andy was here.

Andy, oh my Andy. Such a nice boy, but such a pain in the neck. I had such high hopes for this night, but Andy went to see *Rambo* and then I chased him away. Right at the end, before he walked out the door, I thought he might kiss me, like I wanted him to, but he just turned away and walked out that door.

It made me so sad, and for a second I thought that maybe it would be best if we didn't go out anymore, because he cannot deal with the attention I bring, and he cannot understand that I'm not a big deal. I'm just a girl that wants to be kissed. By him.

But now as I write, I've never been so sure about anything as I am about him. He just needs some help, and I'm willing to give it. I may be the only one who really knows how.

And I have a gift that I want to give Andy. I think that he'll love it, but he won't get it for free. He'll have to give up something of his own. Something he's had all of his life.

Until tomorrow,

Terri.

I read that last part three or four times, until I felt like Burt Ward's Robin in the old *Batman* show, trying to figure out riddles that Frank Gorshin's Riddler had left. Then I smiled and thought back to my third Halloween when Auntie M had walked Johnny and Rachel and me, for that one night doubling as Batman, Batgirl, and Robin. How she'd yelled "Pow!" and "Bam!" at each opened door while us kids showed off our batfighting skills. "Pow!" "Bam!" "Boom!"

What kind of gift could she give that I'd love? Anything, actually, as long as it was from her. But what could she possibly want in return? Something I'd had all of my life? That narrowed it down, because I didn't have much. Except for old Nat, and surely . . . Oh no, that must be it, she wanted my Nat King Cole, and as much as I liked her, or loved her, I guess, that album was more than an album to me. It was . . .

The door slowly opened, and Terri appeared, her wet auburn locks framing her face. Gone was the blood along with her makeup. And she shone with a beauty so natural and clean that I surely knew if she asked me for Nat I'd give it up quick, with no questions asked.

And the shirt she wore. Just a white long-sleeved shirt, but man it looked good. Unbuttoned down so I could just barely see a hint of ripe cleavage.

She sat on the bed so her bare legs touched mine, which I wished right away were not covered with jeans.

"Did you read it?" she said, and pointed her finger to the last paragraph, the one with the riddle.

"Yes, yes I did."

"And what did you think?"

"Um well, I'm not sure I get it."

She then placed the finger a little bit up and said, "How 'bout this?"

"What?"

"Did you read it?"

"I did."

"And what did you think?"

My eyes focused in on the words by her finger, and my heart nearly dropped when the words got through to my brain. I opened my mouth to speak, but those eleven words, and the thought required to analyze them and make some small sense, was almost too much for me. I couldn't be asked to think and then speak at the same time. It was sensory overload. So when I opened my mouth, not a whole lot came out. Just "Uuughh, ughhhmuh."

"Andy."

"Uughh."

"Andy."

Her hand, which had been in the harmless upper-knee area, had just swept to the right, and was now bordering on dangerous inner-thigh territory.

"Yes."

"Read it to me."

"Read it?"

"Yes, read it to me . . . please."

I took a deep breath. Hoped for some strength and read. "I'm just a girl that wants to be kissed. By him."

"Andy?"

"Yes?"

"I am."

"You are? . . . What?"

"Just a girl . . . that wants to be—"

And then I was kissing her. A magic moment in time. When my body just acted, paying no heed to my mind. A kiss of such sweetness. I had to do it again. And my lips met hers, and pressed firmly ahead, and I opened my mouth, just ever so slightly, and our tongues gently touched, and performed a small dance, until her tongue won out and entered my mouth. In an instant, I knew, all my practice had paid off. I had kissed Terri and I knew . . . I . . . Was . . . Good.

She withdrew her tongue and pressed her forehead to mine, until our eyelashes touched. Kept it that way, then jokingly said, "See, that wasn't so bad," and then, "Andy, lay down."

She took hold of my hand and gently pushed on my chest, easing me down on her tiny soft bed. With a sweep of her arm, she scattered stuffed animals, until just she and I were finally alone.

She straddled my torso and leaned slowly down, so that her small hint of cleavage came springing to life. I caught just a glimpse as she lowered her lips and bathed my wounded eye with her kisses. The swelling was huge but it hurt not a bit, her soft tender kisses were life's best medicine.

Then she pulled back her hair and kissed at my neck, her tongue gently darting as she made her way to the place where an ear had once been. My cringe was involuntary, slight but still there, and she read the thoughts of my body and put them at ease. "It's all right now, Andy," she whispered into that stub, then she kissed it so gently while I softly whimpered. And then she rose in a wet blur of auburn and a swell of soft cleavage.

"Terri," I said, in a voice so soft it sounded distant.

"Yes, Andy Brown."

"This is the best."

"The best what, Andy Brown?"

"The best . . . day of my life."

"Andy?"

"Yes."

"It's about to get better."

And with that my eyes grew as, one at a time, button by button, the cloth slowly gave way. And then the shirt parted and I just about died. "Oh

Jesus Christ." It just burst forth from my lips, the words out of my mouth before I could think that maybe her room wasn't the appropriate place for that particular expression.

But Terri just smiled, and she looked down at me, then looked at her cross and put her hand on my mouth.

"Shh, shh," she whispered, then said, "I think it's okay with him if it's okay with you."

"Are you sure?" I said, and she nodded her head.

"Andy, does this feel wrong to you?"

"No, to tell you the truth, it feels pretty good."

"It feels good to me, too." She paused, then said, "I want you to touch me."

"Touch you, touch you where?"

She took hold of my hand and, guiding the way, made an arc for her breast. And then there was contact.

"Oh Jesus Christ." In a chemical reaction that seemed inconceivable, in a period of time that can only be described as instantaneous, my whole body shook. My voice made little gasps, and my face made expressions that I wouldn't want to see on video for a million dollars. Like that (snap of the fingers) I was done. All that planning, all that practice, all down the drain.

I then took on that look that all of us get. That look that we get at the exact moment that great pleasure runs smack-dab into even greater humiliation.

I looked up at Terri, who was smiling at me. A

real smile, too, not just an "I'd better smile so he doesn't feel even worse" smile.

She reached down and kissed my eye, my nose, my forehead. "It's okay, it's okay," she said.

"Are you sure?" I asked, my vulnerability at a peak that mankind may never come remotely close to again.

"No, it's not okay," she said. My heart sank. Then she laughed. "It's better than okay. It means you really like me . . . don't you?" Then, before I could answer, she told me, "Come here," and with a wave of her finger brought me up from my back so I sat up on the bed. "Come here," she said again, and she eased my face into her bare breasts, and she rocked me like a child and placed kisses on my head. And those breasts, which only moments earlier had induced such a spasm, suddenly became the safest place in the world.

She drove me home at ten-fifteen. After having treated me to dinner at Friendly's and a showing of *Pee-wee's Big Adventure* at the previously unthinkable Seven Valley Twelve. No one died in this movie, and even if it didn't offer the emotional wallop of Rambo's "love us as much as we love it" closer, it was nice to see a movie without the soft-drink residue of a previous generation sticking to my soles.

No, on that night, the stickiness was right where it belonged, in my underwear, which I would later wad up and put in my small box of keepsakes as

122

a rather odd souvenir of the most horrifying five seconds of my romantic career.

There in the darkness of the Seven Valley Twelve, life seemed to be pretty good: an ice pack on my face, a huge shiner on my eye, a hand inside my own, a warmth in my heart, and a load in my shorts.

"Andy, when am I going to meet your father?" Terri asked as she pulled into my drive. I had to think about how best to approach this subject. Honesty, as usual, was the policy I went with.

"Probably not tonight," I said.

"How come?"

I looked at my dad's silhouette in the window, moving up and down, up and down.

"How come?" Terri repeated.

"Because he's exercising naked in the living room."

"Really?"

"Yeah, really."

"No."

"Yes."

"Wow." She paused. "I thought my father was the only one who did that." She burst out laughing, and I did too, although the idea of her father's middle-aged balls would come back to haunt me at a later date in a most inappropriate fashion.

"Good night, Terri," I said, and leaned over to kiss her, taking the initiative for the first time in our relationship.

She leaned back, away from the kiss, and extended her arm instead and said, "Let's just shake on it, Andy." A pause, and then another burst of laughter, followed by a meeting of lips. "Good night, Andy . . . you keep ice on that eye."

I walked into the house and tried to keep my right eye out of view, and started climbing the stairs. "Hi, Dad, good night," I said, wishing just a little that my swollen, closed eye was facing him so I wouldn't have to see his penis brushing the shag carpet with each descent of his push-ups.

"Hold on, Andy," he said with a voice that, judging by the slight slurring, seemed to have become acquainted with about its twelfth beer of the evening. "Eight, nine, ten."

"Okay, Dad." I stopped, but stayed in my surreptitious stance.

My dad stood up from his push-up position and cracked open another Genny. Sweat was pouring off his body, but he wasn't breathing heavily in the least. I looked at his deck, saw that only two or three cards remained, and silently dreaded the encore performance that was sure to make its presence felt through the Sheetrock between us.

"All right Andy, tell me why you're so late . . . and hey, tell me about your report . . . I'll bet it was the only one that told it like it really was, huh?"

"Yeah, I think it was, Dad. My teacher was really, um, moved by it."

"Great, great," my dad said, "but hey, why so late?"

"Uh, I went to the movies with Terri."

"Oh yeah?" he said in just such a way that I instinctively knew he had a follow-up question lined up. And I knew what it was. "You get any?"

I tried to get away without an answer.

"Come on, did you? You can tell your father anything."

"Maybe just a little."

"Hey, that's great," he said, acting, I guessed, as some dads would when their kids get accepted to Harvard.

"Thanks, Dad."

"How much did you get?" he said, and I felt my face flush at the mere mention of this whole scenario.

Without really thinking, I turned just a bit, and my father took in the dramatic change in my face.

"Holy shit!" Tietam yelled out. "What the hell happened to you?"

"Just a fight at school, Dad, no big deal."

"A fight? A fight with who?" Tietam asked as he stepped forward to inspect the damage.

"Well, I uh, I uh, read my report in class and the teacher—"

"That son of a bitch!" Tietam yelled. "That son of a bitch! I'm gonna settle this, Andy, goddammit, I'm gonna settle this."

Settling this, I was pretty sure, did not seem to involve a mature and educated debate on the Emancipation Proclamation, but a physical confrontation that would be a mistake of epic proportions. Mr. Hanrahan had already left his mark on Antietam Brown number five. I didn't think adding number four to his collection was something I wanted to be part of. So I tried to stop it.

"Dad, please, he—"

"Not now, Andy, not now. What's his name, Andy, what's his name?"

"Mr. Hanrahan, Dad."

"Hanrahan, huh, Hanrahan?" my dad said as he found the telephone book and started tearing through it. "Haggerty, Handlelong, Hanrahan, there it is. Hanrahan, H. 272 Quaker Path. Son of a bitch!"

"But Dad," I pleaded, "this guy is huge." Hanrahan had to have had a hundred pounds on my dad, and deck of cards or no deck of cards, my father was going to get his ass handed to him. Apparently, he didn't think so.

"That's all right," he said, grabbing the car keys off the mantel.

"He played in the NFL."

Tietam stopped short and looked me in the eye, all semblance of wildness suddenly gone, replaced by the calmest of looks. "Even better," was all he said.

"But Dad," I yelled after him as he headed out the door, "you can't go . . . you're naked."

He stopped and turned around. I hoped that he'd come to his senses, or at least come for his trousers. Instead he opened the door, still nude and still calm, and said, "Give me your pants and tell Mrs. Baskin upstairs that she'd better not wait."

Mrs. Baskin upstairs? Mrs. Baskin? As in Clem Baskin's mother? My dad was nailing Clem Baskin's mother? I laughed to myself and gave him my pants, momentarily oblivious to the fact that my father was embarking on a suicide mission. After he left I walked up the stairs in my history-making underwear. Put on sweatpants and knocked on the door next to mine. "Excuse me, Mrs. Baskin."

"Southern boy, is that you?"

Holy crap! She was the blonde with the red dress. The blonde with the red dress was Clem Baskin's mom. The one who had stuck her tongue in my mouth, who had let me listen to her put on a show. The one who had licked my father's ass. Suddenly I understood, if not completely agreed with, my father's philosophy. I now owned Clem Baskin by proxy, because his mother had licked my father's ass. I had the power.

"Yes ma'am, it's me. Um, my dad had to leave, and he said not to wait for him."

"Is that so?" she said, trying to sound defiant but instead sounding merely jilted.

"Yes ma'am."

"Southern boy?"

"Yes ma'am."

"Call me Amanda."

"Yes ma'am, Amanda."

"Southern boy?"

"Yes m—Amanda?"

"Would you come in here please."

My heart pounded fast. Pounded, yes, because Clem Baskin's mother the ass-licker was requesting my presence, but pounded more so because my father's room was off limits.

"Amanda, I don't think that I should."

"Just for a minute," she said. "Promise. I won't bite."

"All right."

I opened the door and made a quick survey of the room. Clothes and shoes were everywhere. What did he even have a closet for? Then I thought of the sound of the typewriter keys coming, it had seemed, from behind its door. I looked at Amanda Baskin. A pretty face peeking out from under the covers, her hair fanned out on the pillow, the scent of sex and rejection heavy in the air.

"Well hello," she said, trying to sound sexy, and succeeding too. Then, as I moved closer into the light of the room, "My goodness, what happened to you?"

"I was fighting, Mrs. Baskin."

"Amanda, please," then, "Southern boy, you don't look like a fighter to me."

"Well actually, I just got punched in the face. Someone else did the fighting."

"Well come here then, come here. Come here and let your mother take a look at that."

I knelt down beside the bed and let my cavalcade

of emotions fight it out for supremacy. Which one would win out? Disgust? Pity? Sexual arousal? Sexual arousal started to pull away. She touched my eye gently and I could smell the booze on her breath. Booze and my dad's ass? Disgust took the lead.

"Oooh, that's quite a lump," she said, then paused, shifted gears, and spoke again. "Do you think I'm pretty?"

"Yes ma'am." No hesitation in my answer.

"Call me Amanda."

"Okay."

"Tell me I'm pretty."

"Right now?"

"Sure, right now, southern boy, tell me how pretty you think I am."

I hesitated, and somehow realized I was being assigned the rather fragile task of ego repair. Pity made a charge for the lead now, although sexual arousal was hanging tough in the stretch.

"Amanda, you sure are pretty."

"Do you think I'm beautiful?"

"Yes," I said, "I do." And at that moment she was.

"Tell me I'm beautiful."

I didn't know it then, but she was essentially playing a far more subtle version of Tietam Brown's "Tell me what I'm doing to you" game. Planting her ideas in my head, trying to pass them off as my own.

"You are beautiful, Mrs. Baskin."

"Amanda, please . . . Amanda."

"I think you're beautiful, Amanda."

Pity dropped way back, and disgust had pulled up lame and had to be shot. Sexual arousal was now all alone and heading for home.

"Southern boy, your father doesn't think I'm beautiful, does he?"

"I don't know, Amanda." Now pity was back, sexual arousal having slowed down considerably when the word "father" was said.

"My husband doesn't think I'm beautiful either."

"I'm sorry about that, Mrs—Amanda."

"Did you like listening to me the other night . . . with your little glass up to the wall?"

Arousal sped up. Way up. "Um, uh, yeah, I did like it," I said, my voice cracking just a little.

"Did you like the words I used . . . those bad words . . . did you like hearing them?"

"Yes." I was still kneeling by the bed, and her mouth was only inches from mine. For a moment, I thought she would lean forward and kiss me, and to tell you the truth, I think I would have let her. Instead she turned away. Turned away and said, "I liked saying them too, liked knowing you were listening. Liked turning you on. But you know what I really like?"

"No, what?" I could only whisper, having been momentarily shocked by Mrs. Baskin's admission.

"I like to be held." I nodded. She paused and continued. "My husband hasn't held me in years. Ignores me. Your father, he doesn't ignore, but he doesn't hold me either. That other stuff's nice, and your father, he does it real well, but at the end of the night, I just want to be held, and your father . . . well, that's just not his thing."

"No, I guess not."

"Andy," she said, the first time she had used my real name.

"Yes . . . Amanda."

"Would you hold me right now?"

I didn't say yes, and I didn't say no. I think I went into shock, and the next thing I knew, she was lifting back the sheets, exposing her breasts, saying, "Lie down with me, southern boy, it's warm next to me."

I think that I would have, had it not been for her breasts. A beautiful pair they were, too, round and real firm, maybe too firm, as if they were made of more than just flesh. And that's what ruined it. Unfortunately for Mrs. Baskin, she had to compete with Terri—whose breasts, I had decided during the course of my split-second encounter, were definitely real. Mrs. Baskin possessed the second most beautiful breasts that I'd ever seen (which I guess also means they were the ugliest by process of elimination).

"Do you like them?" she asked.

"Yes ma'am, I do."

"Tell me you like them, southern boy."

"I better not."

"Oh why?" she said, her sexy, hoarse voice betraying a little girl's plea.

"I just better not." I started to get up.

"Southern boy."

"Yes."

"Do you know my son?"

"Yes ma'am, I do."

"Do you like him?"

"No ma'am, I don't."

"Did he do that to you," she said, pointing to my eye.

"No."

"But he's not a good boy, is he, he's not good like you?"

I thought of myself only days earlier, pleasuring myself to the thought of her, and wondered how good I really was. "No, I guess not," I said.

"But you won't tell him about this, will you? About any of this?"

"No ma'am, I won't."

"Do you promise."

"Yes ma'am, I do."

"Call me Amanda."

"I promise, Amanda." A promise that would cause me great pain to keep.

"Andy."

"Yes."

"Stay sweet."

"Thank you."

"And Andy."

"Yes ma'am . . . Amanda."

"Can I ask you for one favor . . . a little one."

"Okay, I guess."

"Let me give you a kiss . . . just one, I promise."

I was scared half to death. Scared that she'd jump me, and scared that I couldn't say no. Scared that I'd lie down and hold her and say and do whatever she bid me. I wanted to hold her too. Wanted to hold her and maybe magically transfer a little of my meager supply of self-esteem, because, sadly, Mrs. Baskin had none of her own.

I knelt down again and pursed my lips just slightly, but she took hold of my face and turned it, gently, ever so gently, kissing my swollen eye. Then, with her lips still on my skin, she said, "Tell me again . . . tell me I'm beautiful."

I turned to look at her, my face still in her hands. A tear, I could see, had dropped from her eye.

"Amanda."

"Yes, southern boy."

"You are . . . beautiful."

And with that I heard a car's engine, and I looked out the window, expecting Tietam Brown's Fairmont but seeing instead a late-model Lincoln slowly cruising past our house.

She left minutes later, and for a while I lay in my little bed wondering if I should have accepted her offer and kidding myself that I would have done it just for her instead of myself. I thought of her kiss, and her requests, and her breasts, and of the late-model Lincoln pulling away, looking out of place in the night on our quiet little street.

She was, I thought, the saddest woman I'd ever

seen, and I had a strange thought about her breasts—that if I had breasts like hers, I'd be happy all the time. Then I thought of her blond hair, splayed out on the pillow, and her question about beauty, and I felt a strange sense that I'd just played a scene straight out of *Of Mice And Men*. Then I heard Burgess Meredith say something about "what happened in Weed," and a quick Meredith retrospective ran through my mind. Quack-quacking as the Penguin, then yelling "Down, stay down" at Rocky, then putting poor Lenny out of his misery.

Then I thought about my day and how out of all the events—a first kiss, a first feel, a first punch from a teacher, not to mention Amanda—the one that seemed oddest was my father's report. The clicking of the typewriter keys from inside his closet. Why in the closet? So I rose up and for the second time in my life, as well as the second time in an hour, entered my father's room.

Tietam Brown's closet was a library. Literally. A U-shaped walk-in closet that had been reconstructed into a genuine floor-to-ceiling library. Books were crammed into every available shelf, and large stacks grew like stalactites from the floor for the overflow of volumes the shelves could not contain.

A reading table sat in the middle of the closet with a typewriter, books on Lincoln, slavery, and the Civil War strewn about. I sat down in his chair and looked around, feeling, I imagined, the same way the detective who discovered the bodies in John Wayne Gacy's crawl space had felt upon making that grisly find.

No light reading for Tietam Brown, either. Not a novel to be found. Instead the shelves housed books on subjects beyond my scope of understanding. American history, world history, psychology, physiology, religion, politics, and seventeen different titles concerning Japan. I wondered if just maybe this library had been left behind when Tietam moved in. Part of me hoped so. For considering the alternative meant opening my mind to the very distinct possibility that there was a whole lot more to Antietam Brown IV than met the eye, or met the glass held up to the wall next door.

I stood up from the writing desk and opened a few random volumes. A musty old book on human kinesiology, its margins filled with handwritten notes on almost every page. *The Art of War,* its cover falling off. A King James Bible. Passages were highlighted, pages were dog-eared. Stuck in the Book of Luke I saw a black-and-white photo of a much younger Tietam shaking hands with a man whose face I had seen before. Where had I seen it? The muscular arm answered my question. This was the guy who was feeding the poor. Eddie Edwards. The two of them smiling. I wondered why. And wondered how my father ever hung out with somebody like this man, who was so obviously decent. Or to look at it from a different perspective, why would a guy like him want to hang out with Tietam?

My father had thrown a wrench into the workings of our father-son relationship. A relationship that previously had been so simple. He exercised nude and talked about polished knobs, bareback riding, and the art of the deal. I dismissed him as a man with the emotional depth of a meat-loaf sandwich. Now he'd caused me to question all of this.

And speaking of questions, what had Terri meant with her diary brainteaser? Giving me a special gift while taking away something I'd had my whole life? Then it hit me. As if standing in my dad's library had passed on a secret power of understanding by osmosis. Terri wanted something, all right, but it wasn't Nat King Cole. She wanted *me*.

The thought lit an instant fire in my loins, but the sound of Tietam Brown's '79 Fairmont extinguished it in record time. I turned out the light and raced from his room, then looked out my window at a sorrowful sight.

He emerged from the car a beaten man. Limping, pausing every few agonizing steps to cough up a thick glob of blood. Part of me wanted to race down the stairs and embrace him, to help him. But part of me thought of his pride, the calm look in his eye when he'd walked out the door. Walked out to help me, and returned a beaten man. I lay down instead.

Lay down instead and heard the man who usually hounded up the stairs crawl and paw his way up. Lay down while the man who made his bedsprings bounce and his headboard bang simply lay down with a groan. Lay down while my father paid the price for his love.

Love. A word not usually meant for deadbeat dads. But what else could it be? What could it possibly be, if not love?

Like a sleepless child who counts his sheep, I chronicled the labored gasps and groans of Tietam Brown's breathing, but found no rest. Just a whole lot of questions and a great deal of concern. The concern hadn't waned, and the questions were alive and well, when the sun warmed my face with its first rays of morning.

My dad, I could hear, was sleeping, his loud snores a welcome relief from the sounds of anguish that had earlier seeped through my walls. I entered his room with great caution.

His face was so bad as if to seem somehow fake, as if a Hollywood makeup artist had splashed black-and-blue latex on top of his features. His nose was splattered to the right, the blood that had run out having formed a congealed mass that clung to his chin. His eyes were grotesque in their swelling, the twin softball-like lumps giving him the appearance of some strange insect or alien life-form. Swelling that put mine to shame. Swelling that caused me to fear for his sight, for his brain, not to mention his pride, which may well have been the most serious casualty of all. He lay tangled in his sheets, the same sheets that only hours earlier had been lifted to reveal Mrs. Baskin's body to me. Sheets that were now a canvas to a gruesome smattering of splatters, drips, and stains. A canvas that served to only partially obscure a series of body bruises that made every breath a task.

Antietam Brown IV, I knew, was in this shape because of me. Because of some bizarre sense of honor he felt toward a son he barely knew. But maybe my dad had seen a bigger picture. Maybe the name of all the Browns had been dishonored with Hanrahan's blow. As if the coach had been among the boars tearing my ancestor's dead body to pieces on that Maryland field so many years ago.

I stared again at the carnage and had a sudden flash. A vision, I guess. A vision of Tietam Brown standing toe-to-toe with the monstrous Hanrahan, slugging it out, giving as good as he got. I looked at his hands and realized that my vision was not one of the truth. Tietam Brown lay battered almost literally from head to toe. Almost. But his hands, I saw, were without a scratch. My father had gone down to defeat without landing a blow.

NOVEMBER 7, 1985

I was no longer just the kid with the one ear at Conestoga High. Nor was I just the guy who had a girlfriend that was three leagues out of his ballpark. No, on November 7, 1985, I was now the guy who had been beaten up by Coach Hanrahan. Or, as word spread that day in school, "the guy who got what he deserved."

That at least was the feeling of the Conestoga Togas football team, whose fate in the coming sectional championship lay in the coach's student-beating hands. But to a large group of students, a silent majority, I guess, word spread about the kid who had stood up to Mr. Hanrahan. Who had actually called him a jerk, took a beating for it, but still managed to make it to school that very next day.

Hanrahan's threats of the previous day hadn't left a whole lot of room for interpretation, but I went on with my schedule nonetheless, waiting for the principal, or Hanrahan, or maybe the police to forcibly escort me from the premises.

But the day was flying by without a hitch, and I was enjoying my newfound status as a quasi-celebrity on campus, as well as my status as first-time kisser and first-time breast-toucher. Terri showed up at my locker after second period looking better than ever, and in good spirits until hearing of my father's disastrous dance with vengeance.

By lunchtime, students were taking bets as to whether I was brave enough, or stupid enough, to show up for history. Most bet against me. They lost.

I'm not saying I showed up with any degree of confidence, but at least I did show. I was sweating, but I was there. A history-loving son of a gun, just ready to absorb some learning from Coach Hanrahan, a master of the subject.

I never heard him coming. Don't get me wrong, he didn't sneak up on me and continue his assault, as that sentence might lead you to believe. I just mean that his entrance came without fanfare, without the exaggerated clicking of cowboy boots from way down the hall or his self-led chants of "Togas, Togas, Togas" that usually heralded his arrival. No, in this case, it was just Mr. Hanrahan, his mullet and his muscles, closing the door quietly and saying, "Hello there . . . class."

The football team, of course, cheered their hero, his rep as a badass having been further sealed by his one-punch knockout of a 150-pound kid. A punch that, apparently, Hanrahan had enjoyed talking about a great deal at the afternoon's practice.

As they cheered, I looked closely for a sign. A sign of struggle. A split lip, a bruise of any kind. Just some kind of a sign that a fight had actually taken place at 272 Quaker Path, instead of a one-sided debacle.

I saw my sign! A bruise, or more accurately a series of bruises, on Mr. Hanrahan. Unfortunately, those bruises were all on his knuckles, which apparently had been injured when my dad hit him repeatedly with his face. Hanrahan's face, however, was without damage. None. Whatsoever. So much for my dad being a boxer.

"Okay, class, let's begin," Hanrahan said. "Today we're going to talk about Abraham Lincoln's Army of the Potomac, and some of the key battles that they won, including Gettysburg and Antietam."

The football team laughed, seizing their cue, ready to pounce on Hanrahan's already wounded prey.

He continued, "Andy, I thought that maybe you could help us today, seeing as one of your ancestors fought there."

I tried to detect the sarcasm, but found none. Tried to detect some type of a trap, but came up with nothing. Above all else, I tried to figure out why in the hell he had picked this day, of all days, to call me Andy.

I looked back at Terri, who gave me a shrug. Looked back at Hanrahan, who addressed me again. "Andy, I had a chance to look over your paper last night, and I think that maybe I was a little too tough on you."

Actually, a C minus is "a little tough." A punch in the face goes a little above and beyond.

He continued, "You see, class, in history, there is sometimes more than one side to the story. I hadn't considered another side to the Emancipation Proclamation, but Andy Brown's paper made me think. I thought that Andy might like to speak to the class about his feelings on Gettysburg or Antietam."

I suddenly knew how the Grinch felt when he puzzled until his puzzler got sore, because when it came to what Hanrahan could possibly be thinking—I was puzzled.

So I puzzled and puzzled, till my puzzler got sore, then said "Okay" and gave the teaching profession a whirl.

"Now I'm not really an expert on the battle of Antietam," I began, "but I do know that what could have been the North's greatest victory . . . was hurt a lot by General McClellan, who was on the North, by his uh tendency to overestimate the odds against him."

And for the next several minutes, my presentation continued that way, a stumbling, mumbling collection of facts, put together in an unprofessional but not completely unenjoyable fashion. Sure Clem Baskin shot a few spitballs at me, which prompted a Hanrahan admonishment of "Clem, stop it now" and "Andy's trying to talk," but to tell you the truth, I enjoyed being the center of attention. Enjoyed the laughter after a horrible joke. Enjoyed being seen as more than just "the guy with the one ear," or "the guy with the hot girlfriend." But most of all, I enjoyed looking at Terri looking at me, her smile as warm as a pup by the fire.

"Thank you, Andy," Hanrahan said. "Let's give him a big round of applause for telling us a little bit about a big battle."

As the class applauded, and for the next few minutes, too, I watched Hanrahan. Examined him. His mullet—longer than ever. His muscles—bigger than ever. His face—not a scratch on it. Nonetheless, something had changed. I didn't know what, but something had changed.

FRIDAY, NOVEMBER 13, 1985

My dad lay in bed for most of the next week, ignoring my suggestions of seeing a doctor. By the third day, he was showing some signs of being his normal self, and by Friday he was as good as new—his swollen discolored eyes and Silly Putty of a nose notwithstanding.

"Andy," he said, with more enthusiasm than he had any right to be feeling, "have I ever told you how much I love football?"

"No," I said, "not one time, as a matter of fact you've told me a few times that you hated it."

"Oh come on now, kid, hate's a strong word. Football is a very valuable part of our culture, and we've gotta start enjoying it together."

"Dad, we don't even have a television set," I told him, while wondering if one of the haymakers Hanrahan had tagged him with had altered his thought patterns. In a way, I longed to hear another of his next-door sex operas, just to check on his body's other functions. He had now gone a full week without a visitor in his room—almost six days longer than usual.

Tietam just laughed. "I'm not talking about watching a game on a damned ol' television, kid, I'm talking about you and me, father and son, supporting our very own Conestoga Togas, tomorrow in their quest for the championship."

Surely my father had to be kidding. Just show up as father and son to support the Conestoga Togas? We'd look ridiculous, with our matching shiners, supporting a team whose coach had beaten us both up on the same day.

But he was not to be swayed. "Hey Andy, if not for the team, let's do it for your girlfriend. It's the big game, I'm sure she's gonna be cheering her little boobies off."

I wasn't sure whether to be offended or laugh at how obviously disingenuous my dad was being. So I laughed and got offended at the same time, and said, "First off, Dad, Terri quit the squad, and second, her boobies aren't little."

"Well hell, kid, let's bring her too," Tietam said. "Unless you're embarrassed of ol' Tietam."

"No, Dad, I'm not embarrassed, I just didn't think that you'd want her to see you, like, uh . . . you know, like this."

Tietam looked down at his boxers, the cow having poked its head out of the barn, and said, "Hey, hey she's *not* going to see me like *this*. I'll be dressed to kill when I support my team."

"No, Dad, I meant, see you like this . . . beaten up."

"Oh that," my dad said. "Yeah, I guess you do

145

have a point, but hey, it's not like we got our asses handed to us by just any Tom, Dick, or Harry. No sir, it was Henry Hanrahan who got us. Two-time all-American, NFL star, winningest football coach in section history. No shame in that, son. No shame in that at all."

He paused to give a big cheesy smile, and a genuine, honest-to-goodness Arthur Fonzarelli thumbs-up, then gave me a pensive stare. "Andy," he asked, "why did your girl quit the cheerleading team? I thought she was the captain."

"Yeah, she was, Dad, she was, but she quit because of me, because of what the coach did to me."

The pensive look disappeared, and the other guy was back. The guy with the Fonz's thumb. "Hey loyalty—that's good, that's good. I like a girl who's loyal to my boy. Come on now, Andy, give her a call."

So I did. Called her and invited her on a date with me . . . and my dad, to the championship game. She questioned my sanity but told me that any time with me was a good time, and then asked if my Dad would show up naked. I told her I couldn't guarantee anything when it came to my father.

"Oh Andy," she said, "I was wondering about one other thing."

"Yeah, what's that?" I asked.

"Did you think about my diary at all these last few days, about what it said?"

"Yeah, yeah, I've been thinking about it."

"And?"

"And, I uh . . . think I figured it out."

"And?"

"And, um what?" I said, trying to sound casual. Actually, I was excited as hell, but my dad was listening and I was trying to be as vague as possible.

Terri interrupted my train of thought by saying, "What do you think about doing it, Andy, about really doing it?"

My heart officially stopped and restarted twice during that sentence, but I swallowed hard and said, "Terri, I think it's going to be the best feeling ever!"

I may have spoken a little louder than I intended, because Tietam Brown turned around and with a voice that sounded as if he had a wiretap on my conscience, said, "The best feeling ever? Whatever might you mean, Andy?"

"Dad, stop it," I said, in brilliant whining fashion.

Terri laughed. "What is he, psychic or something?" Then, "I'll see you tomorrow. Pick me up around twelve."

SATURDAY, NOVEMBER 14, 1985 / NOON

I emerged from my house on Elston Court with perhaps the cleanest penis in the continental United States. Hell, maybe the whole world.

Sure, I'd had to handle my father's ribbing, but I paid little heed because I was confident. Confident that if practice does indeed make perfect, I would be pretty damn close to it when the big day was upon me.

I spent the short trip to Terri's house watching my father sing his heart out to "Copacabana" and hoping that by sheer force of will I could make those fuzzy dice disappear.

"Music and passion were always the fashion at the Copa . . . they fell in love."

"Dad, who sings this?" I asked.

"Come on, kid, this is classic Manilow."

"Can we keep it that way?"

"Oh ho," he laughed, "you got me there . . . Actually I wanted Village People, but it's not here. Nothin' like a little People before a big date."

"Dad, you're going to a football game—I'm going on a date . . . and please don't embarrass me."

Just showing up at the game in our condition was going to be embarrassing enough; a father-son team of human punching bags. I didn't need Tietam Brown's unique brand of crude humor making matters worse.

He did his best to assure me. "Kid, believe me, my attention is going to be completely centered on the game. I have reason to believe it's going to be very . . . interesting. The last thing I would do on a day like this is tease you in front of your girl . . . or talk about the four showers you took last night!"

"DAAAAD!"

"Lifting weights in there, Andy? The old clean-and-jerk?"

Mercifully, the car came to a stop in Terri's drive.

"Nice house," my father said. "Preaching must pay well."

Hard to argue with that. I hopped out of the car and slowly made my way up the walk, admiring the shrubbery as I went and hoping for the best on a day that had all the trappings of a disaster. I rang the bell.

"Well hello, you must be Andy," a beautiful woman said. A beautiful woman, early forties, with a face as carefully manicured as the Johnson yard.

"Yes ma'am, I am," I said.

"Well come on in, Terri will be down shortly," she said. "Well I'll be, that is quite a shiner you have. Terri said you were in a little scrape at school."

"Yes ma'am, a little one. Did she say with who?"

"No, Andy, she just said that boys will be boys."

"Oh."

"So you're going to the big game, huh?"

"Yes ma'am."

"We've got to pull for our Togas, don't we?"

"I'll be pulling, ma'am."

"I do wish that Terri was still cheering. What a shame, pulling up lame with only one game to go."

"Yes ma'am, it is a shame," I said. Actually, I was a little surprised. Honesty, I figured out, did not seem to be the best policy in this particular house, especially as it pertained to Terri's boyfriend getting the crap beaten out of him by the beloved coach.

She smiled and said, "That Coach Hanrahan sure has done a nice job with his boys, hasn't he?"

Yes, they are a wonderful group of mean-spirited, bullying, mullet-wearing, steroid monkeys. Actually I didn't say that, but I was sure as hell thinking it. What I actually said was, "Uh, yeah, he sure has."

Mrs. Johnson then offered me a cup of tea.

"No thank you, Mrs. Johnson. My dad's probably getting pretty anxious in the car about now. He's really looking forward to the game."

"Your father!" she exclaimed. "Well isn't that sweet, a father and son going to the big game. Well I'd like to meet him."

My heart momentarily froze. Although my powers of telepathy had failed to make the dice

150

disappear, I called on them once again to make Terri herself appear in front of me so I could spare Mrs. Johnson the pleasure of making ol' Tietam's acquaintance. And I have to admit, I did momentarily, just momentarily, picture this beautiful, demure woman licking my father's ass. She was definitely his type; rich, attractive and . . . married.

Unfortunately, my mental powers were a bit off on that day, as I was unable to make Terri appear before me, but I was able to summon her voice from upstairs. A voice that said, "I'll be down in a few minutes."

I went out to get my dad.

"Dad, please don't embarrass me," I said. "And don't hit on Terri's mother."

Tietam smiled as we walked toward the door. He said, "Andy, I told you I wouldn't embarrass you, didn't I? But as far as the mother, hey I can't guarantee nothin'. Wow they've got quite a few pumpkins here."

Mrs. Johnson met us at the door with a forced smile that did little to hide her shock and, I thought, disgust. She opened the door and said, "Well hello, you must be Andy's father."

"I sure am, ma'am, I'm Tietam Brown," he said, and leaned in and gave Mrs. Johnson a firm kiss on the cheek.

"Well, Mr. Brown, that was nice of you, although to tell the truth, I think a handshake would have sufficed."

"Yeah well, myself, personally, I try not to shake

hands too much, you know, for sanitary reasons. People can be a little gross, right? Like say I was out in the car adjusting my sac and then shook your hand. Well, I'd pretty much be slapping my sac in your hand, wouldn't I?"

I thought I was going to die. I looked at Terri's mom and thought she might die, too. Two deaths at the hands of Tietam Brown's words.

Fortunately, Terri came down, somehow managing to look both wonderful and feminine in a denim jacket, jeans, and work boots, her long wet hair drawn back in a ponytail.

"Hi," she said. "You must be Andy's father. He said you like to be called Tietam."

"That's correct, and may I say, Mrs. Johnson, that you have a lovely daughter, and may I say to you, Terri, that you have an exquisite mother."

"Thank you," they both said in unison.

Tietam smiled broadly, and for just a second I thought I saw what women saw in him, even with his smashed nose and still horribly swollen face. His smile turned to a sly grin, and he said, "Hey where's Mr. Johnson, I could probably use a man of God in my life."

"We could all use him," Mrs. Johnson said, although I couldn't tell if she meant him or, you know, *Him*. "But unfortunately, Mr. Johnson is at a meeting with Billy Graham right now in Charlotte."

"Really," Tietam said. "Billy Graham the wrestler?"

"No," Mrs. Johnson replied tersely, "Billy Graham the reverend." She paused briefly. "May I ask, Mr. Brown, what happened to your face?"

My dad's eyes, the whites of which had turned red over the past few days, registered surprise. "You mean you don't know?"

"No, but I sure as the dickens would like to."

"Well Mrs. Johnson, I guess I was spoiling for a fight and I got what I deserved."

I breathed a sigh of relief, as did Terri. Mrs. Johnson breathed a sigh of indignation. "The Lord tells us to turn the other cheek," she said, her tone pure holier-than-thou condescension.

"I did turn the other cheek, Mrs. Johnson," my dad said. "And he punched that one too." With that my dad burst out laughing, and I guess his laughter was infectious, because Terri and I joined in too. The infection didn't spread to Terri's mother, however, who just glared. Finally, my dad broke the silence.

"Well Mrs. Johnson, as the Good Book says, all have fallen short of the glory of God. I guess I just fell a little shorter than usual on that day."

"You know your Bible, Mr. Brown—"

"Tietam, please."

"Mr. Brown, may I suggest that you live its words."

"That's very good advice, ma'am," my father said.

"I will pray for you, Mr. Brown. For you and Coach Hanrahan, so that he may make this town proud."

"Well thank you, ma'am," my father said as he walked to the car. "I need those prayers . . . and I have a feeling the coach will too."

With that my father departed the house, climbed into the Fairmont, batted the fuzzy dice for emphasis, cranked up the Manilow—yes I did just write "cranked up the Manilow"—and waved good-bye.

I studied Terri's mother through the windshield as Tietam backed out of the drive. A mixture of puritanical and capitalistic values. Dedicated to God's word and the surgeon's knife. A woman, I guessed, who would not be licking my dad's ass anytime soon.

My father was the first to speak. "I hope I didn't offend you, Terri, with my reference to the Bible."

"No sir, but my mother offends a little bit easier than me."

"But I was a little surprised that your mother didn't know about the, uh . . . origin of my face."

I was surprised as well. Terri must have lied about four times to her mother, which didn't seem to fit in well with the Christian motif of the house.

"I know," Terri said. "It's just that there are two things that you don't question in our house. God and Coach Hanrahan. I'd like to, but I . . . just . . . can't."

Tietam laughed. "You just pay attention to the coach today. I have a feeling he's going to surprise a lot of people."

Terri held my hand in the backseat as we made

our way to the big game, as Barry Manilow provided the soundtrack to our own little love story. My dad, of course, sang along. But true to his words, he caused me no embarrassment, the fuzzy dice notwithstanding.

He even gave us our distance as we walked to the field, allowing us a hint of intimacy as the Togas stretched and the band played "Tusk" off in the distance of the playing field on the campus of Cornell.

Amid the pomp and circumstance, Terri leaned in close and whispered into my ear, "How does two weeks sound?"

"Two weeks?" I said, not quite catching her drift. "Two weeks for what?"

"Two weeks until . . . you know."

"Two weeks? Really?"

"Really."

She leaned forward and kissed me. I looked at my dad, who gave me a big thumbs-up and a silent, fist-shaking cheer.

The game itself was marked by some rather odd choices on the part of Coach Hanrahan, who was sporting a dramatically shorter haircut for the big game.

Three times the Togas tried to run the ball up the middle on third and long situations. A little strange maybe, but hey, who were we to question the winningest coach in section history?

A punt on third down, however, did raise a few eyebrows, and another punt on second down had the Conestoga fans screaming in anger, a reaction that three quarters earlier would have been unthinkable.

Still, the Togas rebounded, and with the team driving late in the game, trailing 12–7 with only a minute left on the clock, the Conestoga faithful had every reason to believe that Hanrahan would use his mighty arms to snatch victory out of the jaws of defeat.

First and goal for the Togas on the nine and the crowd was in a frenzy. A give to the halfback, who followed a Clem Baskin block for a four-yard gain.

First and goal on the five. A give to Baskin, who, with chemically enhanced legs churning, lunged to the one.

First and goal on the one, only eight seconds left. A time-out by Coach Hanrahan, who appeared to have shaken off whatever psychosis was responsible for his earlier gridiron goof-ups. He looked poised and calm, ready to guide his boys to a fourth straight title.

Yeah, the coach sure looked calm. Until he looked our way. At my dad to be exact. At my dad, who amid the hoopla just stood at ease, his hand serenely waving as if he was England's Queen Mother out for a Sunday stroll on the streets of old London. I swear they made eye contact, and I also swear that something happened to the coach. He began to cry. Softly at first, almost imperceptibly, but then harder. Harder and harder, until Coach Henry Hanrahan lay shaking inconsolably in the middle of the Conestoga sideline.

I looked at my dad, who seemed to be savoring some euphoric high. Eyes closed and smiling peacefully.

The whistle blew, but the coach was still down. Delay of game. Five-yard penalty. Fourth and goal on the six, but still the coach could not be helped. His team rallied around their fallen leader, but the 270-pound behemoth, who by this point had assumed the fetal position, was a tough one to handle. Another whistle, another five yards. Fourth down, eleven yards to go, and the Conestoga fans, including an irate, powerfully built red-faced man who I guessed to be Clem Baskin's father, were ready to riot.

But then the coach was on his feet. Still trembling, but on his feet. Tears streaming down, but on his feet. On his feet and waving wildly. Motioning for the field goal unit to take the field. Now I'm no football expert, but even I knew that a field goal couldn't possibly win that game. The team needed a touchdown. So if I knew it, everyone knew it, including the three-time defending champions, who were not all that happy with the field goal suggestion. Not happy at all.

Clem Baskin was the first to show his displeasure—by swinging his helmet full force into the back of Coach Hanrahan's skull. The coach went down, and the Togas pounced upon him like hyenas with protruding foreheads, punching and kicking, striking and pounding.

Clem's father was the first one out of the stands, sprinting with short, powerful strides and diving on top of the pile as if joining a World Series celebration. He then joined the boys in pummeling the coach. I looked around quickly and saw no sign of sad Mrs. Baskin.

And then there were more. Parents and players, and students and police. Some fighting, some breaking things up, entrants all into a very odd version of a new Superdance, boogying away to the sounds of sirens and screaming.

Believe it or not, I felt sorry for Hanrahan. Even after the taunts and hatred and the punch. When I looked at him crying, even before Baskin's brave blast, I saw a defeated man. A hulk of a man, who somehow seemed very small. In a way, I thought, he was kind of like Samson of the Bible, his powers lost without the benefit of his mighty mullet.

As for Tietam Brown, he might as well have had a blanket and lotion, for he looked very much like a child at the beach; all glowing smiles at the wonder before him. That smile then turned left, to a brown-haired young woman who'd been trading looks with ol' Tietam throughout much of the game. She'd looked merely average when the first kickoff was launched, but with each passing glance, she changed in my eyes, so that by the time things turned ugly, she was decidedly pretty, bordering on beautiful.

So while I held hands with Terri and watched the field fill with bodies, my father got up, took a stroll toward his girl, and within thirty seconds returned arm in arm with her. Just like that. (A snap for emphasis.) Like watching Houdini.

"Come on," Tietam said, "let's beat the traffic," and the four of us walked, two couples, to the welcoming arms of the Fairmont's cracked seats. And then, once inside, that woman filled the car with conversation and laughter. She bonded with Terri like a long-lost best pal. She treated me like a son that she loved. And as for ol' Tietam, she reduced him to tears. Tears of huge laughter that welled in his eyes as she questioned his Manilow and hid the blue dice.

Ten minutes tops was all that we shared, but we seemed like a family when we stopped at her house. Or her sister's house, actually, a small shingled ranch where she was staying for two weeks before moving along. Where? She didn't say, just "somewhere other than here."

"Will I see you?" said Tietam, with enough of a stammer so that I saw myself in him. He seemed suddenly shy with a woman like this. Self-assured as she was, Tietam Brown was slightly out of his element.

"Sure," she replied. "I think that would be cool. But don't fall in love, because I don't have too long."

"Should I call you?"

"No, my sister will flip if an old guy like you calls," she said with a laugh. "She'll tell all her friends at the bar. But I'll give you a ring. You're listed I hope."

My dad just nodded his head.

"Brown, Antietam, I think I can find it. Now heal up that face. Bye Terri, bye Andy."

And with that she was gone. A streak of bright sunshine, in a flurry of fringes.

"Wow," my dad said as he headed for Terri's. "I've been around, but I've never seen anything quite like . . . her."

I had to agree, and Terri did too. In the mirror's reflection, I could see him smile. A smile that belonged to a man who had never done nude push-ups or perfected the art of the deal.

He drove on in silence, just savoring her smell; a hint of magnolia in a soft summer rain. A comfortable silence that really felt right, as if no words were needed to fill in the gap.

When we pulled into Terri's, the silence was broken by the sound of good-bye and a thank-you from Terri to my newly smitten dad.

"Don't mention it, Terri. Did you have a good time?"

"The game was . . . different. But you were really great. And I like your new friend. I know that she'll call you."

"I hope so," he said, and meant it too.

"Can I ask you a favor?"

"Sure."

"When I get to my door, can you turn your head and close your eyes."

"I guess so," he laughed. "Why?"

"Because your son is going to kiss me."

The old Tietam Brown would have whipped up a reply to ruin the day. But this Tietam Brown, the new Tietam Brown, just nodded his head and did as he was told. I walked with Terri to her door, and he turned his head.

Terri fulfilled her end of the bargain with a wonderful kiss, first soft and then deep. Then she added a little surprise. She touched my balls. Touched them and rubbed them in a secretive way, so that only my boys and I had even a clue.

"Andy?"

"Yeah." A voice as high as my penis was hard, but thankfully practice had paid off and my undies were spared.

"Did you like that?"

"Yes," and actually wished it hadn't been so brief. Wished it was still going on as we talked.

"I'll bet no one else has ever touched you like that, have they?"

"Only my foster dad," I said. Damn. The truth really sucks. All I had to do was lie. One simple lie. Lie, lie, lie, lie. Lying doesn't make a person bad. Hell, I'd heard Terri tell a bunch of them, and she was the nicest person I knew. Why didn't I have the power to lie?

"Andy. We're going to talk about that soon. That and your quarters, and all your other little secrets. But right now you're going to kiss me one more time, reach up real secret and feel my breast, and go home. Okay."

"Okay."

"So give me that kiss."

I did. A nice one too.

"Now that other thing."

I did that too. All of the pleasure with none of the spasming.

"That was nice. Good-bye Andy."

"Good-bye."

I watched the door close and walked away, doing my best to walk naturally, despite the telltale signs of arousal in my trousers. I got in the car and started to whistle. I think everyone whistles when they're afraid they'll be busted. If our policemen just looked for random whistlers, crime would be extinct in no time.

I looked at my dad. "Okay, let's go," I said.

Tietam just kept smiling that new Tietam smile.

"Andy?"

"Yeah Dad."

"Did you just feel her breast?"

"Yeah Dad, I guess I did."

"That's a good boy."

"Thanks, Dad."

And away we went.

NOVEMBER 14, 1985 / EVENING

Later that night, as I often did, I thought of the day. Meeting Terri's mother, watching the game, my dad's mystery girl, and my good-night kiss and feel. But my mind kept returning to Coach Hanrahan's face. When he saw my dad. That look on his face like he'd just seen a ghost. Or worse. I knocked on Tietam's door.

"Dad."

"Yes, Andy, what is it?"

"Can I talk to you?"

"Sure, son, come in." A room that was always off limits, up until now. A tone to his voice that exuded happiness.

I walked into the room and saw my dad, under sheets that were now clean and white, a smile on his face, a Bible in his hands.

"Good book?" I asked.

"The best," Tietam said. "You know I read it a lot, usually looking for loopholes, but tonight I'm not."

"No?"

"No, Andy, tonight I'm looking for truth."

"Did you find it?"

"Sure, kid, it's all around. You just have to sift a little to get to it."

I saw the black-and-white photo faceup on the nightstand. I didn't want to be pushy, but I needed to know. Who was this guy. I needed to know.

"Dad . . ." I tried to sound casual, even if our day had been anything but.

"Yeah."

"Who's that guy in the picture, the one next to you?"

Tietam glanced down and took the old photo off the table. He looked at its image, and I saw a slight sign of sadness hidden in a small smile. Without looking up, he said, "His name's Eddie Edwards."

"Were you two friends?"

"Yeah, I guess that we were."

"Do you guys still talk?"

Tietam looked up from the photo. "No, the last time I saw him . . . we didn't leave on good terms. But I've been thinking of calling."

"Maybe someday you should."

"It better be soon."

"How come?"

"Edwards is dying." He swallowed hard. "Hey Andy."

"Yes, Dad."

"Did you like that new girl?"

I smiled. Thinking about her caused me to smile. Still does. "Yeah, Dad, I liked her a lot."

"Me too," said Tietam.

"What was her name?"

"I never did ask . . . Do you think that she'll call?"

"I do, Dad, I do."

"I hope so," he said, and he seemed suddenly small. Not small like the coach, but like a cute little child with a secret to share. Then, "Remember that night when I gave you the picture?"

"Yeah, I do," remembered it well. His trembling hands and the tears on his face.

"Well, she reminds me of her."

I nodded in silence, and suddenly knew. The answer to the question I'd been asking myself since meeting my dad. What did my mother see in this man? Because I saw it now too.

"Dad?"

"Yes, son."

"What happened that night?"

"What night?" he said, and he sat up so quick that his Bible fell to the floor.

"Well you, you know," I said, "that night at the coach's house."

Then Tietam relaxed and said, "Andy, sit down," and I hauled myself onto Tietam's big bed. He looked at me for a long time, too long it seemed, and said, "Why do you ask?"

"Well because, it uh, just seemed to me that, uh, Hanrahan looked right at you before he, you know, flipped out."

"Yes, Andy, I think he did."

"But why?"

"Andy, let me ask you this. How did you feel when you went to school that next day . . . after you were hit by the coach?"

"I guess I felt pain."

"No, I mean, inside. How did you feel?"

"I guess kind of weird."

"Weird in what way?"

"Self-conscious, I guess, because you know, everyone was talking about it."

"And how did that make you feel?"

"I don't know, a little weird, I guess."

"Ashamed?"

"No."

"Then weird how? Try to explain."

"Weird because . . . I . . . uh, well in a way I guess I was proud."

"How did you feel today at the game? About your face?"

"I guess kind of cool."

"And what do you see when you look at me?"

"I don't know."

"About my face. Try describing my eyes."

"They're really red in your eyeball."

"And how 'bout under the eyeball?"

"Swollen."

"Would you call it a black eye?"

"Yeah, two of them."

"How 'bout my nose?"

"It's broken."

"And up here," he said, pointing to his eyebrow.

"It's cut pretty bad, probably should have been stitched."

"Well there you have it, son."

"I don't understand."

"I went over to his house and look what he gave me. Two black eyes, a broken nose, a gash over my eye. All badges of courage, right?"

I nodded my head as if it made sense, but all that I saw was my beaten-up dad.

"Andy, he *gave* me all these things, but I went over there and *took* something from him. Understand?"

"No, Dad, I don't understand." But part of me did. Understood it too well, and it filled me with dread . . . and pride.

"Andy, when I went over to his house, I took something from him. His will to live. I took it that night."

NOVEMBER 27, 1985 / AFTERNOON

A very strange couple of weeks saw Hanrahan's teaching and coaching career work its way to a pitiful conclusion. First, a team of experts concluded that the Conestoga riot should not entitle that team to their last eight seconds of game time. As a result, the final score remained 12–7, and the Togas had to settle for second place.

Next, a very beaten and battered Henry Hanrahan was placed under suicide watch at Cornell Medical Center as a bevy of witnesses came forth with pieces of knowledge about the coach's past. In truth, it was mostly old news, but for some reason racial slurs, assaults, and statutory rape charges that seemed to slide off the winningest coach in section history now seemed just a little stickier to the laughingstock of Conestoga.

The principal, it seemed, had been informed of all previous complaints but had done nothing, and as a result was suspended pending further investigation.

Our house even served as a backdrop for some of the proceedings, as an unfailingly polite detective named Riley paid us a visit three days after the game.

"Mr. Brown," the detective had said, "Mr. Hanrahan claims that you assaulted him, and intimidated him. Is that true?"

"Well I did try to intimidate him," my father replied. "But I guess it didn't work out too well, huh?"

"I guess not," the detective said. "Were all these wounds the result of your visit to Mr. Hanrahan's house?"

"Yes sir."

"And why did you visit the home?"

"Because he assaulted my son in his classroom, sir."

"Is that a fact?"

"It sure is. Hey Andy, come here."

I showed up, the detective looked at my face and winced.

Tietam said, "And that's over a week old. Should have seen him when he came home. Any father would have done the same."

"Yeah, I suppose he might have."

"Damn right," Tietam said.

"So then you didn't assault him?"

"Did that big monster look like he'd been assaulted?"

"No, not a scratch on him."

"Probably just in his head. You know, his conscience catching up with him."

"Probably so, Mr. Brown, probably so."

Thanksgiving came and went without much fanfare, at least for us Antietams on Elston Court. Terri had gone with her parents to a town called Horseheads, which made me think of the first *Godfather,* while I gave thanks and washed dishes at the diner.

Gave thanks for all the wonder that was filling up my days. And thanks for that next day to come, when I'd have Terri all alone. I hoped I would be ready. If our hot-water bill was any indicator, I would be.

I gave thanks too for my father, who hadn't seemed himself. Since meeting up with what's her name, he'd been living in a fog. A happy fog at first, it seemed, but with each passing day, his chances for a call seemed to shrink, and he looked a little sadder.

He still had his women, but he wasn't nearly as loud. And he'd stopped doing his deck. He even bought an answering machine so he wouldn't miss her potential call.

The phone rang at three on Friday afternoon, the day of my big date with Terri. The one I'd been dreaming about. The one I'd been practicing for.

I heard my dad's voice light up.

"Yes, this is Tietam, is that you? Oh it is . . . Jeez, I thought you might be gone . . . Oh you're leaving tomorrow . . . Well what is your name, you left without telling me . . . Holly? That's nice . . . Yeah, I'm free tonight, what would you like to

170

do? . . . Sounds good to me. Hey I'm glad you called. Yeah, I'll pick you up . . . Five sounds great. See you then."

I thought he was going to do a jig right there in our empty living room.

I looked outside as a truck dropped off lumber at our curb and a team of carpenters pulled power tools and sawhorses into our yard. Usually the only hammering I heard was in my father's bedroom, but on this cool afternoon, with a few tiny flakes of snow floating about, the hammering was loud and the hammering was often in our little front yard, on our small quiet street.

I looked at my father, who was actually now dancing, singing a rendition of "A Holly Jolly Christmas" that would have made Burl Ives scream. "Oh ho, the mistletoe, hung where you can see. Somebody waits for you, kiss her once for me, rin ta tin ta da."

"Dad, what's going on?" I said.

"Revenge Andy, sweet revenge."

"What kind of revenge, Dad?"

"Revenge with a holiday flair. Andy, look outside, at Sugling's house. What do you see?"

"Lots of Christmas stuff."

"That's right, Andy, lots of stuff. Stuff that glows, stuff that lights up, stuff that causes a few cars to drive by, right?"

"I guess."

"But it's really just stuff, and stuff is just a fancy word for crap, right?"

"I guess so."

"Well tonight, Sugling will pay the price. People will be driving by our street all right, but they'll be driving by to see our house, Andy, our house."

"But Dad, we don't even have any lights up."

"Well, you and me are going to go out now and put two spotlights in the ground, okay?"

"Okay, Dad, but that doesn't sound very fancy."

"Andy, I'll tell you what. You go on your date at what time?"

"Terri's picking me up around five."

"Hey same time as your dad. Did you ever think it, Andy, two Browns on the town, at the same time."

"No, I've got to admit that I never did, Dad."

"Where are you going?"

"To the movies, I think."

"Which one?"

I had to think on this one. Our elaborate romantic plan had not involved an alibi, and I knew that my dad could detect a lie a mile away, so I just played dumb and told what might be considered a little half-truth.

"I'm just going to go where Terri wants me to go," I said. Which was straight to her bedroom. Yes!

"Well, Andy, when you come home from your movie, you will get one heck of a surprise."

And then he was off, bounding up the stairs at a pace usually reserved for a coming interaction with a drunk married woman. But this time I heard no bouncing of springs, or banging of head-boards. Just Tietam Brown butchering "A Holly Jolly Christmas" as the carpenters banged out a tune of their own.

By the time Terri arrived, darkness was falling and a shell of a building stood on our lawn as our neighbors, including Gloria and Charlie Sugling, stood silently, by turns shaking their heads, shrugging their shoulders, and covering their ears. I asked the carpenters what they were building, but they were apparently sworn to secrecy.

As we drove away, Terri grabbed my hand and squeezed it hard.

"Are you ready?" she said.

"I hope so," I replied, but even as I said it, the word "ready" triggered a thought. Protection. I didn't have any. Oh how I wished I hadn't thrown my three-pack out. Oh what a pimple on the ass of pleasure.

Mournfully I told her. "Terri."

"Yes, Andy."

"I don't have any, um uh."

"Protection?" she said.

"Yeah."

"Don't worry. There, look in my bag."

I did and was rewarded immediately with the familiar sight of a blue three-pack.

"Where'd you get these?" I asked.

"I drove almost to Binghamton so no one would know me."

"Cool."

"I bought a bunch just in case."

"In case of what?"

"In case you really like it."

The moon was full in the sky when we got to her house, and the flakes were now flurries, the first of the year.

"Do they have snow in Virginia, Andy?" Terri asked.

"Sure, once in a while. But never this early. And never this pretty."

She looked up at the sky, caught a flake on her tongue. "Andy, this night would be pretty if it was raining down turds."

"Maybe," I said, "but you wouldn't catch them on your tongue."

She laughed and I kissed her.

She said, "Let's go inside, you can kiss me more there."

I did, and we did. Went inside and then kissed. On the mouth and the cheek, and the neck and the head. Kissed her until my mouth started to hurt and then kissed her some more. She looked into my eyes, kissed me once more, and said, "Let's go to my room."

My heart was pounding wildly as I stepped inside. Anticipation and visions of grandeur played havoc with my senses. My fingers felt electric, at least the ones on my left hand. My legs were weak. My mouth was dry. I closed my eyes and envisioned her. Stepping out of her bathroom, just a few weeks ago, the shirt with the buttons, with no bra underneath. The purest, sexiest thing I had ever seen.

My open eyes proved me wrong. For Terri Lynn Johnson at that very moment, in her green sweater and blue jeans, cast a vision of pure beauty the likes of which I'd never seen.

She turned on a cassette, and I heard Rod Stewart's rasp singing "Don't say a word, my virgin child, just let your inhibitions run wild." Looking back on it now, the song's a little obvious to be truly romantic, but at the time it seemed perfect. Hell, it still seems perfect.

"Tonight's the night, it's gonna be all right, 'cause I'm in love with you, woman, ain't nobody gonna stop us now."

No, nobody was gonna stop us now, especially when Terri shut off the lights, leaving only a candle by which to admire her, and said, "Why don't you undress me, big boy." Then, "And Andy, take those stupid quarters out of your pocket."

I took out the quarters, three dollars in all, all minted in 1977, and placed them on her bureau. Then went to work.

I'm not going to claim that I was smooth, but I could have been worse as I lowered her jeans and let her step out, then pulled the green sweater, which I guessed cost more than my dad's Fairmont, over her head.

Oh my goodness, she wasn't just wearing a bra and underwear. This was black lingerie, picked out especially for me. Silk. And this woman was going to give me her body, and a memory for life. An honor really. A lifetime honor.

Rod was still singing, assuring me that it was "gonna be all right," and the candle still flickered, casting sweet shadows that licked at her skin and danced on the walls.

She looked at me and smiled, drew my head to her breast. Kissed my bad ear and whispered, "Now it's my turn, lay down on the bed."

I kicked off my sneakers and she slid off my pants, exposing a pup tent that I'd pitched on the way over to her house.

"Andy, I'd like to feel your skin on me, but you can leave your shirt on if you want."

I pulled it off myself, that "skin on skin" idea being too good to pass on, pigeon chest or not.

Now Rod was singing "spread your wings and let me come inside," which sounded like awfully thinly veiled imagery to me.

Then I sat up and took the initiative for the second time in my life, and laid her down on her bed.

"Andy, rewind the song and play it again, and we'll, you know . . . do it."

Sounded like a pretty good idea, so I hopped up off the bed, just me and my pup tent, and rewound Rod to the proper lovemaking spot. Then turned around and saw Terri looking up at her cross, at the flickering image of Jesus, who had died for our sins. Man, I was dying for one of those sins myself, so to speak.

I said, "Can I take that thing down just for a

few minutes?" But by that time Terri was under her sheets, so the son of God wouldn't see her in her black lingerie. She was crying. And the pup tent was gone.

"Andy, I'm scared," she said.

"Hey it's okay," I said as I rushed to her side. I got down on my knees and I pulled back her sheets, exposing a little girl's fears wrapped up in big girl's clothes. "It's okay. It's okay."

"I've never done this before, and I want to, but it's just a little scary."

Personally, I thought this was great news. Not the part about her being scared, but about her having not done it. I thought she hadn't, but she'd never confirmed it, nor had I asked. And even though I would have been spit on and laughed at by any self-respecting horny teenager, I didn't try to talk her out of the way she felt.

"Terri, Terri, Terri, Terri, come on now, don't cry. I'm scared too. And I'll tell you a little secret. I've never done it either."

She laughed right out loud, the sniffle in her nose making it sound extra cute. "Wow, that's a real shock. So I'm not one of thousands."

"No, you're one in a million." Corny but effective, and straight from my heart.

"What about your foster dad?" She laughed just a little but quickly felt bad. "God I'm so sorry, that was really not nice. Forgive me. Okay?"

"Sure, you're forgiven."

"Andy."

"Yeah."

"I feel really dumb."

"Why?"

"Well, I went out and bought condoms, even bought lingerie. I worked out this whole night. And I wanted it so, wanted you to, uh you know, be my first . . . But I just feel so scared, like maybe we should wait . . . just a little while longer. I'm sorry."

"Don't be," I said.

"But I wanted you so much. Wanted you to love me."

"I already do."

The tears in her eyes in the flickering light cast a bright beauty that stays with me still.

"Andy, come here." She lifted her sheets and patted her chest, and I slipped underneath and she pulled me so close.

"Terri?"

"Yes, love."

"Can I lay my head here?" pointing to her breast.

"Sure you can, Andy, lay your head down."

And I did and I loved it, and I told her why. "Right now this feels like the safest place in the world."

"Then stay there, my love, stay as long as you want."

And I stayed there for some time while she stroked my hair, and with my head in her bosom, I unearthed my past, leaving no stone unturned. My mother. Auntie M. My foster dad. Mrs. Delanor. Stolsky and Majors. All the grisly details.

THE RAGE / 1981

Three for three is a tremendous day at the plate for a major league baseball player. Hell, a guy who averages one hit in every three at bats is considered a superstar. I was three for three. So why didn't I feel good about it?

I had loved three women in my life (prior to Terri)—my mother, Auntie M, and Mrs. Delanor. All three were dead. I guess, more specifically, all three were dead because of me. So I guess it would be safe to say that I carried a considerable amount of guilt around with me as I graced the grounds of the Petersburg Home for Boys on a continuous basis from August of 1977 until October of 1981.

Yeah, following the Delanor incident in '77, I was never placed in foster care again. I sometimes blamed Mr. Delanor, and wondered whatever became of that one-eyed prick, but for the most part I blamed myself. Because, after all, I was Catholic, and that seems to be part of what being Catholic is all about. At least that's how the sisters at the home sometimes made me feel.

The Petersburg Home for Boys was not a place that was conducive to forming deep friendships—

179

at least not for me. Some kids laughed it up and seemed to have a heck of a time there, although if given the choice, they would rather have had parents, I was pretty sure. But as for me, well, I just kind of stayed to myself. Sure, I made the occasional crack that resulted in disciplinary action, but for the most part I just sat around, mired in a sea of guilt, trying to learn about God and making mental lists of what I did and didn't believe when it came to *him*.

An orphanage, you see, is not the type of place you want to stay in long. Staying in defeats the purpose, which is, after all, to get out. Get out to foster care, and maybe, if the Fates are smiling on you, even find an adoptive family. But hope for adoption, even under normal circumstances, wanes with each passing year. And my circumstances weren't exactly normal.

So by the time I turned thirteen, in 1981, I had seen a lot of kids come and go. The ones that remained were the ones no one wanted. Like me. And Richie Majors. And Mel Stolsky.

Majors and Stolsky had become something of a dynamic duo over my last two years in Petersburg. Majors was tall, maybe six three, and lean, with a pockmarked face that spoke of previous acne, and a prominent Adam's apple that seemed to have a life of its own whenever he opened his mouth. Which was pretty much all the time. His day didn't seem complete unless he hurt at least one person's feelings, which he did in a manner that made up for in crudeness what it lacked in creativity. He got away with it, too, for while Richie may not have been the toughest guy at Petersburg, Mel Stolsky certainly was.

I rarely saw Stolsky's eyes, as they were in a constant state of subterfuge beneath a shock of long greasy hair. On those rare occasions I did, they seemed dead to the world. Already beyond caring at the age of sixteen. He didn't talk a whole lot, just laughed like hell at Majors's crude put-downs. He backed up Majors's words with his thick arms and short temper, and I sensed by the nuns' reactions around him that even they thought he was beyond hope.

I guess for lack of a better term, I would call them white trash, but I wouldn't want to offend actual white trash by doing so.

But up until I gave my heartfelt lecture on kettles boiling over and the sin of Onan, I did not have much of a history with the two aspiring thugs. I mean they had tripped me when I was walking down a flight of stairs in '77, had given me a world-class wedgie in '78, and occasionally spit on me or punched me in the arm for no reason, but other than that, things were cool between us.

But after getting big laughs on the subject of Onanism, things changed. We become closer. They ate with me one day. Tried to teach me to smoke the next. Asked me how I knew "all that Bible shit." Cracked up when they got a close-up look at my ear. I guess you could say we bonded. So when they invited me into the bathroom and locked the door, I thought nothing of it. I thought maybe they were going to catch a quick smoke before proceeding to not learn anything in class.

I still suspected nothing when Stolsky pulled down his pants. After all, there were urinals all around us, even if most urinal users weren't in Mel's apparent state of arousal when eliminating urine from their bodies.

I should have caught on when Majors spoke. Yeah, his "Hey Brown, how 'bout suckin' Mel's dick?" should have been a giveaway. But it wasn't. I mean, after all, we were tight, right? And besides, Majors's tone was so uncharacteristically polite that I actually thought this was a simple yes-or-no question. As if I could just say, "Oh no thanks, I don't feel like sucking Mel's dick today," and that would be the end of it.

Actually, I did say no, but unfortunately, that wasn't the end of it. And about the time Majors hit me in the back of the head with his forearm and Stolsky started pushing down on my head as if he were doing a perfectly executed triceps extension, I suddenly realized that I was in a world of trouble.

Majors was punching me in the ribs from behind as Stolsky continued to practice his unique form of isometrics. A form of isometrics that he was pretty damn good at, as gradually my face got closer and closer to its intended destination.

That's when Majors started in with his talk

about making me squeal like a pig, and telling Stolsky about what a pretty mouth I had. Sure, he was just spewing lines straight out of *Deliverance,* but I didn't know that at the time. I actually thought he was being original for a change. Original and terrifying.

Stolsky kept quiet the whole time. He just applied ever-increasing pressure to the back of my head and neck while Majors became ever more specific as to what the duo's plans for me were. Majors was going to treat me like a dog for one thing. I was going to put Mel's balls in my mouth for another. And according to Majors, I was going to like it too.

I guess if I had to go back and figure out exactly where Majors went wrong, it would be in changing his tenses—the way he switched them from future to present. You see, he stopped telling me what was *going* to happen, and began telling me to do it *now.* Which in this case was the difference between saying "You're gonna put Mel's balls in your mouth" and "Put them balls in your mouth now!" The difference might seem negligible. But not to me. No, for me, the difference was between feeling terror, and feeling rage. And make no mistake about it, in that bathroom in 1981, I suddenly felt a whole lot of rage.

So what exactly did I do in this rage? Well, to begin with I put Mel's balls in my mouth. And the moment I felt those nuts in my mouth, I clamped down with my teeth and I started throwing my head from side to side like I'd seen my old pal Shakes the dog do so many times.

At that point Stolsky ended his silence. Ended it with high-pitched screams that still make me shudder from time to time. I guess it's not so easy to be the strong silent type when your scrotum is being treated like an old slipper in the clamped jaws of a golden retriever.

Majors was trying to pull me off his beleaguered buddy, but I could have held on all day if I had so wanted. I did not so want. What I wanted was Majors, whose sick plan this no doubt had been. I released Stolsky's battered balls from my mouth, and as I did so, I was reaching for my quarters. Those same quarters that had spelled the end of Mr. Delanor's left eye. The same quarters I had carried with me every day since then.

I grabbed those quarters tight, wheeled around as fast as I could, and put every ounce of energy into smashing Majors's nose, visualizing it exploding as I did so. But I missed. Miscalculated his height, I guess, and missed his nose completely. Instead the punch caught him square in that Adam's apple of his, and he dropped as if he'd been shot, gurgled once or twice, and then fell silent for good. I had no idea that he was dead. Never could have conceived of the possibility.

Stolsky didn't look all that tough writhing in pain on the soiled blue-and-white tiles of the Petersburg bathroom. He looked kind of pathetic, actually. Unfortunately for him, I wasn't feeling real pathetic myself at the time. Not sympathetic. Not empathetic. Not even apathetic. No, all I felt was rage, and my emotion wasn't quite spent. Even as I heard the banging on the door. Even as I heard voices screaming on the other side. I knew for certain that I wasn't quite done with Mel Stolsky. Not yet.

Amid his moaning and screaming, I heard Stolsky mumbling. Praying. I put my right foot on the inside of his crotch and thought of Stallone in the first *Rocky,* saying "You shoulda planned ahead" to the poor SOB on the docks.

Stolsky made the sign of the cross as I put my other foot on the other side of his crotch.

I heard the jingling of keys on the other side of the door, and I heard Stolsky begin the Lord's prayer as I reached down with my left hand and squeezed those balls as if they were the quarters that had been my sole companions over the last four years. I lowered myself into a squatting position and listened to Stolsky's weak attempt at spiritual consolation. "Forgive us our trespasses, as we forgive those who trespass against us. And lead us not into temptation, but deliver us . . ."

The door opened. "Andy Brown, you let that boy go!" I turned to see Sister Fahey, the same nun who had taught me about the kettle boiling over. Over the years I've wondered about whether Sister Fahey thought I was touching Mel Stolsky in an impure way.

"Andy Brown!" the sister yelled. "For God's sake, don't—"

I exploded out of that squatting position and took Stolsky's balls with me. From what I was told, Stolsky would have died had it not been for Sister Fahey, who stopped the blood flow, which I heard was pretty extensive.

It was a historic day for me, and not just because I had put a man's testicles in my mouth. No, it was also the day that I stopped being an orphan, and instead became a criminal in the eyes of the state of Virginia.

NOVEMBER 27, 1985 / EVENING

The line of cars extended out onto Elm Street. A line that I saw was turning into our little dead-end street and then snaked its way back out onto Elm.

My thoughts first turned to disaster. Maybe someone had died. No, that couldn't be it. Sure, motorists slowed down and rubbernecked at casualties, but as far as I knew, they didn't turn into dead-end streets specifically to check them out.

But wait a second, my dad had said that people drove by the Suglings' house just to see their Christmas display, didn't he? That had to be it. I explained the situation to Terri, who had done a pretty impressive job of holding my hand throughout the many gear changes.

But as we got closer, it became apparent that the Suglings' house, despite its considerable holiday illumination, was not the attraction. My house was.

"Andy," Terri said, "there are camels on your lawn."

Indeed there were. Three of them to be exact. But of course there had to be three, one for each of the wise men, who were also on my front lawn. Caspar, Melchior, and Balthazar. Yeah, they were there.

But I guess they had to be. To visit the kid in the crib, who was being fawned over by Mary and Joseph in the manger that had been erected in my front yard. Actually, the newborn king turned out to be a doll, but Mary and Joseph were very much real, as were the two sheep who munched happily on the hay that made up the floor of the manger.

All of it illuminated by the spotlights I had helped ol' Tietam with, which revealed him and Holly, the mystery woman, rocking contentedly on new rockers on our tiny front porch. Looking very much like an old married couple, instead of two strangers on a first date.

When Terri pulled into the drive, after a good ten-minute crawl, the odd scene turned surreal. Actually it had been surreal to start with, so I guess it turned surrealer. That's probably not even a word, but it's the only way I can describe it.

Because as I looked into the white light of this December night and saw the flakes falling ever faster, I heard my father's voice.

"Okay boys, break time. We've got some hot chocolate and cookies inside."

And out of the manger and into our little house walked three wise men, a shepherd, and the mother and father of Jesus. The door closed behind them, momentarily leaving a trail of disappointed motorists behind, but before seasonal depression could set in, the door opened back up and three new wise men, a new shepherd, and a new mother and father of Jesus strolled toward the manger, polishing off cookies before taking their posts.

As I reached the porch, Holly stood to embrace us simultaneously with the type of hug usually not meant for ten-minute acquaintances. But Holly wasn't a usual woman, and her hug felt right at home amid this bizarre Winter Wonderland/Town of Bethlehem scene.

"Isn't it wonderful?" Holly said, and her beam seemed a perfect companion to Tietam Brown's shy, little-boy smile.

Tietam got up and gave Terri the politest of handshakes and embraced me warmly. He said, "How was the movie, son?"

"Well how was your movie, Dad?" I asked, walking that tightrope that separates lying from simply not telling the truth. A tightrope I didn't feel all that comfortable walking.

"Andy, we didn't make it to the movies."

"You didn't?" Had my dad taken her back here and gotten his first strike already? Had she told him what he was doing to her? Had she licked— no, I refused to even think it. She was too sweet. Too nice. Had too much going for her. Plus she wasn't drunk or married.

Fortunately, my dad cleared up the situation.

"Nope, when I told Holly about my little plan here, she suggested that we head back right away."

"That's right," Holly interjected. "I told your dad that those boys and that girl were going to be cold and hungry when they took their breaks, and that we needed to take care of them."

Now the interjection belonged to Tietam, who said, "Yeah, so we stopped at the store and headed back to make hot cocoa and bake homemade cookies."

The cars kept on coming. Until ten o'clock, at which time Tietam shut down the set, paid his performers (including what looked to be a whole lot of money for the camel handlers), thanked all of the remaining cars on a one-by-one basis, and basically looked like how I imagined Walt Disney had at the opening of Disneyland in 1955.

He came rushing back to the house, announced the night a complete success, and decided to celebrate by treating us all to the best restaurant in town, J.R. McClean's.

On this special night, with the season's first snow laying a white carpet across town, we had the steakhouse just to ourselves, save a family of four who talked about "seeing camels in Conestoga" and a man and woman barely visible in the dim light of the bar.

In the plush atmosphere of oak tables and aged beef, Tietam Brown was out of his element but in his glory. "Whatever you want," he said. Words that seemed strange coming from a notorious cheapskate like my dad, even more so in a place where a bowl of soup cost an Abe, and a burger a Hamilton. You know, as in five dollars and ten. At that rate, he might go through a couple of Benjamins on one meal.

I studied my menu in shock, lifting my gaze only when a somewhat less than macho waiter rattled off a list of specials that I had never heard of. Finally, I said, "Dad, isn't this an awful lot of money to spend?"

My dad put his arm around Holly. "Son, you can't put a price on memories. Or family. A night like this doesn't come around too often in life. And when it does, would it be fair to crush these memories with the foolish grasp of stinginess? No, Andy, I couldn't do that to you, or us, all of us. Besides, son, it's time that you started eating better."

As if I was the guy who had placed the Brown family on a weekly fifty-dollar food budget that deemed chicken nuggets a luxury item.

But I just nodded my head, and we all ordered huge steaks while Tietam Brown dreamed out loud about big things to come.

"Sure it was great, but we can do better," he said. "We need some music for atmosphere, and maybe a Santa to collect for the poor. Why he'd clean up on those cars crawling down our street. It would be a pretty cold heart indeed who wouldn't reach into their wallet and give a buck or two in the name of Jesus."

Terri's eyes lit up at the name of the Savior, the same guy who had cost me my big date with destiny, but whom I still thanked for all the good in my life. I thought she might take offense. Instead she said, "Mr. Brown, I think that is a wonderful idea. Your Nativity scene might touch the heart of people who've forgotten what this season is all about. And to have a Santa Claus there to help out those less fortunate really evokes the spirit of the true St. Nicholas."

"Wow," my dad said, "you sure make it sound good. To tell the truth, I was thinking of our Santa as more or less one of those squeegee guys in the city. You know, pressuring people. But please, call me Tietam."

"Okay, Tietam, but do you mind a little constructive criticism?"

"Let's hear it," said Tietam.

"Well, it just seems to me that Joseph, the father of Jesus, shouldn't really be smoking cigarettes in the manger."

Our table exploded in laughter. Holly slammed her fist on the table and said, "Tietam, I told you he was smoking. You just said it was his breath in the air."

I looked at my father, who looked like he'd just been called out on strikes to lose the World Series. "Damn," he said, "I'll fire his ass." Two bad words from Tietam in a single sentence. But I guess it just showed his dedication to producing the most realistic live Nativity scene possible.

Holly admonished her balding new boyfriend, a man who I guessed was at least twenty years older than her, maybe a little more. But damn if they didn't look downright cute together. "Tietam, he's just a college kid, he probably needs that job."

But Tietam was not so easily swayed. "Do you know how much I'm paying those Cortland kids?" he asked. Holly shrugged her shoulders. Tietam decided to answer his own question. "Twelve dollars. Twelve dollars an hour. Three times more than they make at the local fast food joints and bars. And double what they'll make as gym teachers in the real world. Oh yeah he's fired," my dad reiterated.

"You'll need to find a new Mary too," Holly said.

"Why?" Tietam asked.

"Because she said she needs to start studying more. Says she can't spare the time."

"Damn."

Holly continued, "Now, as for the wise men, they're supposed to be Middle Eastern, right?"

"I guess," Tietam said. "But wasn't one a black guy?"

"Well those guys look like they just got off a bus from Long Island."

"Holly," Tietam said with a long extended whine, so it came across like HOLL-LEEE, "come on, give me a break, I'm not exactly drawing talent from the University of Karachi here. I mean let's get real, I could search the whole college and not find three wise men. Look, there's a perfect example."

My father pointed to the window and we all looked out at a large figure walking in the driving snow, about six feet four, maybe 230, dressed only in jeans and a cutoff red flannel. "Look at him," my dad said. "His parents send him off to college, and he's too stupid to even wear a coat . . . All right, here's what I'm going to do . . . I'll fire Joseph, we'll find a new Mary, but I'll keep the wise men, okay?"

Holly raised her hand.

"Yes," my father said.

"Uh, Tietam, if you fire Joseph, who's going to take his place on short notice? You can't just stick the same people out there all night."

Now it was Terri's turn to raise her hand.

"Yes," my father said.

"Tietam, what about me and Andy?"

"You and Andy what?"

"What about if me and Andy were Mary and Joseph?"

My eyes lit up. So did Holly's. So did my dad's.

I had to admit it was a good idea. I didn't smoke cigarettes, and Terri was a virgin, even though part of me wished she weren't.

Holly spoke first. "That would be wonderful, Tietam. Just imagine, your own son, and his Terri, looking down on the Christ child in your own front yard."

"Yeah," Tietam said. "That would be cute. But now we have to get a real kid in that crib, because that doll's just not making it."

Holly pulled playfully at his ear and said, "Tietam . . . you . . . can't . . . have . . . a . . . baby . . . in that crib. He'll freeze."

"Not if we shuttle about four or five kids in and out. Maximum exposure time . . . fifteen minutes tops."

"No real babies," Holly said.

Just then I got a quick twinge in my stomach and realized the whole Joseph role might be impossible to pull off. "Frank 'n' Mary's," I said. "Damn, I work two nights a week."

"Quit," my dad said.

"I can't, Dad, I have to give two weeks' notice."

"Not me," said Tietam. "When I'm not cool with something, I just up and leave."

I had a quick thought of my father "just up and leaving" when I was three months old, then looked at him holding Holly, who became more beautiful with each passing minute. I wondered how she'd ever seemed average at all.

I said, "I'll work out something, but at least until Thursday, I'll be your new Joseph."

NOVEMBER 27, 1985 / 11:10 P.M.

The steaks arrived. Steaks of a thickness that I'd never seen, and a flavor the likes of which my taste buds had never known. So good was the steak that I barely detected the rising voices at the bar, and a short, powerful figure moving out of the shadows. Didn't detect it until it was right behind my father, nostrils flaring, eyes glaring. And in just that instant, it all fell into place. The car. The car that had pulled silently down my street on the night of my first kiss. The night of the coach. The same car that I saw as we pulled into J.R.'s. And that short, powerful figure. I'd seen that same man vault onto the field and dive onto the pile. The man I felt then was Clem Baskin's father. He must have found out.

"You Tietam Brown?" the man practically yelled.

Holly turned to face Baskin, who looked to be five six, 220, and thick and muscular inside a white dress shirt and a pair of tan slacks.

Terri turned and let out a gasp, obviously startled by this crew-cutted bulldog who reeked of bad intentions.

My dad never turned. Just chewed his steak

slowly, then swallowed and said, "I'm having dinner with my family. I would appreciate it if you'd leave us alone."

Baskin was turning redder by the second, his fists were clenched and his body was tensed, ready to strike. "You'd appreciate that, huh?" he said. "Well I'll tell you what, you bald, skinny piece of crap, my wife and I are trying to enjoy our anniversary. But we can't do that because there is a smell over here that makes me sick. So I'll tell you what I'd appreciate. I'd appreciate you and your one-eared son getting the hell out of this place. You got me?"

Holly stood up. "Now stop it," she said, but Tietam held up his hand as if asking a crowd for silence at a championship game. Terri was scared, and to tell the truth I was too, because Mr. Baskin looked about ready to burst at the seams. But Tietam Brown's expression never changed. Instead he began cutting his meat, and with great calmness said, "Like I said, sir, I'm having dinner with my family. I would appreciate being left alone. If, however, you would like to address this problem afterward, we can do so in the parking lot."

A waiter tried to make peace, and a bartender offered to buy a round. But Baskin seemed to be appeased. "It's okay," he assured everyone. "We're going to settle this . . . later."

He turned to walk away, and life momentarily seemed to go on, but in an instant Baskin reached for a solid oak chair, wheeled around, and brought the heavy wood down on Tietam Brown's head.

"Dad," I screamed, just an instant before contact, and my father brought up an arm. But the gesture seemed futile, and like a wounded deer, my father fell to the floor, obviously hurt.

Holly was the first to act, jumping up from her seat, rushing to defend this man she barely knew. "You bas—" she yelled, but the word never got out as Clem Baskin's father let loose with a powerful shove that knocked her over a vacant table.

Now I shot into action, but before I could grab him, I was met with the smash of a water glass to the top of the head, a shot that dazed me and sent me down to one knee.

"Andy," Terri yelled, and she rushed to my aid. Another voice yelled, a voice from the shadows, and when she emerged, I saw Mrs. Baskin in that familiar red dress. "Stop, Brock, you'll kill him." And as my eyes struggled to focus, it appeared that he might, as he was down on his knees throwing hard punches at my father, who showed no sign of movement.

Maybe I was still reeling from the blow to my head, or maybe I couldn't see through the blood that now flowed from my wound. Or maybe the move was so sudden that only trained eyes could see. Eyes that could pause and slow-motion the scene. But all I saw was a flash of an arm and a hook of a neck, and then a human constrictor wrapped around its prey.

A human constrictor wearing a mask of bright

crimson, so thick and so wet that it stood in bright contrast to the whites of its eyes. Eyes that were calm.

My father was hooked around Baskin in a sickening way. A way that held the man's body at angles that bodies won't go. But the sounds. The sounds I think were most sickening of all. Low guttural wheezes from way back in his lungs. Animal noises from a prey that was done.

In the dim light of J.R.'s, I saw Brock Baskin's face. Impossibly red, and ready to burst. Through the blood in my eyes and the fog in my brain, I saw it. Amid the screaming of women and the panic of men I saw it. The face of Brock Baskin as it lost all will to live.

Mrs. Baskin screamed loudest. "Let him go, let him go. Tietam, please let him go."

I'm not sure anyone else saw it. It was just a small glance. So subtle, it seemed, that for a long time I questioned whether it was real at all. My father's white eyes. Incredibly calm. Incredibly calm and looking at me. Only at me. Then one eye gave a wink, and Brock Baskin screamed. And a terrible smell fouled the air of J.R.'s.

Mr. Baskin, it turned out, was right. There was a bad smell in our general vicinity. But it wasn't my father. No, the smell came from Baskin's tan slacks, which were now kind of dark, at least in the middle.

Then Tietam Brown stood, bloodied but unbowed, and walked to his chair and calmly sat down, where he was embraced by his girl, whose white Cortland sweatshirt turned instantly red.

Then Terri helped me up and gave a hug of her own, and although my blood wasn't as thick or as abundant as Tietam's, I too stained a garment. Terri's beautiful sweater became smeared with my blood as, for the second time, she cradled my bloodied head in her warm, loving arms.

Mrs. Baskin, too, embraced her man. A man without a scratch, but far worse injured than we were. No red badge of courage for Brock Baskin. Just a brown smear of shame. And a wife who was crying, only feet from our table. "Goddamn you," she said, in a voice low and shaking. Over and over, the same simple phrase. "Goddamn you, goddamn you."

At first I thought her husband was the target at which her words were aimed. But as her voice grew in volume and the words grew in number, she left little doubt. "Goddamn you, Tietam Brown. If it's the last thing I do, I will get you for this. Goddamn you, Tietam, I will get you for this." Then she broke down in sobs and her words ceased to make sense, but whatever they were, they didn't seem to be nice.

Then the police arrived on the scene, their lights splashing blue on Cortland's white canvas. Made me think of Auntie M, with her beautiful smile on her poor severed head.

They tried to slap handcuffs on my bloodied dad, but a quick word from J.R. himself, in his black cowboy hat, seemed to change their minds.

So the Cortland police, who usually broke up college fights at the Dark Horse Saloon, now took with them a very smelly prisoner. A prisoner who no longer possessed any will to live. And next to him, a wife with nothing left to lose. With only a promise of vengeance to hold the broken pieces of her life together.

My father, I must say, stayed remarkably calm. Even when an ambulance tried to whisk him away. "Twenty stitches at least," one EMT said. But Tietam Brown was not to be swayed. His steak, he explained, was only half eaten. He would finish it here, and then his girlfriend would take him to Cortland General.

"Are you sure?" he was asked.

"Yeah, I'm sure. I can't let one guy . . . poop on my party."

He finished his steak and then he was gone. Gone in a trail of blood drops. A red badge of courage that he wore with great pride. Earned in a fight he hadn't looked for, but that he had ended with force. A fight he hadn't started, but one that he had caused nonetheless. A fight that a sad lonely woman had promised to avenge.

I was bleeding too, but not nearly so bad. Bad enough maybe for stitches, but if so, just a few, and I couldn't quite rationalize a three-hour emergency room wait on a night such as this.

A night when the snow was now five inches deep. A night of kisses and hugs and black lingerie. Of sexy plans that gave way to a much deeper love. Of camels and mangers and chain-smoking Josephs. Of thick steaks and laughter and the stale scent of fresh blood. Of a father in love with a wonderful girl, and the whites of his eyes and the foul smell of shit. Of the sudden realization that a balding middle-aged man might very well be the toughest man on the planet. A true father for a kid who always wanted one, and a hero for a kid who never believed heroes existed.

The drunks were just starting to stumble out of the Horse as Terri and I drove by. Still a few hours away from the mass exodus onto Main Street where mom and dad's hard-earned money bought their kids late night breakfasts at the place where I worked. Damn, I had to work out some kind of deal so I could be a father to Jesus and still wash those dishes.

I saw the cutoff red flannel, dusted with white, the large frame standing motionless among the night revelers, who now lobbed snowballs and tried to work out late night sleeping arrangements in willing new arms. I followed his gaze, and I saw a young woman grabbing the ass of some drunk. And in that ass-grabbing instant, I knew right away that she once had been his. And within his snow-covered flannel, I could almost see his heart break.

My two-hour walk was but a ten-minute drive. Those minutes did not offer much conversation, but volumes in the way of understanding. As if I was really hers, and she was really mine. Like

Rocky and Adrian. Like Zucko and Sandy. Like Joanie and Chachi.

"Good night, Andy," she said as we got to my drive. I looked at the lawn, where only hours before Bethlehem lived. But now only cigarette butts where Joseph had been. Only camel poop where once wise men had stood.

"Good night, Terri, we had . . . quite a night."

"You're not mad at me Andy, are you?"

"Mad?" I asked. "At you? No, why would I be?"

"I hope you don't think I'm a CT."

"Of course not," I said. I had no idea what she meant. College transfer? Colorado Tech? Cookie Toll House?

"Maybe I can T your C next time I see you."

"That would be great." What did that mean? What did that mean?

A good two hours later, I heard the Fairmont pull up, Springsteen drifting out into the quiet December night. "Show a little faith, there's magic in the night, you ain't a beauty, but hey you're all right . . . and that's all right with me."

I heard laughter heading up the stairs, then I heard the bedroom door close, and then I heard something rather odd. No, not beds bouncing, or boards banging, or tape recorders clicking, or voices moaning, or deal-making. What I heard, what I swore I heard, was the sound of Antietam Brown IV cuddling. Actually cuddling.

And maybe the strangest sound was one I didn't hear at all. Strange because it didn't exist. I never heard the telltale sounds of the push-ups and free squats downstairs, or feet heading out after the second act was done, or a slamming door, or a departing car. Holly, the mystery woman, was staying the night.

DECEMBER 12, 1985–
DECEMBER 23, 1985

Tietam and Holly spent all their nights together after that, and not once did I hear the signs of my father's special brand of lovemaking. Maybe that word was the key. Lovemaking. Maybe my father was actually making love next door instead of exploiting the vulnerabilities of lost souls. Apparently he'd dropped his "three strikes, you're out" rule as well, because Holly, the mystery woman, was pretty much a fixture at the Brown house for those next couple of weeks.

One morning I awoke to hear them singing (and I'm not kidding here) "(They Long to Be) Close to You." You know, the Carpenters song. Which was horrible except for the way they were looking in each other's eyes while they did it, which was anything but. But then Tietam had to try to go soprano for the "ahh ahh ah ah ahh, close to you," which really wasn't a pretty sight . . . or sound.

When the serenade was through, he wrapped his arms around Holly and said, "Tell me 'bout ol' Tietam."

"Oohh I need 'im," Holly sang back.

"Holly, you're a poet and my thing shows it, it's a Longfellow." Then, "Let's bake some cookies."

My father had managed to be cute, charming, crude, and innocent all in one sentence.

As for those cookies, they were everywhere. The smell of gingerbread, chocolate chips, and peanut butter was with us practically around the clock. Not just for the performers, who were always around between six and ten, but for the tourists as well. Yes, tourists. Word of Tietam Brown's live Nativity scene had spread to the point where people not only from Conestoga and Cortland but Syracuse, Binghamton, and Ithaca as well were regularly lining our block. And they bought cookies while they were there. All of the proceeds from which went to our local Salvation Army, as did the money Santa collected at the foot of the drive. Sometimes Tietam took his turn inside the Santa suit, and I'll be damned if he wasn't the best, albeit thinnest, Santa I'd ever seen.

When it came to his scene, good just wasn't good enough for Tietam Brown. True to his word, he brought in music for atmosphere. Actually went out and bought speakers, a cassette deck, and some cassettes (I think eight-tracks were strictly in pawnshops by then) and filled the cool air with the classic holiday sounds of Como, Crosby, Sinatra, and others every evening for four hours.

But he didn't stop there. Not my father. No, he had an elaborate stair system built in the rear of the manger so that an angel could climb up and stand on a special perch he had made. A perch that he painted black, so on certain nights the angel really did appear to be flying.

Hey, let's not forget about the drummer boy. Not the little drummer boy. My dad actually went down to Wheeler Elementary School and obtained the services of two drummers from the school band, who took turns standing in the cold for hours, pretending to drum.

As for me, I threw myself into the role of Joseph with reckless abandon. Studied for it, lived it. I became Joseph. In the words of Stan Kellner, the creator of basketball cybernetics, who I once heard lecture at a basketball clinic in Richmond, "See the picture, think the picture, be the picture, don't be afraid to make mistakes." Granted, there was not a whole lot of demand for one-handed point guards, but I was able to use Stan's cybernetical knowledge to become the best Joseph I could be.

But my two weeks of manger bliss came with a heavy price at Frank 'n' Mary's. In return for two weeks off, I had to work midnight till 8 a.m. on the twenty-third, twelve to 6 p.m. on Christmas Eve, and twelve to eight on Christmas Day. Damn, that was cutting things close, especially as I had been invited by Terri for Christmas Eve dinner at the Johnson house—my first face-to-face meeting with the reverend.

Holly had been especially upset over the scheduling. She said, "Andy, we want to spend the holiday together. That's the way families are supposed to do it."

Family. She had referred to us as a family. I liked that. "Holly," I said, "does that mean you're not heading 'somewhere other than here'?"

"Well now, Andy, your father has convinced me that 'here' is exactly where I need to be."

When she said it, I had this corny idea that Holly should have been the angel atop the manger, because I really thought she'd been sent down from heaven to rescue my father.

"Holly, don't worry," I said. "I can still spend Christmas morning with you, and I can still be Joseph on the twenty-third, before I go to work. But I think we'll have to find someone else for the twenty-fourth, because I'm going to Terri's after work."

"Well I think that's wonderful," she said. "Besides, I would never want anyone to stand outside on Christmas Eve. We'll just leave the manger open."

My father, who'd been stringing popcorn for our Christmas tree, obviously had other plans.

He said, "Holly, Christmas Eve is going to be the biggest night of the year for us. Do you know how disappointed people will be if they drive by ol' Tietam's and there's no one out there? It will ruin their Christmas. No, the show must go on."

"Come on, Tietam," she said, "all the college kids go home on the twenty-third. And even if they were able, we wouldn't allow it. No, Christmas Eve is for family."

"I'm offering a lot of money. Twenty-five an hour."

"I don't care if you're offering fifty. No means no."

I'd heard Robert De Niro say the same "No means no" line in *The Deer Hunter*, but somehow Holly seemed even more forceful with hers—in a sweet angelic type of way.

My father smiled and put his string of popcorn down. A mischievous, little-boy smile. "Holly, look what I've got," he said as he pulled a piece of paper out of his pocket and waved it in the air.

"What do you have there, you naughty old man?"

"It's an ad I just wrote. I'm going to put it in the paper."

Holly walked to the couch and snatched the paper from his fingers. She read briefly, then put her hand over her eyes and shook her head. Then she laughed, paused, laughed again, and said, "Tietam, you can't print this."

"Why not?"

"Because it's a little offensive."

"How come?"

"Because it reads 'Attention: Jews wanted.'"

I burst out laughing. Tietam seemed confused and said, "What's wrong with that?"

"I told you, hon, it's offensive."

Tietam got up from the couch, threw up his

arms in disbelief, walked in a few circles on the same shag carpet that his penis had once brushed on a regular basis, and let out a loud sigh.

"I don't get it," he said.

"What don't you get, hon?"

"Well throughout history, the Jewish people have never felt wanted, right? Now I make up an ad that tells them, Hey you're wanted, and you tell me it's wrong. I don't get it . . . So look, if I don't print the ad, then maybe I'll just offer the dough to anyone who wants it, and we'll weed out the people who need the cash more than the family bonding."

Holly went over and kissed her confused man. I thought momentarily that my father was going to start making out with her, but then I remembered that this was the new Tietam Brown, and the new Tietam wouldn't do that in front of his son.

Holly said, "I'll tell you what. Why don't I make up a new ad that doesn't use the word 'Jews' in it. Then I will put it on the bulletin board of the local synagogues, along with our telephone number. When we get a call, we will explain what we're doing with our Nativity scene. And if, by, say . . . the twenty-second, we don't have anyone, then we'll run your ad. How does that sound?"

"Pretty good, I guess."

"Oh, and Tietam."

"Yeah, baby?"

"I'm a Jew . . . and I know that you want me."

DECEMBER 24, 1985 / 11 A.M.

Christmas Eve. But at 11 a.m., it wasn't quite eve yet. Which made it, I guess, Christmas Eve day. I'd been lucky enough to thumb a ride almost straight home, and had crawled into bed at 8:30 a.m., where I'd drifted off immediately, and sometime in the night dreamed of Terri's bare breasts springing from her bra, like a wire snake from a salted peanut can.

I awoke with a start and realized that my kettle had boiled over. I'd been so caught up in Christmas that I'd neglected to pour some out on my own. I looked at the clock, got up from the bed, rolled my shorts in a ball which I tossed in the trash, and then hopped into the shower to wash the sleep and other stuff from my skin. Actually, I stepped into the shower, as no hopping took place.

I walked down the stairs to see Holly curled up on the couch, a book in her hands. "Good morning, sleepyhead," she said. "Care for some tea?"

"Anything but cocoa." I was all cocoaed out. Cookied out too. Even now the smell of fresh cookies brings me back to my manger. "Where's my dad?"

"Your father is out. Shopping. He claims he's getting something special. But he wanted me to tell you that he has ordered a cab to take you to work. And a cab to take you back. It's his treat."

"Jeez, I hadn't even thought of that," I said.

"So tonight's the big night, huh?" she said, and she put down her book and walked to the kitchen, where she poured me a cup of hot tea. Raspberry Zinger.

"I guess so," I said.

"Well aren't you excited?"

"I guess. Probably be more excited if I wasn't so tired. And didn't have to wash dishes for the next eight hours. What kind of people would eat at Frank 'n' Mary's on Christmas Eve anyway?"

"Andy, there are a lot of people who think going anywhere is a treat. Or maybe they have no one to spend Christmas Eve with."

I nodded my head. "Yeah I know how that feels."

She brushed my cheek with her hand and said, "I know that you do."

We stood in silence for just a moment, but that moment, it seemed, was a moment too long. Long enough to think back to all of those years with no mom or dad with whom to share Christmas Eve. Then Holly spoke.

"He loves you, you know."

"Yeah, I know that he does."

"And he's so happy to be with you at Christmas."

I looked down at my cup.

"Andy," Holly said.

"Yeah."

"Try not to dwell on the past too much. Think of tonight. And all the great days to come."

"Holly?"

"Yes, Andy."

"You know this is our first Christmas together, don't you? Me and my dad."

"Yes, Andy, I know."

"Holly?"

"Yes."

"If you're Jewish, why do you . . . uh . . . you know, why do you . . ."

"Why do I celebrate Christmas?" she asked.

"Well, yeah, I guess."

"Well Andy, it just seems to me that lots of people have been killed trying to prove that their religion is right. And I've got to believe that through all of this, God is shaking his head, thinking, This is not what I want. I think that there is a danger to anyone who thinks that they alone know God's plan. So instead of seeing people as Jew or Christian, Buddhist or Muslim, I try to divide all people into two groups: those who are good, and those who have the potential to be good. I celebrate days that give people hope. Christian and Jewish, and Halloween too."

I took a long sip of tea as I leaned on our counter and gazed at the mustard yellow refrigerator, which, had it been a dog, would have been taken out back and shot. I savored that tea, not so much because I liked tea as because it was Holly's. And like everything she touched, the tea seemed full of goodness.

"Holly?"

"Yes."

"Why'd he pick now? I mean this Christmas?"

"Because people change, Andy. People can change."

"But that's been your doing."

"No, he already was changing. I just came along and kind of sped things up."

She stopped talking for a moment, but I could see her mind at work. Pondering as she spoke, she did so haltingly.

"Andy . . . your father is a little difficult . . . to know."

I nodded my head.

"I think that there are a lot of different layers to him."

I nodded again, thinking of his layers and just how many I had gotten through . . . and how many more were left.

"And I think that if you got through all those layers, you would find a lot of pain there in the middle."

"Pain?" I said. "Why pain?" I felt there might be something to this, but to tell the truth, I was kind of enjoying Holly's sympathy. And now that sympathy was Tietam's.

"I'm not sure," Holly said. "Your father doesn't

open up a lot. You can't pry him open either, or else he just clamps down. So instead I try to be patient, nurture him, so he'll open on his own, like a flower."

At later times, I would envision Tietam Brown as a flower, his head swaying in the breeze, like a daffodil on a brisk March morning. But on this particular date, I just nodded and said, "Does he open up to you?"

"Not too much. He opens up a little, and then I try to fill in the blanks myself."

"Can you tell me what he said?"

"Well no, not everything, Andy, because some of it's just for me."

Holly touched my face. A touch I think of often. A touch of understanding. She then put her hand on my shoulder. I think of that touch too.

"Andy, your father is forty-eight years old, that's nineteen more than me."

"Yeah." I had no idea what she was getting at.

"He grew up poor in Albany, toward the end of the depression. Winters are cold in Albany—"

"Holly, I don't really see where you're going with this."

"Okay, okay, I guess what I'm trying to say is that Tietam's first memories of childhood were of his father bringing strangers home as a way to pay the rent."

"Oh." I didn't know what else to say.

"Andy?"

"Yeah?"

"From his little bed, he could hear his father next door . . . cheering."

"Oh."

"And that's all he said. But like I said, I try to fill in the blanks myself."

"Uh-huh."

"And I think that Tietam was afraid to be a father, because he was afraid he'd be like his dad."

I looked at her close. The way she looked in the winter sunlight, which flowed through the window and painted her face with a brush of warm gold. And for just a second, I swore that I saw the vaguest of halos surrounding her face.

"Holly?"

"Yes, Andy."

"I had a wet dream." Holy crap, had I really just said that? I didn't mean it as sexual. I was just really confused, and I guess that I thought maybe this angel could help ease my mind.

The angel laughed, clearly not offended. Quite to the contrary, she seemed kind of glad. Not glad that I'd shot a load in my shorts, but glad that I trusted her with such a deep thought. "Well," she said, "in a world filled with nightmares, your dream's not the worst kind to have."

"But don't you . . ." My voice trailed off.

"But don't I . . . don't I what, Andy?" she asked.

"Um, don't you think that maybe . . . that it's a little weird . . . that um, a guy like me, you know . . . with a girlfriend and all, is um . . . you know . . . having . . ."

216

"Wet dreams?"

"Yeah."

"Why don't we sit down?"

We sat on Tietam's plaid couch.

She patted my knee, smiled, and said, "Andy, I take it you're not sexually active with Terri?"

I squirmed in my sagging plaid seat. "Not really," I said.

"No, or not really?"

"Well, we kiss, you know, and do a couple of other things, but we haven't . . . you know."

"Done it?" Holly said, finishing my thought.

I nodded my head.

"Do you like kissing Terri?"

"Oh yeah."

"How about holding her hand? I see that you do that a lot."

I blushed and said, "Yeah."

"And you like being around her?"

"Very much."

"So why worry about it? Your body may be ready for sex, but maybe your mind isn't."

"No," I assured her, "my mind definitely is."

"Then I'll tell you what. You keep thinking about it. But don't put any pressure on yourself. And then, when it happens, it will happen on its own . . . and it will be the most beautiful thing in the world. Just take precautions."

Maybe it would happen on its own tonight, Christmas Eve. I had to agree that it would be the most beautiful thing in the world. But then

Andy the dreamer ran into Andy the horny teenager, and the horny guy won. And I found myself saying, "But other kids are doing it."

"But Andy, other kids don't have what you have."

"What's that?"

"Love, Andy, love. I see the way you two look at each other, and I know what it is. It's love. And you don't just love her because she's beautiful, do you?"

I shook my head.

"Or because she's stacked?"

I laughed and shook my head again.

"You love her because she likes you and she loves you and she wants you and because she makes you feel like you're the most special person in the world."

What was this lady, a mind reader? An angel?

I said, "Is that why you love Tietam?"

"No, 'cause he's hung like a hippo."

I fell out of my chair, and she laughed till it hurt, then laughed some more. Finally she stopped, leaned close to me, and said, "Can I tell you a secret?"

"Sure," I said, sensing something big.

"We've never done it."

Had it not been for her arms, I would have fallen again. My eyes were wide and my voice was high as I let out a loud "You haven't?"

She shook her head.

"Why not?"

"Well Andy, if your father is right, then I guess you'd know about his rather odd habits. You know . . . with women."

I nodded my head.

Holly smiled and said, "Do you think he needs more of that?"

"No, probably not."

"I think that he needs something else, don't you?"

I nodded my head, but I wasn't quite sure.

"Andy, your father needs to be loved, and he has never given himself a chance, not since your mother died. And I think that we've found that, found love, together. And just like you and Terri, when it does happen, it will happen on its own . . . and it will be the most beautiful thing in the world."

It all made perfect sense. Perfect, that is, until I threw my dad into the equation, and then it seemed a little crazy.

"Andy." Holly's words startled me from my state of confusion.

"Yeah."

"Do you know what I do up in Tietam's room all those hours?"

I laughed. "Well I kind of thought I did, but now I really don't have a clue."

"I paint."

"Paint, like, his room?" Not the brightest comment in the world, but kind of par for my course.

"No, dummy," she said, in a way that made "dummy" seem like a wonderful compliment. "Watercolors. And I want you to know that I've done a painting for you, and I think you'll love it, and I'm going to give it to you for Christmas."

"Wow," I said, "that's great. Do you do that for a living?"

Oddly my question seemed to catch her off guard, seemed to stun her like a quick jab from a boxer.

"I was painting in New York, the city, working on children's books, but I kind of got . . . side-tracked . . . Hey, your cab is here."

"Thank you for listening, Holly, to my stupid worries."

"Hey they weren't stupid . . . and listen, when you come back from your dinner, we're all going to open one present, and then you know what I'm going to do? I'm going to tuck you in and read you a story . . . do you have a favorite?"

My mind raced back to my dear Auntie M, and the thought of three kids nestled in bed waiting for Santa Claus on a clear southern night.

I said, "There was this one called, I think, *The Happiest Christmas*."

"The one about the missing reindeer? I know it by heart."

And then I heard honking and an old Grand Torino pulled up the drive. A rusted-out chariot to take me to the ball.

"Bye Holly . . . and thank you."

"No, thank you, Andy. And remember, people can change; I'm living proof."

And I heard her exclaim as that rusted-out, cigarette-smelling piece of crap rolled out of sight, "See you later, Andy, it will be a great night!"

DECEMBER 24, 1985 / 6:40 P.M.

The line of cars was backed up nearly a mile onto Elm Street, all coming to get a gaze at Tietam Brown's little yard of Bethlehem. Unfortunately, the yard consisted of only one wise man, a new Mary, and the original nonsmoking Joseph, who apparently either felt a strong sense of loyalty to his job or else didn't care a whole lot about Christmas. But that was it. No drummer boys, no angels, no shepherds.

I looked at the new Mary as I approached the manger. She may not have had Terri's looks, but she seemed pretty and nice, about twenty, I guessed, with dark hair and dark eyes, which were probably a lot closer to the original Mary than Terri's auburn-haired, green-eyed rendition.

My Joseph cohort said, "That's Andy," and she gave me a firm shake and a pleasant hello as I passed by her, accompanied by Mario Lanza's proud tenor as it boomed "What Child Is This" on Tietam's speakers.

The lack of performers meant that my dad and Holly would have the night to themselves as soon as I showered off the layers of Frank 'n' Mary's grease that had built up. True to Holly's word, the diner was home either for families celebrating the night or for solitary souls just wishing for someone with whom to share a holiday meal.

I opened the door and was met with the foreign sound of . . . a television set. I don't mean the language was foreign, like French or German, but foreign as in, you know, new to the surroundings. They looked so cute together on the couch, hand in hand and both smiling broadly, as the Alastair Sim version of *A Christmas Carol,* which I think is called *Scrooge,* flickered warmly in the darkness.

My father sat up and said, "Andy, come in. Come in and sit down." He patted the couch for emphasis, and I took a seat next to the happy couple, who seemed to be gloriously inebriated.

I said, "Wow, this is great, a television set." I later found out that not only was this movie in black and white, but all else was as well, as the set was a black-and-white one, and an old one at that. Still, as I looked at the TV, with the aluminum foil on its rabbit ears, it seemed right at home in Tietam's old house.

Tietam couldn't have been happier. "Holly gave it to me early," my dad said with pride. "So, you know, we could enjoy it tonight. Hell, if you weren't having dinner at the big house, you could watch this with us. It just started, you know. It's a heck of a movie. Been years since I've seen it."

Holly leaned in to Tietam and whispered into his ear. My dad nodded his head.

She said, "Andy, your dad got something for me, too." She was nearly crying from joy. She took her hand from behind my father and thrust it at me, and even in the dim glow of Jacob Marley's ghost, I could see her diamond shine.

"Oh God," I said. "It's beautiful. Is it a, um a . . ."

Just as before, Holly finished my thought. "An engagement ring. Andy, yes it is. Yes it is."

"Which means you're going to be—"

"Married," my father said. "We sure as hell are."

I don't know who was happier. Holly or Tietam. Or me for that matter. A kid with a family, what more could I want. Possibly it was a three-way tie for first.

Holly stood up, but still kept her hand in the air. She positively glowed with beauty, and a touch of strong alcohol as well, as she said, "Come Andy, have a drink with us."

I thought about my one drunken exploit with my father, and had no desire to relive it, with or without the porno film. I said, "I'd better not."

"Come on, young man," Holly said as she took hold of my hand and pretended to drag me into the kitchen. "You have one drink with us. Now do as your mother tells you."

Against my better judgment, I let her pour me a shot. I think of Wild Turkey, though I'm not really sure. But it was brown, it was strong, and it made me shake like a leaf while my father laughed and said, "Thatta boy, now chase it with this," and handed me a Genny Light, which I promptly chugged down.

My father was laughing when I set my beer down. "Now take off those clothes and let's do some push-ups," he said, and the three of us laughed until I regained my wind to find one more shot in my hand.

"Dad, I shouldn't," I said.

"Andy, this is important. This is a toast."

I raised my glass, as did Tietam and Holly.

"To the memory of my wife, who brought into this world a fine son. To the grace of God, who let me have a second chance. And to my future wife Holly, who believes in me."

We all said "Cheers," and I downed my third drink, and took a deep swig from a new Genny to stop my body from shaking. My head was floating in a wonderful way, and part of me longed to stay in this warm loving room for the rest of the night. But then I saw Terri, or her vision at least, by the glow of the fire in her black lingerie, kissing me softly before peeling off clothing and making sweet love, and then carving a turkey. Hey I know the turkey doesn't make sense, but it was my vision, and that's what I saw.

Damn, it was getting late. After seven already, and I still smelled like French fries with gravy, which was the perennial Frank 'n' Mary's favorite, day or night, Christmas Eve or no Christmas Eve. I ran up the stairs, two at a time, like the Tietam of old, with the remainder of my Genny in hand.

While the water streamed down, I thought of this night, and the magic it held. I couldn't have been more excited if I'd seen Santa himself, with that smoke encircling his head like a wreath much in the way an alcohol buzz was encircling mine. Was it really a good idea to be drunk at my girlfriend's house on Christmas Eve? Probably not, I decided as I swigged down the remainder of my beer.

A quick change of clothes and a dash of cologne, and I was back down the stairs, where Ebenezer Scrooge was choosing money over love. What a jerk. I thought of Bob Seger and a song that wasn't a hit but hit home with me nonetheless. "I ain't got no money, but I sure got a whole lot of love." Then I had the sudden feeling that I'd forgotten to do something, but I didn't know what.

Holly was holding two small presents in her hands. She said, "Andy, it's probably better that you don't drive right now, and even better if we don't drive you."

"Yeah I think that's safe to say," I laughed. "Plus with this traffic outside I'll probably be able to walk to Terri's house faster than I could drive."

"So your father and I got you these." She handed me the first gift. "This is for all the walking you do."

I opened the gift. A personal cassette player. I'd say a Walkman, but in fact it wasn't. Some other brand, I can't recall which.

"Thanks Holly, thanks Dad, I'll be able to use this a lot. But I don't have any tapes."

Holly handed me the second gift, which was about exactly the size of an audiocassette. Nat King Cole, *The Magic of Christmas*. She started to cry. Just a little. "I know that this won't take the place of your mother's, but I thought you could listen to it in times when you can't get to hers. And I know I can't replace her, but I thought I could be here in times when you need me."

She gave me a hug and I tried not to cry, but man it was tough and I just laid my head on her shoulder and closed my eyes hard. Because remember, crying's not crying unless a tear falls from the eye. And how could one fall if my eyes were clamped shut. Eventually the feeling subsided and I managed to walk out the door without shedding a tear.

Holly held open the door and shouted, "Remember that story, Andy. I'm tucking you in."

And then it was Tietam's turn. "I love you, son," he yelled, which was all but drowned out by Dean Martin singing "Let It Snow! Let It Snow! Let It Snow!"

I said goodbye to Joseph and "Nice to meet you" to the new Mary, who said, "Why are you crying?" in a gentle, sweet voice. Damn. Then, just as I reached the end of the drive, a delivery truck put on its brakes and a driver jumped out and said, "You Antietam Brown?"

"Sure am," I said.

"Then sign right here."

I signed and thanked him, I looked at the

package, which weighed a pound or so. Magazine, I guessed, but as I started to open it, I read the full name on the label. Antietam Brown IV. Not mine. So I walked back across the lawn, where Mary checked on me again, and slipped the package between the storm and front doors. Nothing, I thought, was important enough to disturb them on this night.

Then I turned up the collar of my denim coat and walked past the manger again, where Mary once more made sure I was all right. Then, once free from her care, I put on those headphones and pressed PLAY on the Walkman. Yeah I know it wasn't a Walkman, but "personal cassette player" sounds a little goofy. Yeah I pressed PLAY on that Walkman, and . . . nothing. Absolutely nothing. No batteries. Damn. I needed my Nat. Needed it bad. Was jonesing for Nat.

But then my thoughts turned to Terri, and Nat slipped into the back of my mind. Thoughts that were jumbled together. Man, I was having trouble focusing as I walked at a quick pace, and I looked at the sky and saw stars spinning around, which I was pretty sure wouldn't have been the case without my four drinks. Probably not a wise decision to arrive hammered at the reverend's house. But a brisk walk with Jack Frost nipping at my nose ought to sober me up.

So once more I thought of Terri, and let her various images slug it out in my mind. Green eyes, tight sweater, holding hands, good-night handshake, "Backstreets," bare breasts, black lingerie, deep kisses, bare breasts, black lingerie, black lingerie, bare breasts.

By the time I got to Terri's door, we seemed to have had a tie in the visionary battle of supremacy. Yes, black lingerie and bare breasts had ended in a dead heat, but more importantly my brisk walk had served its purpose. No longer was I just a boyfriend showing up drunk at the reverend's house. No, now I was a boyfriend showing up drunk and with a visible hard-on. In my hurry to get dressed, I'd sensed that I'd forgotten something. That something, it turned out, was my underwear. Quickly I arranged things in a more clandestine way.

Dingdong. In a moment, Terri was at the door, and man, she looked beautiful. Her hair cascaded down her shoulders in deep luxurious curls, and her eyes shone in a way even more beautiful than Holly's new diamond. Her dress hugged her form, not too tight, but just enough, a green velvet number that, like her sweater, looked to have cost more than my father's car.

I saw the reverend approach with an outstretched hand, and I thought of my father's handshake analogy, and momentarily I contemplated pulling my nuts out of my jeans and slapping them into his palm. Thankfully, no nuts were slapped, but I did let out a little dopey laugh as I shook the reverend's manicured hand.

"Have you been drinking, son?" he asked. Not quite the greeting I was looking for.

"Just a little, sir."

"What in blazes is any teenage boy, let alone my daughter's boyfriend, doing drinking on the eve of the Lord's birthday?"

God please let the truth suffice. "Well sir, my father just got engaged tonight, and they asked if I'd join them in a toast."

Terri squealed with delight, which seemed to take some of the heat off me. "Oh Andy, that's great. I'm so happy," she said.

The reverend relaxed, and smiled a bit. A fake, forced smile, but a smile nonetheless. "Well, maybe that did call for a drink," he said in his rich baritone that had saved many a soul.

"Dad, rest assured, Andy is not a drinker," Terri said.

"Is this true?" the reverend asked as he ushered me inside. It smelled simply divine inside their fine home, like pine trees and cinnamon, and the fire crackled away in a blaze of deep orange while Alastair Sim danced at his nephew's house on an awfully big screen. A screen that stood next to a huge Christmas tree. Ten feet at least, and as white as the snow. With a mountain of presents piled up underneath.

"Yes, Mr. Johnson, it is. This is only the second time. And there won't be another for a long time, I'm sure."

"May I ask what that first occasion was?"

"Yes sir, my father took me to a movie for my last birthday, and he gave me a beer before we saw it." Not only had I left out the part about him not having seen me in sixteen years and nine months, but I hadn't mentioned the porno flick either. Also, the six beers had conveniently become one. Maybe not technically lying, but pretty damn close.

Mrs. Johnson appeared, looking seasonal in a red dress which showcased cleavage and a pair of breasts that seemed to have all the pliability of a pair of croquet balls. She extended her hand, which of course made me think of my nuts, but I swallowed my laugh while still trying to lose the images of Terri's bare breasts that were sashaying in my mind.

Just when things seemed at their very worst, I saw my salvation, so to speak. Tiny Tim. "I love this part," I said, and we all turned to look as Tim, who didn't look tiny at all in this particular version, said, "God bless us every one."

The reverend put his arm around his wife, who put her arm around Terri, who put her arm around me. We just stood there while the credits rolled, until the reverend finally said, "That's what it's all about." I was dying to say something about the hokeypokey, but wisely refrained. Thankfully, both my buzz and my hard-on seemed to be subsiding.

Then we sat in the living room, a big happy family, and things settled down nicely. Mrs. Johnson brought forth tray after tray of holiday snacks. Fresh-baked cookies and pastries, which made Tietam's selection look positively sparse. We talked of the snow, which had just started to fall, and of Santa and reindeer and Christmases past, and I mentioned a place in New Hampshire where I'd heard it was Christmas all year. A little kids' park, but one nonetheless that I wanted to see.

Terri said, "Do you like roller coasters, Andy?" to which I replied, "I'm really not sure."

"Not sure," she said. "What do you mean?"

"Well I've never been on one."

"Never?"

"Not ever."

"Mom, Dad, maybe Andy could come with us to Lake George this summer. They've got that great old wooden roller coaster."

"Sure," the Johnsons said in unison. Said it in such a way that I knew they'd rather die a horrible painful death than have me take part in their vacation.

"So it's a date?" Terri said, and silence prevailed until Mrs. Johnson leapt up and said, "Time to eat," and I imagined a boxer being saved by the bell.

The reverend and I sat down at a table of mahogany with eight hand-carved chairs, surrounded by photos that hung in gold frames. One of the Johnsons on their wedding day. One of young Terri in pigtails and bows. And one of the reverend shaking hands with the coach. A black wig and a mullet sharing a smile. Then the Johnson women brought out plate after plate of mouthwatering dishes. Sweet potatoes, peas, corn, squash, a casserole of some kind, fruit salad, and fresh rolls. Four of them were foods I'd never even seen, but man they looked good. Then last but not least, a turkey. What a turkey it was. The type of turkey that Scrooge might send to Bob Cratchit, or his nephew's house, depending on what version you watch.

The reverend spoke up, and filled the room with his velvety baritone once more. "Terri, would you please carve the turkey?"

My vision! It was coming true. My vision of Terri, it was all coming true. In reverse order, sure, but coming true nonetheless. Hey reverse order was fine with me. She could carve the turkey first, then we could make love, then she could put on her lingerie and place soft kisses on my lips in front of the fire. Nothing wrong with that order. Nothing at all.

"Dee-licious," said the reverend, clearly savoring his food, and I made the mistake of taking a swig of my milk as he started to speak again. "Whew-ee, I'll have to work off this meal. Maybe some push-ups after—"

But he never finished the sentence, because in a flash of mental lightning, I thought of the reverend in the nude doing push-ups, and I spit out my milk.

"What the devil," said Mr. Johnson, and he looked awfully mad, but I just couldn't help it, and I laughed hard again. "What in Sam Hill is going on here, young man?"

All eyes were upon me, and an answer was needed. The truth or a lie? Which one would do? I looked at Terri. No help there. I did a quick eenie-meenie-miney-moe in my head and decided to pick this very one. Uh-oh. The truth.

"Well sir, I momentarily visualized you doing those push-ups naked, and it seemed kind of funny."

The silence was deafening. So I decided to break it. "I'm sorry, sir, but I think that drink I had has made me think a little strange tonight. But like I said, I'm not going to drink again for a very long time, maybe forever, so I don't think you'll have to worry about that anymore."

"Well let's hope not," the reverend said, adjusting his tie. "The Lord doesn't want us to be thought of naked. That's why he gave us clothes."

He did? Jeez, I must have skipped that chapter where the Lord handed out the clothes. Then I thought of Jesus saying, "Taketh ye this custom-tailored one-thousand-dollar suit and weareth it," and almost laughed again.

Unfortunately, the dinner conversation continued its religious theme, which didn't bode well for me. The reverend opened the conversation.

"Andy, to be honest, I was a bit apprehensive about letting Terri participate in your father's little Nativity scene, especially as the Virgin Mary. Taking into account that some of our religions tend to place the Virgin almost on the level of our Lord, which borders on blasphemy."

"Yes sir, I respect your opinion."

"Do you agree with it?"

"Um, no, not really . . . sir."

"What religion are you, Andy?"

"I'm a recovering Catholic, sir."

"Which means what exactly?"

"That I don't believe in everything that I was taught."

"Including the Virgin?"

"No sir, I do believe in her."

"But not in a place near the Lord."

"Yes sir, I believe she's pretty close to the Lord."

"You do, Andrew?"

"Actually, Andy is short for Antietam, Mr. Johnson."

"Oh I see, like the battle. Did you have ancestors who fought there?"

"Yes sir, my great-great-great-grandfather did."

The reverend contemplated my answer and mumbled "Interesting," then seemed to shift gears and headed back to my lawn.

"Yes sirree, Andy, I had a few doubts, but then I thought, Heck, anything that honors the spirit of the season can't be all bad, isn't that right, hon?"

"It sure is, William," Mrs. Johnson replied. Speak when spoken to, I guessed, was the rule of this house.

The reverend chewed a piece of turkey, swallowed, then turned his attention back to me.

"But now tell me, Andrew, sorry Andy, did your father have trouble finding good Christians to stand in his manger on the eve of the Lord's birth?"

"Yes sir, Mr. Johnson, he did have some trouble."

"So may I ask, how did he adapt to that situation? I heard from one of my congregation that he had quite a line of cars tonight."

"Yes sir, he did."

"Well then, Andy, what did he do about his trouble with Christians?"

"Well sir. Most of the manger was empty. Just one wise man and Joseph. I'm not sure if they were Christians or not. And Mary was a Jewish girl."

The reverend let out a deep sigh, a sigh of disgust. "Can I be honest here, Andy?" His voice was picking up passion, as if he was saving a soul.

"Yes sir, you can be honest with me."

"Well as a Christian, I am offended by that. Deeply offended."

"I'm sorry you feel that way, reverend."

"You're damn right you should be sorry, son. The Jews killed our Lord, and for you, or your father, or his wife or whatever, to dress up a Jewish girl and parade her around as the Virgin is offensive to me."

"Well, I'm pretty sure that the Virgin was a Jewish girl."

I did a quick scan of Johnson faces. Mrs. Johnson disgusted. Terri scared. Mr. Johnson, contempt, pure and simple.

"Mr. Johnson, if Mary had been a good Christian girl, well there wouldn't have been a whole lot of need for Jesus, would there have been?"

Mrs. Johnson screamed. Terri fought back tears. And the reverend. Well, he spewed forth a form of venom from way down in his gut. A big fat serving of fire and brimstone headed my way.

"May I suggest, Mr. Brown, that you leave this house now, collect your father and his new bride, attend your midnight mass at St. Catherine's, and pray for forgiveness."

"Well, uh, actually, my father's not Catholic, and his fiancée is Jewish."

Terri tried to help. "Dad, she really is nice." Her father wasn't listening. Instead he brought up John 3:16 in a menacing, shaking baritone.

"For God . . . so loved the world . . . that he gave his only begotten son . . . that whosoever believeth in him . . . should not perish . . . but have everlasting life! Which means it is easier for a camel to go through the eye of a needle, than for a Jew to enter into the kingdom of God."

This talk had sobered me up in a hurry, but I had to fight off the temptation to laugh in his face. Instead I slowly put my hand in the air, as if he were a teacher and I had to go pee.

"Mr. Johnson?"

"Yes! What is it, an apology?"

"Um, that's not how the verse goes."

"It most certainly is."

"No, really, it's not. It is actually easier for a

camel to go through the eye of a needle, than for a rich man to enter into the kingdom of God."

I saw him lurch forward slightly, as if he was poised to rise up from his seat. I saw his lip start to shake, as if he was getting ready to mangle more scripture. Instead he sat back and closed his eyes softly, waiting, I guess, for the return of his good Christian sensibilities. He opened his eyes and then spoke in carefully calculated prose.

"Young man, I want you out of this house. You have brought shame to my home. I will say to your face what I've told my daughter for weeks. She deserves better than you. Much better by far. She deserves a Christian and an athlete as well."

I looked over at Terri, thinking that surely she would come to my rescue. Instead she did nothing. Just looked at her plate.

I stepped outside into the cold, snowy night, and walked off into the darkness. About two hundred yards down the street, I heard her. Terri. Yelling. Yelling my name and running as fast as her heels and the weather would allow. In her arms she held something. My coat. Thank goodness. And I knew that my arms would soon hold something too. Her body. Real close.

I met her halfway, and hugged her hard. Wrapped my arms around her and didn't let go. I kissed her, and kissed her again, waiting for the heat of her tongue to melt the ice in my blood.

That tongue never came. Instead she yelled, "Stop, Andy, stop," and burst into tears. I tried to hug her again, but she pushed me away.

She put her head down and wiped at her tears. How I wished she would have let me wipe them myself. Slowly she looked up and regained control.

"Look, Terri, I'm sorry, but—"

"Shut up, Andy, shut up. It's my turn to talk. You've said enough for one night, don't you think?" She paused for a while, and took several deep breaths, as if breathing in courage for what she'd say next.

"Put your coat on, Andy, I don't want you to freeze."

"Why don't you wear it, Terri, you're—"

"Just wear it, Andy, I'll be safe at home much quicker than you. What I have to say won't take long."

I feared for the worst . . . and got it.

"Andy, I had three things in my life that I loved. My God, my family, and you. You disrespected the first two and now I can't have the third. Do you understand?"

"He led me into it, Terri, he—"

"Shut up, Andy. You came to my house drunk. You humiliated my father. I love you, Andy, but I can't see you anymore." She brushed at new tears, and I just stood frozen, unable to move, unable to believe that she and I were no more.

"But Terri," I said, "can't you forgive me? I'll make it up to you, I'll—"

"God will forgive you, Andy . . . But I won't. Goodbye."

I watched her get smaller as she walked toward her home. She never looked back as she mounted her steps. Never looked back as she opened her door, stepped inside, and disappeared from my life.

I stood still for a minute, maybe more, then looked at the sky, at stars that were no longer spinning, at a world that no longer turned. And very clearly I felt my heart break in two.

DECEMBER 24, 1985 / 11:25 P.M.

Emptiness consumed me as I made my way back home. A home that was filled with love and the Christmas spirit. I imagined the millions of children who, as Nat sang, "would find it hard to sleep tonight." Children who knew that Santa was on his way. With lots of toys and goodies on his sleigh. I wondered if Santa had anything for me on that sleigh, like a new heart. I looked up at the sky, as I had for so many years as a child, hoping to hear the faint jingle of bells signaling St. Nick's imminent arrival, but realized that Santa, like love itself, was just a figment of my imagination, an ode to a more innocent time. Like maybe an hour ago.

Well, I thought as I trudged through the mounting snow, at least I have my family.

An hour's walk turned to two as I slowly retraced the route that a few weeks ago had been filled with such hope. She had wanted me to kiss her. Yeah, I guess she had, but that seemed like a long, long time ago. Now, she just wanted to never see me again.

How does a kid comfort himself in times like

these? Well, it's pretty damn hard. My only shot was to try to think of something negative about her. Let's see. What could I dig up on Terri? She was beautiful. She was kind. She was funny. She was a good kisser. She had beautiful breasts. Damn, like I said, this was hard. Then I thought of looking at her after sharing my thoughts about the virgin. How I'd looked to her for backup and she'd given me none. She'd picked her father over me. Well, it was not much to go on, but I decided it would have to suffice as I walked the last horrible yards to my house.

Gloria Sugling was outside on her lawn, looking sad and somewhat older in the glow of plastic snowmen and Santas.

"Merry Christmas, Mrs. Sugling," I said with as much holiday enthusiasm as I could muster.

"Hi Andy," she said, without a whole lot of Christmas spirit on display in her voice.

"Mr. Sugling working again?"

"Yeah, but he'll be home by morning, in time to open our presents."

"That's good, well, uh, good night, Mrs. Sugling."

"Good night, Andy."

Then, as I was walking up the drive, she spoke again.

"Sounds like they're making up," she said, with a motion to my father's bedroom window.

"Excuse me," I said, a little confused.

"Well I heard some pretty loud voices a few

hours ago. But it sounds like everything is fine now . . . Good night."

"Good night." I walked up that drive slightly confused, and a little bit sad for Mrs. Sugling, all alone on this night. She didn't fit the profile of a Tietam Brown strike, but perhaps her living next door and being married to a cop made up for the fact that she wasn't rich. The old Tietam Brown would have liked that a lot. As I got closer, I could hear thumping coming from my father's room. Which meant . . . well I'll be darned, my dad and Holly, in the throes of passion.

I could feel the stairs vibrating as I made my way up, into my room, where the wall between my room and Tietam's had never seemed thinner. It was like listening to one of those movies in Sensurround, with the headboard and the box springs threatening to land right in my lap. And the language. Whew. Holly knew her verbs, or at least one of them, real well.

I'd enjoyed the sounds of them cuddling a whole lot more than this particular scene, which didn't seem to fit the promise of "the most beautiful thing in the world" that Holly had predicted.

Still, I tried to excuse my dad's rather graphic performance next door. After all, he'd been saving up his urges for almost a month, which had to be almost a month longer than he'd had to save up before, so who was I to begrudge him his fun, especially on his special night.

All the same, I didn't feel like listening, partially

243

because I didn't like what I heard . . . and partially because I did. And I didn't want to think of Holly that way, especially when I heard the faint sound of my dad's voice saying, "Worm that tongue, baby, worm that tongue!" Didn't want to think about her that way at all. No, when it came to Holly, I preferred to think of her with a halo, not my father's ass, surrounding her face.

Luckily, I still had Nat in my jacket, and I summoned him to the rescue. With the help of a couple of batteries I found in my desk drawer, Nat's kind, caring voice was soon doing its best to both soothe my sorrow and drown out the acts taking place in Tietam Brown's bed.

A few minutes later, silence prevailed in the room next to mine and Nat was singing about "the dear Savior's birth." God it was so beautiful, even without the scratches and pops of my mother's old album, that I felt myself fading off to sleep, despite the events of the evening.

I didn't hear the door open. I only saw a small flash of light. Light from my father's room that cast him in the darkest of shadows as he stood in my doorway. I caught the strong scent of alcohol and sex as my tired eyes strained to capture details in the darkness. A bottle of whiskey in my father's right hand, a red Santa hat perched on his head, and a smile I didn't like glued to his face. The Santa hat was all he wore.

A sudden movement to the right side of my bed, and then I wasn't alone under my sheets. My dad was now laughing and I felt something strange. A mouth on my penis.

I guess it's strange how the brain works in times like these. When the whole world seems to freeze for just a moment or two, just enough time to squeeze out a thought. Those thoughts can be strange in times like these. And my thought? Hey, she's doing more than just tucking me in.

I turned to my side, away from that mouth, shut off my tape, and heard Tietam laugh. The laugh of a sadist watching a fish on dry land, gasping for air, flopping in vain.

But that mouth was persistent, and it stalked its weak prey until I turned on my stomach and it gave up the chase. Then the figure slid out and threw up its hands, and a voice I'd heard only that night filled the small room's tense air.

It said, "I give up, the kid's way too scared." But then Tietam's laugh stopped, and then his voice was heard stabbing the night with cruelty and hate. He grabbed at an arm that was still raised in the air, gave it a turn, and I heard a sharp scream. And in the dull glow, I knew her face and placed her voice as Tietam Brown yelled, "Suck that dick."

Then, with a push, the Virgin Mary was free, a Mary now trembling with fear and with pain. I could hear her small sobs as she crawled under the sheets, and Tietam's laugh filled the air as I lay silent in bed.

I don't know why I didn't try to stop it. I wish

that I'd tried. At the very least, I could now say that I tried. But I can't, because I didn't. I just stayed there instead and rolled onto my back, with a body that, to my great shame, had become greatly aroused.

When her mouth took me in, I instantly thought of the dual nature of man. Just for a moment, I thought of my father, who'd gone from hero to hated in the course of one minute. And his son, who was experiencing both the best and the worst feeling of his entire young life.

Did I want it to stop? Yeah, part of me did. But I knew I was helpless, so I just didn't fight. What I wanted to stop was my father's cruel laugh, so with a push of my thumb I made that laugh stop, and let Nat King Cole try to take me away. It didn't take long, I didn't outlast the song, and my whole body shook with both pleasure and shame. And I tried to hold on to that pleasure for as long as I could, for I knew that once it ended my new life was done. That nothing I loved would ever love me again.

I saw Tietam's face as whiskey dripped down his chin, which he backhanded away before swigging again. A face of contempt and smug satisfaction. As if he'd proved that the world was his after all. The king back at his castle after a brief detour in love.

The Virgin Mary just lay there, hugging my leg as if it was the last respite before returning to hell. My right hand gently stroked her, as best it could, and though I could feel nothing, I hoped that she did.

Then she finally let go and slipped out of my bed, still cloaked in the robe she'd worn on our lawn. In a manger that was meant to give hope to the world. A world that seemed hopeless from inside my sad, tiny room.

I saw the clock turn to twelve, Merry Christmas to all. Mary walked out, with a sad final glance. In fact, I saw nothing; but I didn't have to: I knew. Sadness hung from her like a rusted steel chain. I could sense that she wanted to walk downstairs and leave. Away from that house, and that street and that town. But a snapping of fingers and a point toward his bed let her know with no doubt that her night wasn't through.

His bedroom door closed, and then I heard him walk down, where he turned on a light and staked out his claim to a world that revolved around the cracking of beers, the flipping of cards, and nude push-ups and squats on the Lord's day of birth.

DECEMBER 25, 1985

I heard my father leave the house at a little after nine on Christmas morning, the last of many sounds he had initiated since closing the door to my room and shutting out hope from my world. Sounds of bedsprings, and headboards, and small sobs, and loud cries, and cruel laughs, and hurried shameful steps, and a car's engine, and tires burning rubber on a cold winter night. But most of all, I heard my conscience scream, begging me to do something, anything, to make the madness stop.

Instead I did nothing. Just lay there in the darkness, cursing my cowardice and mourning my memories of happiness. I almost drifted off at 6 a.m., a time when overeager children would be waking up, tugging on their dads' pajamas, getting an early start on the best day of the year.

Sleep, however, didn't come. For as the first rays of Christmas morning came peeking through the window, I heard my father sobbing.

Three hours later, he was gone, in his crappy car with its music blasting, its dice hanging. Leaving me alone in a house I couldn't stand, in a world I couldn't change.

school, and she'd fall into my arms. And we'd be back together, we'd be back in love.

What now seemed oddest of all was that when things were at their worst—at Terri's house, that is, because things certainly went downhill from there—I had thought of my dad. Like he was going to come riding in on a white horse and save the day for Andy. But maybe Andy didn't need to have his day saved. Maybe Andy could have saved it himself. He could have just gone into a rage and saved it himself.

I grabbed hold of my quarters and pictured the scene. Throwing my left with the change and the rage. Making beautiful contact with the reverend's big mouth. Seeing those white caps fly like pieces of Chiclets. Watching his wig fly off into the fireplace. Causing his wife to break into wrinkles that no surgeon could fix.

Now those were thoughts of comfort. And comfort me they did, to the point where I was actually smiling when I made it to work. Where no one was there except Mary and Frank. Who made me a waiter for the very first time.

A one-handed waiter, but hey, I did my best serving up Frankie specials and lots of desserts. A one-handed waiter with a crooked smile and a broken heart, gorging himself on slice after slice of Mary's homemade pumpkin pie.

I got off ten minutes early, with a ten-dollar bonus from Frank and a ride from a new Cortland teacher named Thompson, who dropped me off at the Seven Valley 12 after telling several stories about some guy named Bochco.

I bought a Coke and some popcorn, and took in *Rocky IV* amid families and young lovers, a group that only one night earlier I had been a proud member of. I was watching Stallone, but it just wasn't the same. He was once again fighting for democracy, but still, it wasn't the same. What was missing was Terri and her hand in mine.

I arrived home around midnight. A few cars were driving down my street, obviously looking for just one more evening of Nativity magic to celebrate the Lord's birthday. But the manger was empty.

I opened the door to find the Christmas tree still adorned with the various images of Holly. I looked once again at the empty place under that tree where her special present had been, and then I looked at the couch where only one night before, she had glowed with such beauty.

But now the living room was void of all the love that had, for too short a time, made the small house a home. In love's place there were beer cans and the fresh scent of sweat mixed in with new sex. But intermission was over and a new act had begun. An act that seemed almost tranquil when I got to my room.

I briefly considered playing the tape of Nat, but that would have made me think of Holly, which would have been too painful to bear. Maybe my mother's album. No, maybe this just wasn't a night for Nat. Not that I didn't appreciate "the dear

Savior's birth." I did. I just didn't know if I would feel like celebrating it ever again.

The tranquil act gave way to harsher things: the sighs that seemed vaguely familiar turning to labored grunts, my father's questions becoming demands. Amid this scene, I tried to sleep, but my conscience kept me up. I thought I heard some choking, then an anguished cry of "Stop," and now my conscience screamed. My heart pounded, my adrenaline raced, and I realized I had to make a stand. I could not stay still while this scene played out. Could not just die inside while a braver man begged to be set free.

I heard her voice scream "Stop" one more time, and I heard Tietam let loose his laugh. And I sat upright, then sprang to life and bolted down the stairs. I thought of the basement and its rusty ax, but then grabbed the telephone instead. Dialed 911 while I slowly climbed the stairs.

I guess I could have waited, just sat back and let Cortland's finest handle things. But I heard him laugh, and I heard her scream, and I decided not to wait. I put my shoulder down like I'd seen TV cops do, and I charged at Tietam's door. It gave way and let me in, but not without some pain that caused the phone to drop and go skidding across the floor.

"It's over, Dad," I said. "The police are on their way." The words barely got out, but they felt so good to say. Letting him know that I couldn't be bullied, wouldn't give in to his crap, that I could

253

stand up to him. I looked at him for some kind of sign. A blink or a shudder. Just one little thing. Any small sign to let me know he was scared. Instead he just smiled. On his knees, on his bed, naked and smiling.

"Hell, that's okay, son, let the cops come. Maybe Officer Charlie can be leading the charge. He can say hello to his wife, and then I'll play him a tape of her tongue in my ass. How does that sound to you, son?"

Gloria Sugling. The voice that I knew. She'd seemed so lonely last night, and now she lay naked before me, her face hidden in shame, her body shaking with sorrow. She'd had her three strikes and now she was back—my father relaxing his rules for the sake of exploiting more sadness.

"Is that what you want, Andy, or do you want something else? Don't you want to pick up that phone and tell the police it was all a big joke? Don't do it for me. Do it for poor Mrs. Sugling. Do it for her. Do it for the Halloween pumpkins. Or the scarecrow. Don't you want to see a scarecrow next door instead of a 'For Sale' sign, which officer Charlie will surely put up if he finds his wife here."

I dialed the number.

"Get out," my dad said, when my short call was through. I started to leave, but then he snapped, "No not you. I was talking to her. You're going to watch while Miss Gloria leaves."

She slowly sat up, her face full of black tears. A

face that was equal parts sadness, pain, fear, and shame. She reached for her panties, but Tietam got to them first, saying, "I'll keep these here."

Then Mrs. Sugling reached for her bra. Once again, Tietam was quicker, snatching it up and throwing it into the hall. "You can put on your clothes when you get back to your house. Now leave."

Mrs. Sugling's knees buckled. I thought she might fall, so I rushed to her side, and helped keep her up.

This time he yelled, "I said leave! Get out! Get the hell out of my house. Take your fat ass, and your saggy little tits, and get out of my house!"

I walked her home. Against my father's demands, I walked her home. I draped a sheet over her trembling shoulders, and while my father showered me with insults, I walked Mrs. Sugling home. While I was walking, I looked up at the sky, and I wished that somehow, I could summon my rage. Wished that I could have it at my disposal to take care of my father. I didn't know just how useful it would be against Tietam Brown, but I grabbed hold of my quarters and opened my mind up to the fact that it might happen soon.

He was playing his tape when I got back to my room. Gloria Sugling. He was playing it. The whole ugly thing. Sang while he played it. G-L-O-R-I-A!

I listened to him play her mind like a maestro of frail psyches. Selling modern-day snake oil; his hairy ass as a cure-all for loneliness. Plotting a course from fun to brutality, and not allowing departures until the whole trip was through. Using her own voice as insurance. I lay down in my bed and wondered how the same guy who had sung Burl Ives a few short weeks ago could now be so filled with hate. In a strange way, I was thankful, for that hatred made it harder to think of Terri. Or Holly. As odd as it seems, my adrenaline rush had served to drown out my despair. And now, as that rush gave way to exhaustion, I simply could not fall asleep sad. For I had stood up to my father. Stood up to him twice. I'd seen the worst of what lurked within him, and I had faced it down.

I woke up a short time later feeling something wasn't right. Hot breath in my ear. A figure at my bed's right side. The breath came hotter still, right next to my stump, and suddenly I realized that my father had my arm hooked in a way that wasn't natural. His lips were now touching what was left of my ear, whispering, "If you ever threaten me again, I'll kill you. Do you understand?"

I nodded my head, for I was too scared to speak. Then slowly, deliberately, my father tore my shoulder from its socket.

I walked to the bus stop at 4:00 a.m., my right arm throbbing. No longer out of its socket, but still hurting like hell. The best I can figure is that sometime after I blacked out, my father must have popped it back in, an odd but useful talent he must have picked up along the way. I thought back to my father's visit from the detective, my father asking if "that big monster looked like he'd been assaulted." The detective saying "not a scratch on him." As if pain and suffering didn't exist without the benefit of evidence. No harm, no foul, as they say in pickup basketball.

I had stayed in my room for most of the twenty-sixth, while my father stayed in his. He went out about nine, in pursuit of yet another night of spiritual fulfillment, and I went downstairs to use the phone. The presents still lay unopened beneath the tree. The tree of Holly. She deserved better than to be on display this way. It was as if she'd been lynched and was hanging, left to rot. So I took her down. All nine pictures. I felt the sour taste of vomit race up my throat, but swallowed it down. There was something very odd about those pictures. I studied one. Her face. Especially her eyes. Despite her environment, Holly, I saw, still had the eyes of an angel. I tore the photos up. They had caused enough suffering already.

My finger had been trembling when I dialed New York City information. I didn't want to count on strangers, but I had nowhere else to turn. Somewhere deep down inside, my dad had snapped, and I longed to know what had caused it. I guess because I was full of fear, for both my father and his victims. Fear for my own safety, too. I think that fear was my biggest. God I dreaded the coming night, and what surprises it might bring. A guy like him could probably kill and not leave a trace of evidence. I guess I feared for my dad's soul too—I hope that doesn't sound too preachy. For although the decision isn't mine to make, abusing women didn't seem like the quickest route to heaven.

So I asked the operator if an Eddie Edwards was listed in New York. Not just one but three, he said, so I gave all of them a try. As the saying goes, the third time was a charm, and a warm laugh put my nerves at ease. He said that he'd love to see me, and that tomorrow would be fine. He even offered to wire me bus fare, but I said I had it covered.

I had saved up almost ninety dollars during my tenure at the diner, and I thought that if I could do without little things like food, I could just squeak by with that amount.

Mr. Edwards lived on 132nd Street, a real long walk from midtown, where the bus had dropped me off. But I had no clue about the subways, and a taxi wasn't in my budget, so I walked almost ninety blocks. Ninety blocks to think about the cards the last few days had dealt me. Ninety blocks of Terri. Ninety blocks of Tietam. Ninety lonely blocks.

I wish I could say it didn't worry me when white faces stopped appearing. But uptown was a whole new world, even for a kid with a past like mine. Luckily I had one ace in the hole—a dad I thought might kill me. I slept next door to a monster, so why sweat a walk through Harlem?

Mr. Edwards greeted me with a big smile and a root beer. I liked him right away. He'd aged greatly since his picture, but still looked full of life. He may not have been quite the specimen I'd seen in Tietam's picture, but his handshake was firm, his shoulders were wide, and I thought that if the situation called for it, this guy could still kick some ass. I didn't know a whole lot about death, but Eddie Edwards did not appear to be residing on its doorstep, as Tietam's words had led me to believe.

His apartment was small, but tasteful and neat. A black-and-white portrait of a beautiful black woman hung over his mantel. The room's centerpiece. His wife, I guessed, but didn't ask. Two smaller black-and-white photos stood under it in wood frames.

One showed a group of soldiers, all black, with

the exception of one white guy who I guessed must have been an officer. The other was Eddie Edwards, holding up his fists, his body lean and strong. He must have seen me looking, for he chuckled just a bit and said, "That was me in my prime, in '63, the same year I met your dad."

I had thought of so many questions, but now none came to my mind. I had so many questions that needed answering, so many things I had to know. Finally all my thoughts produced one small word. I asked Eddie Edwards, "Where?"

"Down in Mississippi," Eddie said. "Worked the territory there. All the cities, small towns too."

Which cleared up . . . absolutely nothing. He might just as well have been speaking a foreign language.

"We once did twenty shows in eighteen days, not much time to rest. Long trips through back-water towns."

I didn't want to insult him, but I got the distinct impression that he thought I knew a lot more than I did.

"Um . . . Mr. Edwards?"

"Yes, Andy, and call me Eddie."

"Okay, Mr. Ed—uh Eddie."

"Yes?"

"Uh, I don't want to sound naïve, but what is a territory?"

Eddie smiled in disbelief. As if he hadn't real-ized that I barely knew my dad.

"Jeez, I'm sorry, son, I guess that I forgot. You

grew up without your dad. So you don't know what a territory is?"

"Not really."

"Do you know anything about him?"

"Besides the fact that he exercises naked with a deck of playing cards, no, not a whole lot," I said.

My attempt at humor failed. I had been hoping for a laugh, but my remark hit Eddie Edwards like a big hook to the gut. It seemed to stop him in his tracks for just a second, then he said, "So he still goes through his deck?" I nodded in silence, not sure what it all meant.

"Do you know what your father used to do for a living?"

"No, to tell the truth, I still don't."

Eddie hesitated just a bit, as if he didn't want to shock me. But at this point nothing Tietam did could shock me. "Well Andy, he and I were wrestlers."

I was shocked. "Wrestlers?" I said, then breathed out a laugh—a laugh I regretted right away. I didn't want to insult Eddie Edwards, but damn. Wrestling?

"Wrestlers?" I repeated. "Like the kind that's on TV?"

"Well kind of," Eddie said with an understanding smile. "Of course the business has changed a lot since then."

"I'm sorry, I didn't mean to laugh, it's just that my father's just a little guy, I can't see him screaming, throwing punches."

Eddie nodded in agreement with everything I

said, then backed up his nods with words. "Well Andy, you're right on all counts. Your father was a little guy, at least by wrestling standards. He didn't scream, and in all the time I knew him, I only saw him throw one punch."

I nodded in silence.

I felt ashamed of my presumptions. Eddie Edwards deserved better than to have me laughing at his life. He was about the nicest guy I'd ever met, I can't think of any nicer. But a certain sadness clung to him, maybe cancer, or his wife. I wondered if she was still alive and my gut feeling told me no. I took a swig of root beer and no longer laughed when Eddie talked.

"Well Andy, I came back from Korea with a purple heart and a court-martial. Not a whole lot of opportunities for a Negro with a court-martial back in '54. So when I got the chance to wrestle, I took it. Had already put in nine years when your dad came in from England."

"England?" I said.

"Sorry Andy, I forgot, just thought he might have said where he came from."

"I thought he came from Albany."

"Yeah, yeah. I guess he did. But I think he moved when he was twelve, maybe thirteen, I forget, but it was with some guy his mother met. From what I remember Tietam saying, and your father never said too much, at least not about his past—the guy kind of promised wealth in London, and wound up mining coal in Wigan."

"What the heck is Wigan?"

Eddie laughed. "It's not a real nice town. I'm not sure Diana's ever been there. But Wigan is the place where your dad learned how to hook."

"Hook?"

"Hook," Eddie confirmed.

"What is hooking?" I was wide-eyed and listening hard, hoping to latch onto something that could help me understand my father.

Eddie got real serious as I could sense him collect his thoughts. "Hooking," he said, "is the . . . art of . . . causing pain."

"And was my dad good at it?" I asked, even though I knew the answer.

"Yes . . . your dad was good. Pound for pound he may have been the best."

Eddie Edwards, I sensed, wanted to talk, almost needed to, it seemed, and I was going to let him. He took a seat in an easy chair, one with a Bible on its arm, and he told me of my dad.

"Yeah, your father sure could hook. Practiced it, studied it . . . Kind of like a scientist, discovering new ways he could cause pain. Read books about the body. Big books. In the gym no one could touch him. But in the ring, in Mississippi, well that wasn't quite the same. 'Cause in the ring you're only as tough as the promoter lets you be. And lots of times, in the business, the promoters had a hard-on—'scuse the language—for a guy who could go for real. Wanted to teach them respect, which is really just a way of saying they

263

treated him like crap. Until November twenty-second, that is, the day the president was shot."

"You mean you wrestled the same night that the president died? Wasn't it canceled? Wasn't like it a national day of mourning?"

"In Mississippi?" Eddie asked, one eyebrow raised.

"Well, uh, yeah," I shrugged.

"Andy, the only reason they would cancel is to have a celebration."

"You're kidding," I said, in a voice just above a whisper. But I already knew he wasn't. I had been raised in towns right outside of Richmond, where the Confederacy was based. I had seen the southern generals still standing tall on Monument Row. I had done my time in Petersburg, home of the famous siege. I even had a name to honor a man who'd shed his blood on southern soil. But I'd never even entertained the thought that the Civil War still lived and breathed in 1963 in the state of Mississippi.

"No," Eddie said, "I'm afraid I'm not. Although I wish I was. No, the president wasn't too highly held by a lot of folks in Mississippi. Caused them a lot of problems about a year before down at the university."

I nodded, but really didn't know what it was he was referring to, although I made a mental note to check.

"Most of the boys in the dressing room felt pretty bad, I guess. We all shared the same dressing room, all got along okay for the most part. Couple guys weren't shy about letting people know they didn't want any niggers in their business. On this night in particular, they were laughing about the president, loud enough to hear. Wanted me to hear. Called Kennedy a 'nigger lover,' were glad that he'd been shot. Now, most black folks in the South loved JFK, ever since he'd called up Mrs. King while her husband was in jail. Personally, I thought he could have done a little more to help. Your father didn't even give him that. Said he was like Abe Lincoln with better hair, only acted 'cause he had to."

I made another mental note.

"In spite of that, your dad got up, walked over to where I was. At this point I hardly knew him; and I sure don't want a problem, especially with him."

"What did you do? Did he start a problem?"

"No, he asked me for a ride."

"Was that a bad thing?"

"No, not bad, but kind of shocking. Colored folks just didn't ride with whites back then, at least not in the business."

"Why do you think he asked?"

"Well to make a statement most of all. Didn't like the South at all, didn't like the people in it. But he later told me he just thought we were quite a bit alike. Read the Bible, didn't drink, didn't whore around."

"Are you sure you're talking about my father?" I said, laughing.

"Yeah, that's the way he was back then. Changed, though, over time."

"Did you give him a ride?"

"Sure. That night and then on. Got along real good. Stayed at the colored hotels, ate at colored restaurants. Was a hero to the black folks, once word got around. Black section would chant his name, white folks wouldn't make a sound. Didn't stop the promoter, though, from beating him all the time. With guys who couldn't lace his boots. Really bothered him."

I felt lousy for my father. And touched by what he'd done. Despite what had happened since that fateful Christmas Eve, I was rooting for my dad.

"A promoter name of Fuller took a chance and brought us to Alabama as a team. Thought a black man and a white man preaching civil rights would draw some heat."

"Did it, you know, draw some . . . heat?"

Eddie's face lit up. He sat forward in his chair and let out a hearty laugh. "Heat? Hell, I guess it did. We had a riot in Montgomery. Our first town after television aired, when we wore our Dr. King shirts. Oh boy! That ring filled up with rednecks, and man, the shit was on—sorry 'bout that. I'm throwing wild punches, Tietam breaks a few bones, most of the boys run out to help. Old Man Fuller was there, even his nutty kid Robert, who'd been selling programs . . . Plug got pulled on our tag team, afraid someone would be killed. Come to think of it now, your dad took a knife

266

in the thigh. Ugly wound too. So after that, things went back to the way they had been. I wrestled the Negro match and your dad never became the star he could have been."

"Wow, that's a shame." Maybe not the most insightful of comments, but it's the one I gave. It was a shame too.

"Yeah, after that, somewhere around '66, we went our separate ways. No hard feelings, just the way of the business. I went to work in Georgia, where I met my wife. Studying medicine in Atlanta. Tietam went north. Minnesota, New York, Indianapolis. But the knock on your father was always the same. Too small, no gimmick, wouldn't get blood, no good on the mike. Really bothered him, that he never made it up north. Finally I heard that he went to Japan."

"They have wrestling there? I mean I know they have sumo, but—"

"Yeah, wouldn't your father look good in those suits?" I smiled as Eddie sat back and breathed deeply; this conversation had tired him. I thought of my dad in one of those sumo things, even though many times I had seen him wear less.

"Actually, Andy, wrestling is big business there. More of a sport, not as much of a show. Your dad had lots of chances, he just never would go. Which is crazy, because guys from Wigan were like royalty there. Lots of respect for their skills. Not like the States. But until '66, for some reason, he just never would go."

"Why do you figure he changed his mind?"

"Your dad, he was pretty tight with a dollar, pinched pennies so hard he could make Abe Lincoln scream. Good with investments too. Saved every dime and put it to use. Lots of other boys made more, but they went through it like water. Cars, women. Your dad had been saving since way back in England. Used to claim that if he could just have a couple good years, he could live off his investments for the rest of his life . . . if he kept his overhead low. He said that was the key."

"Like if he had a small house and a crappy car?"

"Yeah, something like that."

Suddenly my dad's financial situation and lack of any noticeable employment made a little more sense to me.

"Your dad called me some months later. Said Japan went well, though he didn't like the people. Said he could pretty much write his own ticket there. He tells me he's married, to a beautiful girl he met there. Says she's just gorgeous, and better yet, she's with child. I guess that child would be you? Andy, I'll be real honest, until you showed up, I thought you were, you know . . . Asian. Then, next thing I hear, he's working in Florida. Your mama died giving birth, sorry, and he doesn't have you with him."

I nodded my head.

"I'm still working in Georgia. Kind of their token Negro, I guess. I keep my mouth shut, and I keep my ears open. And I hear things, you know?

"What did you hear?"

"Well, I hear that Tietam's changed."

"In what way was he different?"

"He'd taken to drinking, and whoring around. Hooking guys in the ring. Hurting the boys, just 'cause he can. So your father gets fired. Catches on in Charlotte. Same thing there. Drinking, whoring, hurting the boys. Charlotte gives him his notice after only a week. All of a sudden no one will hire him. For some reason, he outright refused to go back to Japan, even though the door's wide open.

"Your father couldn't find work because word had gotten around on him. About how dangerous he was. So he calls me, tells me he needs help, needs a place to work. Not so much for the money, by now he's got plenty, but to take his mind off your mama . . . and you. So I make a call to the office, put in a good word for your dad. Except they're not interested. Like I said, word had gotten around about him."

"So is that when he quit?"

"No, but God I wish it had been. I put myself on the line for him. Told the office I'd look out for him, I'd talk to him, keep him in line."

"Did they go for it?"

"Well kind of."

"Kind of?" I asked. "What do you mean?"

"Well they said they would hire him, but they wanted to change his look to something more marketable."

269

"Like?"

"Downtown Tietam Brown, kind of like a flower-power-hippie-type guy."

"They wanted my father to be a hippie?" I said, trying to picture something so ridiculous. "Why?"

"Because that's what promoters do, Andy. They take care of the guys that they need, but take advantage of the ones they don't. Understand?"

I tried to. But my dad as a hippie. He barely had hair, even back then.

"You see, Andy, I think they wanted to be known as the guys that humbled Tietam Brown."

I thought I understood. "Well did he do it?" I said.

"Yeah he did. Didn't like it, though. As if the name wasn't bad enough, they were beating him every night, trying to get your father to get blood for no good reason, except they know he hates it, thinks it turns the business into a circus."

I thought of the steakhouse, where my father had bled. He hadn't seemed to mind it. Even liked it, I thought.

"Now some boys loved bleeding, we called them 'queer for the blade.' But Tietam won't do it, won't let anyone else do it either. Says if they want him to bleed, then they'll have to do it hard-way."

"Hard-way?"

"Hard-way is done with hard shots to the eyebrow. Punch it till it splits. Dangerous as hell. But Tietam would tell the boys that if they wanted juice, they'd have to get it the hard way. And he'd let 'em, too. He'd just stick that face out, let them try to bust that eye. Take shot after shot. Sickening to watch."

I shrugged with disgust. Why would he allow that to happen? I thought of the thick scars that zigzagged through his eyebrows, and wondered how many blows it must have taken to earn them.

"Well those first few weeks weren't so bad. It was good just to see him. The South had changed just a little, so us riding together didn't seem quite as strange. But your father was different. Not just the pain of losing his wife. That I expected. But something was different. He started bringing home girls. Every night he's bringing home girls. We always split rooms so we could save money, so I have to lie there listening to him, and watching this new ritual with a deck of cards and some beer."

"Yeah," I said, "I've seen him do it."

"Okay, then, less said about those cards the better. I got to a point where I just couldn't take it. Don't even want him around me. The straw that breaks the camel's back is in August, at one of those little no-name motels he likes to stay in. He comes in late, two, three in the morning. I can't see the girl, but I sure smell her. Perfume. Alcohol. Money. Then I hear punches, figure he's snapped, is beating the girl. Except he's not. She wonders why he's sweating so much, because the room's kind of cool. Except he's not sweating. He turns on the light, and that rich girl is just covered in blood. Blood on her chest, her face, pooled up in her neck. And she sees this and goes nuts. Crying, screaming. Tietam, he couldn't be calmer. The whites of his eyes are just peering out of all that blood running down his face. His eyebrow is swollen like an egg from where he's been hitting himself.

"The girl grabs the bloody sheet and runs out into the parking lot screaming murder, and me and Tietam rush out of the room, fire up the car, and we're gone, leavin' town just as the police hit the scene. Never did come after him. He always paid cash, never gave a real name, but he tells me he's gonna start using a tape player to record his girls from then on.

"Andy, I tell you, it was the hardest thing I'd ever done, because your father was like a brother to me and I felt truly bad about what had happened to your mama. Truly bad about what happened to you. But I told him I couldn't be around him anymore. That my wife and I had a Christian home, and he was no longer welcome."

"What did he do?" I asked.

"He said he understood. Didn't blame me. Just sat in the car as calm as could be, blood sticking to his face, that stale iron smell stinking up the car. He said he was leaving the very next day, after our big show in Atlanta. Says he wants to do the right thing for business on his way out.

"That next day should have been fine. After all her hard work, my wife was finally done. A doctor

272

at last. We made plans to go out. To celebrate. To even have a drink or two. I said I wouldn't be home late, I wrestle early on the card. That this would be a night we'd never forget.

"Well, I get to the building and Tietam's not there. I'm thinking he's no-showed, just left a day early. But he shows up as the first match is hitting the ring. Promoter's hot as hell, decides to make Tietam look bad. Pulls him aside and starts giving him hell, tells him he's going to lose, which is nothing new. But then he says he's pushing a new guy who's debuting that night. Former ballplayer. Young guy, maybe twenty-six. Tells Tietam not to do one single thing on offense, just make the kid look good.

"So Tietam puts on his gear and he heads to the curtain. He sees this big kid, must go three hundred and ten, he's got a huge cowboy hat, and a fringed vest that says 'Texas.' Been in the business a whole month and a half. I see Tietam's face, and I should have known there was going to be trouble. So many times I wish I could have gone back in time and prevented it all."

"What happened, Eddie?"

"Oh God, let me see. Well for a minute or so things weren't going so bad. But then the kid nearly takes Tietam's head off with a clothesline, breaks your dad's nose, blood's pouring out. As your dad's getting up, I see this kid get down in a three-point stance, like he's back on the field. And—boom—this kid just drives your dad to the mat with an unbelievable shot. Like a big football tackle, and the crowd all goes 'Ooh.' So I'm thinking your dad is gonna be hot, that he's gonna get up and hook this poor kid. But instead he stays calm, and I can kind of see him say something. He talks to the kid. Says, 'Good good, one more. But harder this time!' So the kid goes to the corner, he signals with his finger, you know, saying, How 'bout one more. And the kid gets in his stance, waits for your dad to get up. Up comes your dad, and the big kid takes off, fires out of his stance like some kind of a rocket. And your father, he . . ."

Eddie's voice trailed off, and he swallowed real hard. Once, twice, three times, in obvious pain. Pain of the body, but more so the mind, as he struggled to tell me the rest of the tale.

"So the kid, he's charging, he's charging full steam. Coming in low and fast, gonna spear Tietam's gut . . . But your father gets ready, and he starts to move, and he shoots up his knee . . . and I swear as I sit here that the sound of that kid's face as it exploded was like a shot from a gun. It drove him straight up in the air, all three-hundred-plus pounds, landed him back on his butt, and the kid can't move, because his body's in shock.

"His teeth are all gone, at least most of them are, his nose is smeared all over his face . . . and his eye . . . his right eye . . . it's just hanging there . . . dangling down from its socket.

274

"I see your father get up, I'll never know how, because his knee's all swelled up, like a big basketball. And sticking out of his knee I see pieces of teeth . . . just sticking there. And I want to help, but . . . I can't . . . I just can't. I just stand there staring at the teeth . . . in his knee . . . and the eye . . . hanging there. But your father gets down, down on his knees, and again I'm thinking about the teeth stuck in there. But he's down on his knees, in front of the kid, surveying the damage, and the whole world is still. Crowd's just a blur, no one's moving a bit. Except for your dad, who balls up his fist . . . and with one brutal punch . . . he crushes the kid . . . crushes his eye . . . against his very own cheek."

I felt my throat tighten, and I tried hard to talk, but nothing came out. Poor Eddie looked bad, and I felt a twinge of great guilt, like a spear in my side for making him take part in this taxing ordeal. He took several deep breaths and then forged ahead.

"It gets worse, Andy, your father gets worse." He paused, let that fact register inside my shell-shocked mind. "Do you want me to continue?"

I nodded, whispered a weak "Yes."

"I tried to make some sense of it, Andy, I really did. Impossible, though . . . it really was. I just stood there in the locker room while he pulled those teeth out of his knee. Just dropped them to the floor. Didn't even care. And I tried to talk some sense into him, I really did . . . and he just stood up, blew some blood out of his nose, right where those teeth were, and said he didn't need advice from some Bible-thumping . . . nigger . . . I was in shock, Andy, tell the truth, everyone was. All the boys in the back, crowd, everyone. Then Tietam walks out, blood still pouring from his nose, no shirt, just his stupid hippie trunks and boots. Just walks out to his car, bag over his shoulder. Turns to me and, of all things, asks me if I want to grab a beer. Of all things, a beer. I tell him, I'm going to the hospital, gonna check on the kid, who at this point is being loaded into an ambulance. He gives me a nod, says he's hittin' the road. Makin' a quick stop and then he's hittin' the road. He shuts the door and off he goes.

"Well Andy, not too many of the boys made it to the hospital. Kid was new, hadn't had time to make any friends. But I stayed out in that hall, praying, waiting for news. No one from the office showed up, probably figured they can't make money off him, so why bother. I call home, tell my wife to expect me late. Tell her we'll celebrate another time. She sounds kind of funny. Not mad, just different, understand?"

I nodded.

"When I come home, my wife's up. Acting kind of funny, tipsy kind of, she's drinking a glass of wine—probably just one of several. I tell her I'm sorry, explain about the kid's eye, how they can't save it. Kid'll never use that eye again. My wife, who's usually the nicest person in the world, doesn't seem to care. She's distracted, acting funny, like she's drunk. Or something else.

"Then I see it, Andy. It's hidden, but I see it. On the television set. Behind our wedding picture. A deck of cards. Your father's deck."

I thought of my father. Hated his guts. I looked at Eddie, expecting pain or fatigue, but saw only resolve.

"The days went by. I never said anything, but I guess she suspected I knew. We stopped talking much, just passed by each other. The best of friends turned into total strangers.

"One night, my wife is working. I'm home. Home as usual, wishing for the old days, wishing I'd never met Tietam Brown. Hatred is just consuming me. Then I look at her picture, that one right up there, and I swear, Andy, it was like a lightning bolt from up above. Strikes me right in the heart. I get up from my chair, grab my old Bible. This Bible here. Without even thinking, I just open it up. Close my eyes, and I open it up. Put my finger down on a page. Open my eyes. Luke 6:37. 'Forgive, and you shall be forgiven.' Simple as that. The Lord spoke to me. Simple as that."

DECEMBER 31, 1985 / EVENING

I spent three days in New York with Eddie Edwards, seeing the sights and helping out with the homeless. On New Year's Eve, I caught the 5 p.m. Greyhound heading back north, where an uncertain future lay waiting for me. I thought of my father, and whether he cared that his only son had been gone for over four days. I'd left a short message on our new answering machine, just to let him know I was fine. I did not mention Eddie. I just said I was fine.

The kid next to me, from New York to Middletown, had long hair and drank beer, and lent me some tapes to help pass the time. Zebra, I think, and some Blackfoot too. And a band, I forget, with a real ugly singer who sang "We're Not Gonna Take It," which made me think of punching my dad.

He offered me pot, which I politely refused, and much to my amazement, no one said a word, as cannabis hung inside of that bus like thick cumulus clouds.

I gave back his tapes when his turn to leave came, and I sat back and enjoyed what I later realized was a good contact high as the snow blew by my window at an ever-quickening pace.

When that bus pulled into Cortland and I stepped into four new inches of snow, I was high on life and secondhand weed, and was raring to go. Which was a good thing for me, as I had quite a bit of walking to do. A walk that would take me through the last twenty minutes of 1985 and into the New Year, which I hoped to befriend.

I passed by Frank 'n' Mary's and gave a wave as I went. I put my head down, and my collar up, and thought of Bob Dylan in an old picture I'd seen. Something about "freewheeling," except he'd been in New York, with a girl on his arm, and I was in Cortland, and my arm was free.

Funny how quiet it was, without the college kids there. Just a few happy drunks ringing in the New Year. The Dark Horse was near empty, not like those times when I walked home from work and saw lines snaking outward, into the night. Lines of drunk students hoping to meet the girl of their dreams, at least for one night.

I'll never know what made me look there, for I seldom did. Pontillo's Pizza, the best slices in town. But look there I did, and once I did, I just stared. At Clem Baskin and Terri, the two holding hands and sharing a Coke with one glass and two straws. I should have just left, but I was unable to move, as if the sky had dropped big globs of white glue instead of powdery snow. And I saw her look up, and her green eyes met mine. And

279

my heart, my poor heart which just one week earlier had been broken in two, was now smashed to dust by the mere sight of her face.

JANUARY 1, 1986

Icame home that night about twenty to two, feeling as lonely as a boy can get, thinking of forgiveness but finding it an empty concept I was unable to believe in. I saw a red light flashing on the answering machine.

I pressed PLAY, and heard her voice. Terri. Compassionate, yet determined. Soft, but not weak. Saying, "Andy, it's me. I know you're hurt, but you've got to understand. Clem is a Christian. He and his parents gave themselves to the Lord on Christmas Day. I need that right now, for me and my family. Andy, I've asked God to forgive you . . . and maybe one day I will too . . . Good-bye."

I refused to cry. After a ten-year absence, I'd cried too much. Tears of joy and tears of sorrow— far too many of each, in too short a time. Why had my father come along? I was doing fine in Virginia. I wasn't good, wasn't happy, but I was fine nonetheless. No hopes to be snatched, no heart that could break, no father to hate. I longed for those times when every day seemed the same.

JANUARY 2, 1986

God, I dreaded January second, the first day of school. Dreaded the thought of seeing Terri and him. But my mind was made up—I just wouldn't cry. I'd get through that day, and my eyes would be dry.

I entered the school to a few brief hellos. Hellos brought on by my dad, the town's Nativity hero, who had made me his Joseph, which I guess earned me respect. Respect enough, at least, to make saying hello a socially acceptable part of the day.

God, give me the strength to shut off my heart, to keep me from feeling, I thought to myself as I walked down the hall. Because to see her with him would be too much to bear. Her hand in his, it didn't seem right. That hand that had fit so well in my own was now someone else's, and no, that didn't seem right.

But I didn't see Terri before opening bell. Or the bell after that. I heard Baskin's voice, but he wasn't with her. Just he and his friends, talking about what was new in their lives.

"Did you do it?" one said. "Yeah tell us about

it," said another. One after another, their voices rang out, each one talking about "it," those two scary letters that for high school boys could mean only one thing.

Then I heard Baskin's voice. His cocky high voice. Saying words that still haunt me to this very day. "Yeah, I did it," he said, proud as can be. "I fucked her. Fucked her last night, in the Lincoln's backseat." Words of congratulations, hand slaps and hugs. They all seemed a blur as his words drove a stake through what was left of my heart.

"I fucked her." As simple as that. The F word. Used as a verb, a powerful verb. Hateful and ugly.

As I stood in a daze, Baskin passed by, his four or five lackeys all beaming with pride. "Hey Annie," Baskin called. "Yeah you heard me right. I fucked your girl, and she loved it, begged me for more." His lackeys cheered wildly as Clem the good Christian shot his arm in the air. And then just when things looked like they couldn't get worse, they did. Did indeed. "Hey Brown, Annie Brown," Baskin said with a smirk. A smirk that spoke of great hatred, which he then dispensed with great joy. "Oh yeah, she loved it, 'cause I did it so good. Not just one touch and a squirt like you, little boy . . . Hey that's it," he continued, "your new name . . . One Touch Annie Brown." With that he was off, explaining the name's origin as he walked down the hall. The origin of my new name, One Touch Annie Brown.

The seconds ticked by, each one slower than the

one before, it seemed. Each minute a lifetime, until the bell rang for lunch. I tried to sit in the courtyard, which once had offered such hope, and I thought of Terri, back when she was mine, chasing me with her breasts as the fall leaves swirled around. But I was ushered inside by a teacher, who I guess didn't care about things like young love. Inside meant the cafeteria, that cavernous hall where kids ate fried food and tried their best to put down other students who weren't doing as well as themselves. And on January second, I was at least pretty sure that everyone was doing a whole lot better than me.

Still no Terri, which seemed rather odd, but Baskin was making some loud noises up front. Kind of like he was onstage, so that everyone looked as he held a grapefruit quarter aloft with one hand.

He was quite far away but I made out the words as he said, "Come on, kid, give me your best shot." The kid sat still with the other math nerds who frequented that table on a regular basis. But hey, at least those kids were good at one thing, their math, which was one thing more than me on this horrible day.

"Come on," Baskin taunted, "just give me a punch. I'm not gonna hurt you, unless you don't do as I say." So the math nerd got up, rather timidly so, and looked at Clem Baskin, all muscled and hard. "Give me a punch," Baskin said one last time, then let out a roar and bit down on his grapefruit, like Ali in Manila.

He egged on the kid, through clenched grape-fruit teeth. "Come on, ya wuss, let me see what ya got." So the nerd let loose with a feeble right hand that made scarcely a noise as it hit the wedge in Clem's mouth.

"Aaaghh!" Baskin yelled out as he withdrew his wedge. "You are denied, now sit down, you geek." Then he ripped off his shirt and stalked his next victim, his body still white, his back acne still red. "Hey, how about you?" he said to a kid, who I saw was Bill Bradford, the soccer goalie from class, who now ran winter track.

"Whatya say there, Bradford, how 'bout testing your strength."

"I'd rather not, Clem," said the boy, who looked poised to throw up.

"Well now, you've got a choice. Hit me . . . or I'll hit you. What'll it be? It's all up to you."

Bradford tried to decide, but Clem made his own choice and blasted the boy with a powerful slap. When the kid went down, a hush fell over the room except among the lackeys, who were ten or twelve strong. Those lackeys applauded, and chanted Clem's name. His good Christian name. Clem the good Christian, and his disciples of love.

"All right, who's next?" Baskin said with great malice as he picked a new wedge from his table. Then, with one wicked glance, he came toward me. I put my head down, but it was already too late. He'd already seen me alone at my table, alone in the world, with nowhere to escape. I looked at the cafeteria aides, hoping for mercy, or just some sanity in that insane world. They just stared blindly ahead. Had eyes but couldn't see. But they might as well have been spectators at the Coliseum in Rome, with their thumbs signaling down to Baskin the Gladiator, and his weapon, a fruit.

He said, "Hey there, One Touch, how's everything? Think you might like to give me a punch? Or you gonna cum in your pants, just like old times?" His football friends roared, and the rest of the room gave a courtesy "Oohh," even though I doubted they knew what he meant. "Yeah, One Touch here shot his load as soon as he touched Terri Johnson's big tit!" I guess they knew now.

God, this couldn't be happening. Not here, not now. Or anywhere, anytime, because it just was so cruel. But yes, it was happening, was happening there, was happening then. And the kids in the cafeteria were chanting his name. "Baskin, Baskin, Baskin," just like in the big games, and just like in those big games, Baskin basked in the noise.

He yelled, "Come on, One Touch, get out of that seat. Show me your stuff, give me a punch." And he stuffed the wedge into his mouth, bit down on it hard, and offered the room a big yellow smile.

I started to panic and thought of my dad, a real-life hero of sorts, maybe he'd save the day. But alas, he was no hero, just a piece of shit who destroyed human lives.

By now Baskin was flexing, shouting through

citrus flesh. "Get up, One Touch, or I'll come after you." Of those two choices, I thought, I'd settle for number two. It would be better to sit there, just get my shot and go home. I really was ready to just pay the price. Ready to sit there and get smacked in the face. But then the grapefruit came out, and he opened his mouth.

"I know all about her, your mother the whore . . . yeah you heard me right, One Touch, your mother's a whore." And then for the benefit of all in the room, he spread the good news like a disciple of old. "His mother's a whore. She's in porno magazines."

The laughter rained all over me. Stained me with its ugliness, its bitterness, its bile. But while the room was swallowing me whole, I thought of another mother. His. Amanda Baskin, the sad married drunk. I'd seen her breasts, had heard her words through the wall. Had heard her lick my . . . that was it. My father was right! He was right after all. She had licked my dad's ass, and now I'd tell the world. How she'd wormed that tongue, how she'd . . .

I couldn't do it. I just couldn't. Because I had given my word. Her sad, lonely voice making me promise. I was tempted, I was. I had broken my word only one time before, and I'd lost someone I'd loved. The memory of Mrs. Delanor, who I for too briefly called Mom, wouldn't let me give in. Because I knew if I did, somehow I'd pay. In my soul. I would keep Mrs. Baskin's promise forever, and I would keep it today.

So I said not a word, which wasn't the case when it came to Clem Baskin, who was reaching even lower into his cruel bag of tricks. And reaching into his pocket to pull out a page. A page just like the one I had pulled from our tree. A page of poor Holly, and two men with no faces.

"Look at this," Baskin yelled, "his mother in action. Look at her face, all covered with—"

That last word never got out. It couldn't get out, for his mouth became full. Full of my fist, clear up to my wrist. I hadn't planned on snapping. I just did, that's all. Inside a split second, I had gone into a rage. I don't remember grabbing my quarters, but I must have, I guess. Because over a dollar was pumped from his stomach. Along with three pieces of teeth, and a whole one as well.

For a moment I thought my fist was stuck there for good. But I got that fist out, and just stood and stared. At the pieces of teeth lodged deep in my knuckles. Over one thousand miles and sixteen years from that night in Atlanta, but I just couldn't stop thinking, Like father, like son.

Then I was down. Down on the floor of the cafeteria, where a nonstop barrage of knees, feet, and fists made solid contact until the whole room went black.

JANUARY 2, 1986 / EVENING

My hand was throbbing. That was my first thought, as I returned to the land of the conscious, after a seven-hour delay. The teeth that had been lodged in my knuckles were gone, but the damage had been done. Not just to Baskin's mouth, but to my hand as well, which ached despite what I guessed was my pretty heavily medicated state.

I guess there was a certain sense of satisfaction in having lodged my fist into Baskin's big mouth, but the rage that was triggered was so fierce and so quick that I saw it more as a devastating setback. Giving in to demons that had already made my life hell. Kind of like David Banner on *The Incredible Hulk*, saying, "Don't make me angry, you wouldn't like me when I'm angry." I wondered if Clem Baskin liked me when I was angry.

It was my hand. Despite the throbbing, that hand felt alive. Warm, wonderful . . . loved. I don't know if the human mind is prone to premonitions when the body is pumped to the gills with intravenous pain medicine, but I knew without knowing, what that loved feeling was . . . Terri, my Terri, holding my hand.

I tried hard to focus, but it all was a blur, and I tried hard to speak, but the effort was fruitless.

"Andy, Andy, are you awake?" she said. Her voice was hoarse, her nose stuffy, as if she'd been crying for a very long time.

"Andy, Andy?"

I squeezed her hand as best as I could, and opened my eyes so as to take in her hair, and her skin, and her eyes.

She smiled at my squeeze, and got out of her chair. Got down on her knees, put her cheek on my hand. She said, "Can you . . . forgive me . . . Andy please. Can you forgive me?"

Forgiveness? I knew about that. I didn't know much, but I knew about that. Eddie Edwards had taught me about that. But forgiveness, I knew, ran much deeper than words. It had to come from the heart. And my heart was gone. Crushed by this woman, who now held my hand. So, could I do it? It certainly seemed like a lot to forgive. But old Eddie Edwards came back to my mind. Opening his Bible to Luke 6:37.

I closed my eyes and gave her a smile. A goofy, doped up, but wonderful smile. Then using all of the strength that morphine hadn't yet borrowed, I squeezed her hand and pulled it toward me. Put it on my bruised cheek, and then gave it a kiss. Hoping that my message would be clear as a "yes."

Apparently so, for she got up from her knees,

her hand still in mine, and covered my face with soft kisses.

Then she looked into my eyes, and said, "Thank you," those two simple words, that we hear so much every day that they've stopped meaning much. But those two words were special, incredibly so, for they came not from her lips, but straight from her heart.

I then saw the glow, the beautiful glow. A glow from the light streaming in from the hospital's hall. Light that caused her to look, in my narcotic state, like an angel of mercy, sent down from above. Sent down, just like Holly, to help a lost soul, and just like Holly, I knew that soon Terri would be gone. Out of my world, but not out of my life, where she'd live forever, inside of my heart.

To this day, when I think of my Terri, which I do every day, I think of her first and foremost as that angel of mercy. And then I think of black lingerie, and her bare beautiful breasts. But first, the angel. The angel always comes first.

"Andy?"

I gave her a wink, to let her know that I heard.

"I did something wrong, terribly wrong.

"I thought he loved God, but he just . . . wanted . . . me.

"I kept saying no . . . but he was so mad . . . and so strong . . . I just couldn't stop him . . . and I . . ."

Her words just trailed off, and were replaced by her sobs. And I thought back to lunchtime, and my hand . . . and his mouth, and now thought that I liked it. I liked it a lot.

Terri took her head off my chest, which was now damp with tears, and this time when she spoke, she got all of it out.

"I stayed home today, Andy, I was just so, so, so sad, and I couldn't bear to see you, I was just too ashamed. And then when I heard what you did, I was glad. Really glad, Andy, but then really sad. Because I heard you were hurt, and my father said 'Good.' That you got what was coming, and you'd end up in jail. Then I told him to shut up; yes I actually did. I talked back to my father, and said he was wrong. Then I told him about the punch, you know, the Hanrahan punch, and what kind of a man the coach really was. Still, my dad tried to defend him, so I took their dumb picture right off of the wall. I said if he kept it, I wouldn't come home. I blamed him for you, and then I told him about . . . what happened. And I thought my father would care, I thought he would love me. His eyes watered up, and I thought he would hug me, but he reared back his hand and he slapped me instead."

I wanted to leap up out of that bed, to protect her, to hold her, but the drugs in my body had taken over my will, and I just lay there instead.

"The slap wasn't so hard, but it hurt me so bad. Not in my face, but here, in my heart. And while he was calling me names, and putting all the blame on me, I suddenly saw him for what he really was. I saw him the way you did last week at my house. God help me, Andy, it took me seventeen years to find out what you did in one day.

"And Andy, at a time when I needed help most, all he could think of was himself. Saying, How will this make him look, how will this make him feel. I hated him, Andy, and I told him that, too. I told him I was coming to see you and that's when he said he was . . ."

Her voice faded out in a trail of small sobs, and she tried several times to continue, but the words seemed caught in her throat and drowned in her sorrow. She placed her head back on my chest for several moments, then tried again, and this time when she spoke, she got all of it out.

"He said he was sending me away. To a school far away, where I couldn't humiliate him, to a place where no one would know that his little girl was a slut . . . That's what he called me, Andy . . . a slut. He tried to stop me, but I ran past his raised hand and out of the door, and even while I was pulling out of the driveway he was quoting the Bible and damning my soul, and wouldn't you know it, Andy, he got the verse wrong."

The thought made her smile, and I tried to smile, too, although I'm not sure if it registered, for I was fading real fast.

"I drove over here, Andy, but they said I was late. That hours for visiting were already over. But I begged, and I cried, and they let me come in. And I just want to come back, if you'll let me, I guess. I'm leaving tomorrow, I don't even know where, but I just want to come back to your heart . . . if you'll let me back in."

God, I wished I could talk, to let her know she was already there, that she'd been firmly entrenched since she first held my hand.

"I'll write to you, Andy. And I'll wait every day for you to write back. I'll understand if you don't . . . God knows how I've hurt you . . . but I'll wait every day for you to reply."

Then she sat in her chair and just held my hand. She stroked my hair and my face, and what was left of my ear. And held on to my hand.

I don't think that a single day has passed that I haven't thought of that moment, her hand holding mine. Maybe I think about it more than I should. But to me, it meant much more than just human hands touching. For no matter where life might lead us from there, I knew then that she loved me, and that she always would.

JANUARY 5, 1986 / AFTERNOON

I was released from the hospital after three days of care. My injuries, while extensive, did not need much care, just some old-fashioned rest. My father was there to get me, and he played the dutiful father up until his car door shut, at which point all talking ceased.

We pulled into the drive without having exchanged a word. I was busy anyway. Busy thinking about Terri, my angel, and our new start together. Thinking also about forgiveness, and what a gift it was. A gift to others, but to one's self as well. Forgiveness, after all, was about healing. Healing wounds. What about the wounds my father had inflicted, not only physically but mentally as well? Should he be forgiven? Or did he even want that at all?

There was a decency to my father. I had seen it. Seen it enough to know it existed. But it was a side of him that had needed to be coaxed out, by Holly, and I guess to some extent by me. But like some hermit crab, he'd retreated back into his shell of drinking and women, and I wasn't sure if he'd ever want to come back.

The manger still stood in our small front yard. The manger where our substitute Mary had stood, before she fell under the spell of my father's inexplicable charm.

Then, through the door and on my way up the stairs, which I climbed with great effort, I peered at the gifts, which were still under the tree, except for the one empty space where Holly's present had been.

"Hey Andy," my father called up just as I was opening my door.

"Yeah," I called back.

"We need to talk, I'll be up in a while."

A while was an hour. Tietam knocked softly, and I told him, "Come in." I was sore as hell but dead set on defiance, as I had vowed to not let my dad ever unnerve me again. But my heart was full, and my hopes were high, not for my father, but for the letter from Terri, which would surely be coming.

He came shuffling in, looking not like a monster, but like a small balding man. But when it came to my father, I had learned that looks could deceive.

"What do you want?" I said, feigning disinterest and hoping he bought it. I lay prone on my bed, reading a magazine.

"Well, I'd like to say, 'Sorry.'"

I grew quickly defiant. "Sorry for what, Dad— my shoulder? It's a little too late. Or for raping our neighbor? Are you sorry for that? Or for my

Christmas Eve blow job? Or maybe you thought that was cool? Whatever it is, I don't want your sorrow."

"I'm sorry for Terri."

He had caught me off guard, and I dropped my defenses, and the magazine, too. "Terri?" I asked. "What do you mean?"

"I know about Baskin."

I struggled for a second to think of what I could say. While I was struggling, Tietam continued.

"I know what happened that night, and I think it's my fault."

"Your fault, but how, besides, how could you know." I looked hard at my father, and saw a true sense of remorse. But I saw something else, some other emotion. But I just couldn't place it.

"I was there that night, Andy. In the hospital hall, outside your door. I wanted to see you, when I heard what had happened. But I heard your girl-friend inside, and it just tore me up. It tore me all up, because I could have stopped it."

"Stopped it?" I said. "How, you weren't there."

"No, but I knew about his past."

"What past?" I asked.

"Do you remember New Year's Eve, when you came back from New York . . . You came home and heard a message, didn't you? I know you did, because I heard it too, that sweet voice must have broke your heart. Claiming that Baskin kid was a Christian, that he'd turned his life over to the Lord. I knew that it was just a crock about Baskin

297

finding God. But not her words. No, they were the truth. I mean, she wanted to believe."

I nodded slowly, and I sat up on my bed. I forgot all about my pain, and focused on my father.

"Andy, do you remember Baskin's mother?"

"Yeah. How could I forget?"

"Do you remember that first night I brought her home?"

I told him I did.

"You know I didn't think much of it, I thought she'd be just like all the rest. You know, we'd have some fun, I'd do my deck, go back for round two."

"I know, Dad, I was listening."

He smiled for just a second, then said, "That's right, I forgot."

I smiled too. Damn that Tietam. He had that way about him. Sometimes even now, in spite of everything the thought of Tietam makes me smile.

"Well I go to leave, and she calls me back, tears are running down her face. She says she needs someone to talk to. Talking's really not my thing, but I did the best I could.

"She says her son is a real bad kid. Says he has no hope. Strangles cats, things like that, says she's scared of him. Said those steroids made him wild, so he couldn't control himself. Said he forced himself on his own mom, that he was just too strong to stop.

"The whole thing kind of freaked me out. Which is why I took the shower and came into your room. Remember that night?"

"Yeah, I remember," I said, thinking of my mother's picture and the tears on Tietam's face.

"Andy, I think that lady needs some help, needs to talk to someone who can help her. Instead she wants to talk to me. Like I'm some kind of doctor. That was the night you got the kiss from Terri. Remember?"

"Yeah, I do."

"You know, if there's a God, I'll pay for this, might pay for a lot of things I've done. But there she was, drunk as hell, and she's looking to be held. And instead I—"

"What did you do, Dad?" I blurted out. I really had to know. And despite knowing he was a monster, I felt some sympathy for him.

"I made her call me Clem."

Oh man. He was right. God would make him pay.

"I may have been a little rough with her. All she wanted was a hug. Then you came home with your eye all swelled, and I went running for the coach. Thinking I would hook him quick; instead, he nearly killed me. I don't know how I finally stopped him. Some kind of miracle, I thought. When I was driving home, I got to thinking that maybe it was a sign. Maybe I had paid the price for what I did to Mrs. Baskin. So I tried to change my life. Which is why I was so weak, I think, when . . . Holly came around."

I had made a vow that I wouldn't cry, but I found it hard to keep. For my eyes filled up when I thought of her, hanging on our tree.

"You know, she was drawing lots of pictures for books for little kids."

"Yeah, she told me about her art."

"Then her sister calls her. Says she's in a lot of debt. Gambling, drugs, things like that."

I struggled with my tears. Tried not to let them fall.

"Got involved with some bad people. Needed money fast . . . I guess the rest is history."

I thought of Eddie Edwards. Thought of that verse in Luke. "Could you forgive her?"

Tietam smiled just slightly. A smile of sadness and regret. "Sorry, kid. That's something I can't do. Not after seeing her like that."

Now I was a counselor, a philosopher, a shrink. Thinking of all that I had learned during one monstrous week. Thinking of Holly, thinking of Eddie, thinking once again of Luke. "Dad, nobody's perfect. We all make mistakes."

"You're damn right," said Tietam. "We all make mistakes. And I made the biggest." My last words had made him angry, his eyes glared just a bit. I began to speak, but didn't. I let Tietam finish first. I could see his right arm shaking. I knew I'd touched a nerve.

"Do you know what my mistake was, Andy?"

I decided not to ask.

"It was thinking she was different. But she was just the same. Just like Sugling, just like Baskin, just like Terri."

"Just like Terri?" I yelled out. I stood up from

the bed. The sudden move made my head spin and I almost lost my footing. It was just an instinctual move, I didn't want to cause a scene. But my instinct was to defend the girl I loved. "Take it back, Dad, take it back!"

My dad was now a different man. I no longer felt his pain. Now I could feel his hatred as he got close to me, almost nose to nose. For a moment I thought he'd hit me, but I didn't give a damn. Then I remembered Tietam didn't punch, with one notable exception. Instead he turned his back to me and said words in a whisper. So low I couldn't make them out, so I asked him to repeat them.

His back stayed turned, and his voice only rose the slightest bit, but this time his voice got through. He said, "I saw her grab your balls."

He had caught me unprepared. I tried to react in some brave way, but instead I just said, "So?"

Tietam wheeled around and fired his words like bullets, rapid-fire and deadly. "So . . . she let you feel her up, right in front of me. So . . . what if she felt up Baskin, let him grab her tits. Listen, kid, that's carte blanche, he's got the go-ahead. Some girl feels my nuts, I take her home, that's just the way it is. Now maybe 'No' means 'No' to you, but not to me, and I doubt it did for Baskin. She touches nuts, that pussy's his, and don't think that cock-teaser didn't know it. To cry about it afterward is wrong—he was well within his rights."

It was as if he'd thrown a knockout punch, for

301

his words had staggered me. Literally. My knees had buckled and I went down, just collapsing on my bed. But the tirade seemed to comfort him, for when he spoke next, he had mellowed.

"Look, Andy, I don't want to hurt you. I've done enough of that already. And I really did like Terri. But she will break your heart. Over and over. Because that's what women do."

I tried to catch my breath as he walked away. He looked down at my phonograph and stared at it awhile. Just stood and stared without a sound. A pause that filled the air with greater tension with every passing second. I have thought about the way he chose to break the pause. I've thought of it for years. And I have no doubt that in his heart he knew his words would send him past the point of no return. A point from which he knew for sure our relationship was over.

"Nat King Cole." Three simple words. One special name. "I never did care for that nigger."

I dared not say a word. Just sat on my bed looking at my old canvas sneakers, wishing they were ruby slippers so I could tap my heels and get the hell out of my room.

"Yeah," he continued, "never did like him much, reminds me of your mother."

He picked the record up, examined the scratches, turned it gently in his hands. "Hey look there—Kathy Collins, your mother's maiden name. Well isn't that sweet. From mother to son. A gift." And then, with one flick of his wrist, he shot the record at the wall, inches from my head, where it hit with a smack and shattered.

My heart, which had been so full only one night before, seemed on the verge of breaking once again. I wished for a second that I could snap, force myself to. Just thrust my fist into his mouth. Lodge it there so it couldn't hurt me anymore. Instead I felt my stomach get weak, I felt my nerves start to fail, and felt my throat start to close, making swallowing difficult.

"Dad," I cried. "Why?" They were the only words I could get out.

"Why?" my father said, mocking me. "Why? Well I'll tell you why, Andy, my boy, my only boy. Because it's about time that you learned about your mother."

He sat down beside me, put his arm around me. His touch was like ice, the touch of a man whose heart had grown cold. His words, when he spoke, were like lethal darts, sticking in deep, killing me slowly, from the inside on out.

"You think I'm stupid?" he asked. "You must think so, Andy, if you think for a second I don't know where you've been." My stomach got weaker. "So you gave me a call just to let me know you were okay. Well isn't that nice. Had to check out the city, huh, isn't that what you said? Well Andy, do you know how easy it is to check out phone records? I call in a favor, and I find out you were calling from a house owned by an Edwards."

My heart was now pounding, my voice was dry, my throat continued to tighten, and my brain started to hurt. I didn't know where he was going, but I knew it wasn't anywhere good.

"Now Andy, let me ask you, what was a nice white boy like you doing with a dirty nigger like Edwards—what did the two of you have to talk about?"

I looked down at my shoes, afraid to look up, still wishing for a special power to get me out of this room.

"Damn it, boy, I'm talking to you," he said, grabbing my bad arm with just enough force to make me scream out in pain. Pain I wish I could have just swallowed, but it was too late.

"Hey, did Edwards tell you about the little gift I left, my calling card, fifty-two cards to be exact."

I didn't say a word, but he knew nonetheless.

"Funny thing about that nigger, talking about Eddie, not his wife, though I suppose she was one also. Yeah, funny thing is, he's religious, right, thinks sex is a sin. And he lives in Georgia. Believe it or not, they got laws down there. Laws that make certain acts illegal. But nobody pays attention to the laws, I mean why should they, right, kid? . . . Oh I see, you're not going to talk. Well that's fine, just listen. So where was I . . . oh yeah, talking about Edwards. Anyway, Edwards is the only guy who listens, thinks he can't do stuff 'cause it's against state law. Ridiculous, right? Now why didn't he just get his knob polished in Tennessee, is what I'm thinking, right? I mean it's a two-hour trip. Go see Ruby Falls, maybe check out Chickamauga, then go to a hotel, put that black dick in her mouth.

"Except Edwards won't do it. He's too good a Christian, whatever that means. His wife, meanwhile, is dying for it. I can tell. Call it a gift, but I always can tell. So one night in Atlanta, I do a number on this kid from Texas . . . Eddie tell you about that?"

My eyes were still focused on my sneakers, but I nodded my head.

"He did, huh? Wow, you and your nigger must have been best buddies . . . Hey kid, he tell you about the eye? I bet he did, didn't he?"

Against my better judgment, I nodded again. Tietam Brown whooped with joy. He was enjoying himself.

"So anyway, kid, Eddie, the compassionate Christian, goes to the hospital, and I head for his house. See, I had a chance with the old lady once before, but she wasn't a doctor then. Was just going to medical school. No real challenge there. But now she's a doctor, and I get my chance, so I take it. I show up, she's drunk, but she tries to fight it at first. But I know what she wants. So it doesn't take long, and she's fumbling with my trunks. Believe it or not, I'm still wearing my trunks. Balls are all sweaty, but she doesn't care.

Then he laughed and said, "This is where it gets funny," and he started slapping my back.

"The funny thing is, Eddie's wife can't suck a dick. She doesn't know how, she's never done it. The nigger's all teeth, and it's starting to hurt, so I . . . I . . . Hey Andy, buddy, you're not crying, are you?"

I'd kept looking down, but my body gave me away. Sobs that were silent, but sobs all the same.

"Thatta boy," my father said, his voice thick with false compassion. "You let it out. Just let it all come out." A pat on the back completed the sham, and his voice changed its tone again. Now he was a teacher.

"Books are great, you know that, son? They can teach you quite a bit. But sometimes books alone do not suffice, they can't teach you everything. For example, I've done quite a bit of reading on the history of Japan. It's just something that I'm interested in. But during the course of all that research, I never knew that they have a thing for blond girls. Blond singers, more precisely. And I never knew that they hired girls to sing, fly them over on a one-way ticket. Get them there and then let them know that they need to do a little more than just sing for their money. Did you know that?"

I shook my head. My whole body throbbed. My head, my hand, my shoulder, my ribs. It all hurt so bad. But my gut hurt the worst, because I knew in that gut that something was wrong. My father was a lot of things, but a liar was not among them. I knew his next words would be true, and I knew they would hurt.

"So Andy, put yourself in my shoes for a second. Pretend you're me. Just for a second. Pretend you're in love for the very first time. Made beautiful love for the very first time. She's carrying a baby, you sing that child songs. Then one day your wife, who is due in two weeks, she comes into the room crying, says she's got a small problem. Says she's not really sure just what's growing inside her. Who knows, she says, it could be yours, or maybe it's not. Could be a Jap. A nasty, slant-eyed father-torturing Jap. And Andy, tell me, what would you do?"

I felt for him, I really did. Because I knew his pain was real. He was like a roller coaster, taking my emotions for a ride. Up and down, round and round.

"I'm so sorry," I said as I wiped at tears. "God, Dad, I'm so sorry."

Tietam got up from his bed. An evil grin creased his face.

"Hey, don't. Because I don't feel sorry for me. No, Andy Brown, I feel sorry for you."

"Why?"

"Well it's really quite simple. I guess what I'm trying to tell you is your mother was a fucking whore!"

He was trying to provoke me. I was pretty sure of that. Trying to see how much I'd take. Maybe trying to see what my "rage" was really like. But the rage was never something I ever could control. It just appeared every several years, and left great suffering in its wake. Usually I suffered most. I did make a move for Tietam, but not one born out of rage. No, in my tiny bedroom amid broken pieces of my life and Nat King Cole, I was just an injured kid defending the honor of his mother, throwing a wild punch at a very dangerous man. A man who specialized in causing pain. He ducked the punch as if it had been thrown in slow motion. From a hand that he caught in the crook of his arm. A hand with fingers that he snapped like pieces of chalk. First the pinkie and the pointer, then the two middle ones. Finally the thumb, which he pulled from its socket with deliberate care.

The pain was just too much to bear, and I felt myself teetering on the thin line of consciousness before losing the bout. But mere seconds had passed when I felt Tietam Brown's hand slapping my face. Not to cause harm, but to help me come to. Because my father, you see, was not quite through with me yet.

I became vaguely aware that I was prone on the floor, and that my father lay behind me, his limbs seemingly everywhere. Right forearm pressed against my neck, left arm hooked around my right. And his legs were wrapped around my waist in some strange configuration. Firm, but not painful. At least not at first.

He spat out a phony laugh, one of extended exaggeration. "Whoa ho, look at me. After all my lecturing on the big F word, when I finally let it fly, I use it as a fucking adjective. Which we all know that it's not. Of course not. We all know it's a verb. As in Clem fucked Terri. Or did Terri fuck Clem? I guess we'll never know for sure."

Tietam then arched backward and cinched up on his hold, bringing forth a kind of pain I never knew could exist. Pain so deep and sickening that I couldn't even scream. Excruciating to such a degree that I felt something leave. My will to live. It was leaving. I was begging God to let me die. Until my father spoke again, and the will came rushing back.

He didn't so much speak as hiss into my injured ear. Hot breath in my stump, stabbing right into my brain. "Imagine you're a woman and you've got a child inside. Due in two weeks, in this type of pain. What kind of damage would that do?"

My will returned, blocking out the pain, but my consciousness was fading. I fought it off as best I could, but his wrist was dug in deep. Dug into my neck, not letting blood get through. As my world faded off to black, Tietam Brown served up one last dose of hatred.

"All that blood just came gushing out of her mouth and I knew she was gone. Just like I wanted, that fucking whore, she was gone. But how could I know that you would still be alive. Inside of her womb. Goddamn you, boy, you were supposed to—"

I think that "die" was his word of choice, but I'll never know for sure. For just as in my incident with Clem Baskin, that last word never made it

309

out. And just like Clem Baskin, lots of teeth were lost in the attempt. But not in my fist. In the back of my head. In that one bright red split second, I had snapped once again. Wasn't sure how I'd gotten loose, but I'd cost him some teeth. I had leaned forward enough and come firing back with my head. And then he let go with his legs and covered his mouth with his hands, and then I was up on him, all fury and feet. The rage had returned.

A kick to his ribs and a stomp to his head, and Tietam Brown screamed and reached under my bed. Came out with his hands around the barrel of a bat that I kept there just for him. Had kept since the day after Christmas, just waiting for him. I knew he would use it if he got the chance, so I made sure that he didn't with a kick to his face.

"I'll kill you," I screamed. Over and over, the same primal scream. "I'll kill you, I'll kill you."

And Tietam Brown began to scream. "No, Andy, don't, please Andy don't!"

But I kept it up. Screaming I'd kill him and then doing my best to make those words truth.

He looked almost comical, with his teeth broken or gone. Blood spilling out as he begged for his life. But nothing was funny when my feet found their mark. Over and over, my feet found their mark. Kicks to his face, his ribs, his middle-aged balls. All thrown in a rage, but even while caught up in its fury, I sensed that somehow something was wrong.

Yes, something was wrong. My kicks were still landing, but my father still moved. At least twenty kicks, but my father still moved. And though he was screaming, his face, through the blood, didn't look scared. He screamed and begged for his life, but he didn't look scared. The whites of his eyes looked incredibly calm, and as he crawled to his knees, I saw his mouth form a red, jagged smile.

My rage left me then, and took with it most of my strength. Now fear came rushing in, shooting straight through my veins. I knew that I had to act before Tietam got up. I had to act soon.

At that moment I had a premonition of sorts. I thought of my dad and that night in Atlanta, and the big kid from Texas with his eye hanging out. And though I didn't know how, I just knew if I hit him—my knee in his face—history would repeat itself, right there in my room.

So I charged at full speed, and thought of Tietam's eye hanging, and thought that in spite of shattered fingers, I would find the will to make a fist, and that fist would crush his eyeball against his very own cheek.

My premonition was wrong. For right before impact, my father dropped to his side and scissored my left leg with both of his thighs. I went down hard, the impact of my head on hard wood jarring my brain, so that when I regained my bearings, my left leg had already been broken in half. I had two last thoughts as a free man, both of them hazy. Before consciousness left me, I saw a bone sticking out of my sock and I felt my body being thrown down the stairs.

JANUARY 8, 1986

The old man was distinguished, I could just tell right away. Wire-frame glasses he wore low on his nose, and his snow white hair was thick. He had an air of confidence as he told an armed guard at my door, "No, don't worry, I'll be fine," and he let the door slam shut behind him. He put his briefcase on a wobbly table and told me who he was.

"Antietam Brown, I am the chief psychiatrist at the state hospital in Ithaca, and I have spent quite a while looking into your case, and I'd like to tell you what I think."

He wasn't cocky, he wasn't rude, but I was bothered by him just the same. I'd had three days to lie in the forensic unit at Cortland General with a cast from my toes up to my waist, a cast up to my elbow, and four splints on my fingers. Armed guards at my door, who revolved on eight-hour shifts, and not a whole lot of medication. I'd been offered but I refused, I wanted my mind clear to do some thinking. And that's exactly what I'd done for four straight days, except for the few hours I gave in to sleep. No books, no games, no TV, just three days for my thoughts to stew. So I really did not need some quack telling me about his thoughts. I thought I'd share with him my own thoughts instead. And I decided that I'd yell them.

"I think my father set me up. I think he wants me in jail. I think he wanted me to hurt him. I think he killed my mother. And I think he wanted me in here. I think he broke my leg all by himself, not by falling down the goddamn stairs. I think that my father is a rapist, and a murderer, and a lousy goddamn father. And I think I want you out of here."

My chest was heaving in and out by the time my spleen was fully vented. But man, I felt relieved. I looked intently at the doctor, and tried to read his face. What I saw was damn near shocking. Understanding. Kindness. Caring. A little sympathy as well.

"Can I speak for just a moment?" A soft voice, in control. "You may find my thoughts to be of value."

I nodded my head.

"I think, Antietam, that . . ." He hesitated while he pondered how best to share his thoughts. I was going to object to his using my full name, but I decided not to at that time. In fact I never did. To the chief psychiatrist at the state hospital at Ithaca, I would always be "Antietam."

"I think that the odds of five fingers and a leg all breaking during the course of falling down one flight of wooden stairs would be quite astronomical."

"You mean you think he pushed me down the stairs."

"I would not disagree."

"After hurting me himself?"

"Again I'm in concurrence."

"You think he set me up?"

"That is my opinion."

"So I'm not going to go to jail?"

"Well that part is not so easy."

"I don't understand." For just a minute I'd been ecstatic. Like this doctor was an answer to my prayers. Vindication for me. Incarceration for my father. I'd even managed to sit up in bed, no simple feat while a body is in traction. Now, with the doctor's latest words, I lay back down in frustration.

"Well Antietam, there is the matter of the tape."

"Tape?" I said. "What tape?"

The doctor opened up his briefcase. He had a small recorder placed inside. He pushed a button and I heard my voice. A chill went up my spine.

"I'll kill you, I'll kill you," my voice sang out, as did my father's anguished cries.

The doctor stopped the tape and looked at me, waiting for some kind of *explanation*. That chill got ever colder as I searched my brain for some kind of reason. But for several moments, I came up blank, until I thought of Tietam's hand. Reaching for my baseball bat? Or something else, instead?

"He set me up! He planted it. He tried to make

me snap. He said he'd killed my mother, he knew that I would snap!"

The doctor nodded thoughtfully, as if considering my claim. "Your mother's death is a surprise to me, but it bears investigation. As far as the audiocassette in question, it does seem a bit convenient."

"So you believe me?"

"Yes, I do."

"So when can I get out?"

"I fear it's not that simple. There is the other matter that is quite troubling."

"Which is?"

"Antietam, your father nearly lost his life from the beating that you gave him. His liver was severely lacerated, his body nearly drowned in its own blood. Two ribs were fractured, one of which punctured his lung. A testicle required drainage. Down the road he'll need lots of work on what you did to his teeth."

I struggled for some logic, a way to let him know about my dad. About his superpowers. But I was afraid I would sound crazy. I said it anyway.

"My father is like Superman. He just lay back and let me beat him. He even smiled a little."

"I think a jury would have a hard time reaching that conclusion. Taking into consideration the extensive injuries suffered by Clem Baskin. Whose family might still be considering filing charges."

"But Baskin made me do it too!" Now I really did sound crazy. But the doctor didn't flinch.

"I'm not inclined to disagree with you."

"About Baskin?"

"He'd been in and out of trouble. My research on your case has unearthed a student who has chosen to be nameless, who said that Mr. Baskin was quite cruel in terms of how he treated you. This student felt that Baskin received his just deserts. However, once again a court of law might see things differently, if Mr. Baskin was a witness."

"What about my dad?"

"Do you mean do I think he willingly allowed his own body to be sacrificed, so his only son could go to jail?"

I nodded silently, realizing how insane this whole idea must seem.

"Antietam, I'm not . . . completely unfamiliar . . . with your father's . . . superpowers." He said the last word with an empathetic smile.

"You're not?" Total bewilderment.

"I believe you know Coach Hanrahan?"

"Yeah, yeah, I do." A small light in the forest. I might avoid jail time after all.

"The coach is under my supervision at the hospital. He doesn't communicate too well, his head suffered quite a trauma at a ball game. But he knows your father's name real well. So this morning, I decided to pay your father a social call."

"Where, here at the hospital?" I was vaguely aware that two ambulances had been summoned to our house on Elston Court. Just like Creed and

Rocky, after their big battle. Father and son after a small spat, each going to Cortland General. For that first day, in all my agony, I thought the guard was there for my protection.

"No, I spoke with him at your residence. The nature of his injuries required a longer duration at the hospital. Much longer in fact. But as you mentioned, and as I have learned, you father is not an average man."

"What did you find out?" I said.

"Well there were no confessions or revelations of that nature. I don't want to mislead you or raise your expectations. But he made no attempt to hide his intention that as retribution for his injuries, you spend time in jail."

"Do you think it's going to happen?"

"I think the possibilities were strong. But . . ." He emphasized that word. "I had quite a productive talk with your father, and I think we have reached a compromise that is amenable to all parties."

"A compromise?" My heart resumed its pounding.

"Your father would consider dropping charges if I take you on as a patient at the hospital."

Oh my God! I was going to be locked up! "But that's for crazy people," I pleaded. "I don't belong in there!"

I saw the doctor grimace. He adjusted his glasses slightly, and bit down on his lip. Trying to find a way to tell me that I was going to the funny farm.

"Antietam, I will be honest with you. In comparing your mental state with your father's, I think your father has more issues that need immediate attention. He offered only minimal insight into the past few weeks' occurrences. But from that insight I could see the patterns of a man in need of help."

"Did he tell you how he raped my neighbor, or how he made the Virgin Mary perform oral sex on me?"

"No, he did not address that first contention, or the second for that matter. But Antietam . . ."

"Yes?"

"You might not want to speak too much about that second thing, because it does make you sound quite crazy."

The laugh we shared was timely, and it helped create a bond. A bond that would grow strong with time, as I would later share with him all my thoughts.

"Antietam?"

"Yes?"

"He told me about Holly." He paused, waiting for a response. My alert stare served as one. "About how abandoned he had felt. About the pictures that he saw. And I believe that he interpreted those photographs as some kind of personal attack. Classic narcissism; he believes that the world revolves solely around him. And I believe that he took out his aggressions for this perceived personal attack on an innocent party; that party being you. A classic case of displacement, to cite Freudian methodology. Then he went a little deeper into his past."

"You mean about my mother?"

"No, I mean about his father."

"His father?" I said. "You mean the one who died in World War II?"

"Well, he only had one father, and he served in World War II, but this one came home very much alive, in body if not in mind."

I nodded in befuddlement. This news was kind of stunning.

"He was a prisoner of war in the Philippines, from what your father told me. Now I am not a specialist in history, but I believe the prisoners' treatment was harsh. They were subjected to great amounts of torture and did not receive treatment for their ailments. Which in the case of Antietam Brown the Third meant syphilis. Very common, very treatable. But left untreated, can cause dementia, which seems to be what happened. Apparently it got to the point where the poor soul could barely function. He was admitted to the V.A. hospital in Elmira in 1950, and remained a patient until his death. He died there just eight months ago. In all those years, he was never the beneficiary of a single visit from your father."

Apparently, Tietam Brown was not the type of guy who could fast forgive a grudge. He wasn't real keen on forgiveness, a fact which had served to shape his life. I had a simple question, one whose answer seemed quite easy. I thought I knew, but I *had to know,* to best understand my father's actions.

"Who held him captive over there?"

"Why, the Japanese, of course."

I tried to bask in this glow that enlightenment had offered, but I was quickly cooled by the doctor's voice, in spite of its sincerity.

"Antietam, you are not without issues of your own."

"I'm not?"

"You possess quite a bit of anger."

"Well you would too if you'd lived my life!"

"I do not disagree. In and of itself, the anger is not the problem. The problem lies in how you let it out, usually in bursts of great aggression."

"But each time they deserve it!"

"Upon looking at your case history, I would say there is some basis to your opinion. But Antietam?" He paused and looked at me intently.

"Yes?"

"I want you to ask yourself one simple question."

"Okay."

"Who ultimately pays the price for all that anger?"

Wow, he'd hit the nail right on the head. "I uh, guess that would be me."

"Yes, I think it is. And without some type of treatment, I'm afraid that trend will continue."

"What kind of treatment?"

"Therapy, some medication."

"But can't I do that without being—"

"Committed?"

"Yeah, committed."

I could see the doctor struggle to best explain my situation.

"Yes, Antietam, I think it could. Ordinarily. But yours is not a case where 'ordinary' springs to mind. There are victims to consider. One who nearly lost his life. One a jury would be prone to find sympathetic. Another victim, a high school senior, a football star, one with a bright future in athletics. Struck down by you, and your aggression. With the aid of a bunch of quarters, no less, which might indeed be considered a weapon. And let us not forget about the Virginia bathroom incident."

I saw my chances fading as the facts were unveiled. The face of logic was laughing at me. Spitting on me too. The doctor sensed my despondency and helped to ease the pain. Gave me a spoonful of sugar to help the medicine go down.

"Of course that is not my personal interpretation, but I am afraid it would be the court's. You don't deserve to go to jail. You don't deserve to be committed. What you do deserve is treatment on an outpatient basis, but I'm afraid that we don't have that luxury. So I would like to request a hearing that would allow you admission to our facility. In six months' time you will be assessed, and I am confident of dismissal. Your father was looking for attempted murder. I am doubtful that he'd get it. But even if you reached a plea on a lesser charge, you would be facing jail time. A good deal longer than six months, of that I can assure you. So when we both weigh all those factors, I feel that our compromise is quite beneficial to all parties. Beneficial to your father, because he receives his perceived retribution. I get to make sure that you receive the best of care, so your life won't be squandered by your anger. And you, Antietam, will leave our facility one month before your eighteenth birthday, the master of your fate and the captain of your soul. All in all, I would consider my visit with your father to be an overwhelming victory."

"Overwhelming victory" was not the way I would phrase it, but it really didn't seem so bad. I would be out midway through the summer, and I could get a good grasp on all my anger with the help of a doctor whose name I did not yet know. A doctor who, despite his age, smiled now like a child as he reached into a sleeve inside his briefcase and said, "I talked him into something else."

"What?"

"This," he said, with a knowing grin, as he pulled it from the case and handed it to me with utmost care, like the treasure that it was.

"Terri's letter!" I yelled the words, and then yelled them once again. "Terri's letter!" I try not to use the F word except on rare occasions. The only useful advice my father ever gave me. But this was Terri's fucking letter! And it made my heart leap for joy as I lay there on that bed. And then the floodgates opened. I don't want to sound too wimpy, and I know this story is filled with tears. But my goodness, those tears began to fall, and they felt so fucking good. I actually rubbed the letter on my face, the smear lives to this day. And I smelled it, as I would do every day, and that smell brings back that wondrous face. I loved her, how I loved her, I would write her every day.

I was full of such emotion that I didn't see the doctor open up the door. He could have eased out and not been noticed for several hours, maybe days. But I heard his understanding voice when it said, "I guess I'll leave you two alone."

I reached for words to express my appreciation for all this man had done. How he'd put his reputation on the line for me, how he had grabbed my dangling future and placed it in his hands. But the tears just kept on streaming down, and I couldn't think of what to say. So I just went for the obvious, the simplest way of giving thanks.

"Thank you, thank you, Doctor . . ."

"Masters, Dr. Masters," the old man said, and he let the door slam shut behind him.

EPILOGUE / DECEMBER 1991

Dr. Masters died in September. September the fourteenth, 1991, to be exact. He died right in front of Coach Hanrahan, or to be more precise, he died right in back of him, from a massive heart attack. Died right in back of him because he had died while attempting an uninvited act.

The custodian who found him had no formal background in forensics, but somehow seemed to grasp that something wasn't right. Maybe it was the nearly comatose patient, a former all-pro lineman, who lay slumped on the bed with his pants around his ankles. Or maybe it was the chief psychiatrist who lay dead on the floor with his penis severed from the wrath of his own zipper. Which had caused a puddle of blood that had started to run into tiny rivers, like veins from a heart.

My sole confidant was dead. The man who said I would be out by the time I turned eighteen. A man who had pumped me full of Thorazine and used my honesty as a weapon. Preventing my exit by convincing me he had my best interests at heart.

My confidant had been Dr. Lucas Masters, or Ass Masters to his friends. A respected physician and intellectual who liked to ride the Hershey highway. With doped-up patients like the coach, who could only fight him in their minds.

Quite often I have envisioned how Ass Master's life came to an end. I imagined the coach, who I had seen just a time or two while I was under Masters's care. He would offer up a feeble smile from a drooling mouth, for a ghost from his former life. His muscles were gone, along with his mullet, but his hair had grown out over time. I guess the long hair was what sparked my thought, the thought of mighty Samson. Summoning the courage for one last great feat of strength. Causing the walls to come tumbling down around him. That's how I saw the coach. Summoning one last remnant of his former glory and shutting down his ass. Just refusing to let it open. Causing the distinguished doctor to strain too much, and grab his heart.

Masters's last act on earth had been of self-preservation. Trying to defend his good name, his honor I guess. If I put myself in his shoes, I guess I might have done the same. Hmm, if I was a rapist of drugged men, what would I do? Would my last act on earth be to hide the real truth? Would I do like the good doctor and zip up my fly? And like the good doctor, would the teeth of that zipper bite into my penis and rip off the tip?

The circumstances of the doctor's death caused

a rather massive inquiry into just how he'd lived his life. Masters's office yielded nothing, but his home gave up his skeletons. Just handed them over. In the form of meticulous journals he'd kept on a few special projects like Coach Hanrahan.

The coach's case caused quite a stir; he was a media sensation. A *People* cover, a plaque in Canton, and a network movie in the works. Which I'm pretty sure will leave out details like racial slurs and knocking students out, but hey, let bygones be forgotten.

Some weeks went by, and in mid-November another bone was found. Actually, "reexhumed" is more correct, as the bone had been discovered once before, and quickly disregarded. After all, it seemed so innocent, it was just a stack of letters. Twenty-seven of them, addressed to Terri Johnson, none of them delivered.

My trusty lawyer then jumped in, in pursuit of justice and the spotlight. He launched a massive lawsuit, which he claims will bring me millions. But somehow the heroic acts of a football star drew more attention than the kid whose love letters went unsent. So whereas the coach got *People* and a movie, I got a lawyer on a talk show, where he was part of a panel about "not giving up a fight." He should have been an expert on "showing up twice a year and saying, 'Hey, you know things could be worse.'"

But apparently at least one viewer had been moved by the tale my lawyer told. Moved enough to send my guy a package, postmarked in New Hampshire. It read "Attention: Andy Brown." My only mail in five long years, but for two weeks he was too tied up to see me.

When I saw the package, I knew it right away. Still in that same wrapping paper of Christmas 1985. Holly's gift, the one she'd made, and finally it was mine. I waited for my talk show king to leave so that I could open it alone. And when I did, my heart filled up, along with both my eyes. A portrait, a real work of art, of me and Terri smiling. She had made me a bit too handsome, but it was perfect otherwise. Terri every bit as beautiful as my memories of her were.

She had also sent a letter and inside were two things that were welcome, and one that wasn't needed. A phone number, a train ticket to North Conway, and a long apology.

I spent my last few weeks in Ithaca writing down these words. Hoping I can make some sense of what has happened, and trying to exorcise my demons.

I asked my legal ace to help me with two things before I left: to locate my old girlfriend, and to see what became of Tietam Brown. I told him to take his fee out of the millions I have coming.

The Johnsons, it turned out, fell victim to an audit. They could have fought, but they ran instead, and took their daughter with them. I guess a family of their means could be anywhere by now.

My father sold his house in '88 and moved out

of town. He never paid his son a single visit, though he lived just twenty miles away. I try not to think of him too often, and usually I fail.

So now I'm heading through Vermont en route to the White Mountains of New Hampshire. Just a little way from that children's park where it's Christmas every day. So what if I am 23, I still want to ride the coaster.

I am getting reacquainted with an old friend, Nat King Cole. Singing about the Savior's birth. A song that no longer triggers thoughts of empty cans and unwanted acts, but thoughts of happiness instead. Thoughts of Terri. Thoughts about what might have been, and thoughts of what may still be. One day soon I will look for her, and hope that destiny will lend a hand in turning over stones. But for now, I'm happy thinking. Thinking about that autumn night when she'd wanted me to kiss her.

ACKNOWLEDGMENTS

Writing this book has been one of the great joys of my life. Rewriting it—again and again—well . . . that's another story. I was fortunate to have had a great group of people help me out along the way.

Thank you to MacKay Boyer for sharing her knowledge of adoption, foster homes, and juvenile correction facilities in the state of Virginia.

To Dr. Scott Biasetti and his wife, Anne, for their insight into the health and social services system in the state of New York.

To Dr. Mark Lermann for explaining the complexities of the New York State psychiatric system.

To Dr. Russell Hamilton for confirming my theory for the tearage possibilities of a certain part of the male anatomy.

I had the benefit of calling in three of my mentors and friends in the wrestling world: Terry Funk, Harley Race, and Robert Fuller, for their memories of wrestling in the segregated South. An acknowledgment to Sputnick Monroe for his role in changing the way the business was run.

Thanks also to William Regal for filling me in on the history of hooking in Wigan.

To my wife, Collette, who was always enthusiastic about what I'd written.

Barry Bloom, Lisa Bloom, Jennifer Chatien, Barry Blaustein, and Dana Alborella all shared their valuable (and sometimes painful) opinions of my original manuscript, which I could have sworn was perfect when I handed it to them.

Claire Dippell and Lydia Grunstra were both very helpful during my dozens of phone calls with each of them.

A special thank-you to my agent, Luke Janklow, for believing in this book, for finding a perfect home for it, for quite possibly being the only person in his profession to use a Mutt Lange/Julie Miller analogy to make me understand the book business, and for having the guts/nerve/intuition to send this novel to Victoria Wilson.

Having come from a world where huge holes in a story line, implausible plot contrivances, and completely unrealistic characters were not necessarily considered bad things, I found Vicky Wilson's standards awfully tough to live up to. When she let me know I had, I felt kind of like the kid who snatches the pebble from the old man's hand on the old *Kung Fu* show: elated, but a little sad that the journey was over.